SNAP CACKLE & POP

by Carol Kearney

Dedication:

I would like to dedicate this book to my husband Harry and my daughter Emma. Thanks for keeping me fed, watered and topped up with wine whilst I wrote this book.

I would also like to thank Leesa Wallace of Wallace Publishing for giving me a publishing contract. Leesa I will be forever grateful.

CHAPTER 1

It takes Tom just eight minutes to tell me he's leaving me. EIGHT minutes after thirty-eight years together. He didn't even pause for breath; it was like he'd stored up eight minutes worth of puff in his lungs, so he could get it out in one foul swoop. Why tonight, after I'd been to bums and tums? Why not Saturday morning or Sunday night? Why Thursday night? Thursday's our special night when we eat pizza and drink rosé wine. This didn't make any sense to me... and we were going to the Graysons' for dinner the following evening, hadn't he thought of that?

As Tom closes the front door behind him I don't shout after him, I'm stunned beyond belief. I can't cry, I can't scream, I can't sob, so I stand there like a small child and watch him go. Even the dog cocks his head to one side as if he's trying to work out what's happening.

I walk to the fridge in a trance and pour myself a large glass of wine. Tom has left me a large brown envelope on the kitchen worktop and although I want to open it, I can't. I sip on my wine and stare at the envelope. Eventually, I make my way to the lounge and sit on the sofa for hours. It's ten o'clock in the evening, it's dark outside and I haven't turned any lights on in the house. Rupert, our lovely little Bichon Frise, is pawing me for his dinner. I walk back into the kitchen, pour the dog his biscuits and watch him as he eats without a care in the world. The envelope on the side is begging me to open it. I pull out the contents and sit at the table: documents for the car and a small wad of cash; no more than a thousand pounds. A thousand pounds for thirty eight years of marriage! He's also left a post-it note to say that he has closed down the bank account. How thoughtful of him. As I pour more wine, a mixture of bitterness and panic washes over me. Why has he left me? Why hadn't I noticed anything? Has his behaviour changed? If so, when did it change? We were really happy on the cruise last month, weren't we? I can't get my head around any of this so I frantically ring Tom for answers, but his phone is switched off. In a panic I ring a mutual friend of ours.

It only takes two minutes to make Lisa buckle under the stress of my direct questioning. Two minutes to realise that Tom, my Tom, has left me for someone else. I can hear her heavy breathing and I can hear the chink of the ice in her gin and tonic as she says, "I don't want to get involved Cathy, it's between you and Tom... but yes, he has met someone else. I spoke to him last week."

Fury takes over and I slam the phone down on her. *She* doesn't want to be involved? *She* has constantly been involved with everything Tom did. Tom was, in her own words, 'the one that got away,' 'her plan B.' The full story only emerged a year after Tom and I married. Apparently they were 'shag buddies' for years and they also had a secret pact - if they were both still single by the time they were thirty they'd marry each other. I remember Tom playing it down and laughing, saying it was youngsters' talk, whilst Lisa took it more seriously saying she'd meant every word of it. All those sly looks, winks and smiles; I'd seen them all. I felt Lisa had taken great delight in confessing that she'd known Tom was about to leave me for someone else. Who is this woman and do I know her?

My second phone call is to Ginny. I just want to ask if she knows who this other woman is and I do not expect her to crumble. Ginny is a ballbreaker; a director of a large company; a mother ruthless enough to send her two boys to boarding school then say she can't entertain them in the school holidays because she is too busy. She is also a member of the Women's Institute, she runs the local book club and plays bridge with her affluent friends. She can drink any man under the table and yet, when I ask her outright why Tom has left, she cries like a baby.

"You have to forgive me, Cathy. Trevor swore me to secrecy and I didn't want to hurt you."

How did she think keeping something from me was saving me from getting hurt? As for her husband Trevor, she hates him. She's been having an affair with someone at work for the past three years and yet, this so-called intelligent woman was told to keep quiet by her bald, pig headed overweight husband and she obeys? Of all the mutual friends we had, I admired Ginny the most and yet here I am laughing my head off hysterically from the shock. How wrong I've been. In fact, I've been wrong about all of them. I laugh hysterically for what seems like hours until I finally drop to my knees and sob. Why am I the last to know? My thoughts become bitter as I imagine our friends laughing at me. Maybe he's out having a meal with some of them now, maybe they're glad I'm not in the equation any more. Maybe he's telling them what a dreadful wife I am. All this surmising is exhausting so I take a shower. I let the water run through my hair and over my face, it temporarily makes me feel a little calmer. As I get dried, I look around the bathroom and realise how empty it is: there's no shaving foam, hair gel or razors on the side. It actually looks quite tidy and there are no towels on the floor. As I walk into the bedroom a terrible aching covers my whole body and I long for Tom to come home. I want to pretend this isn't happening.

I get into bed, my hair still wet from the shower. I can smell Tom's aftershave on the pillows and my emotions go from longing to hold him to a sickness in the pit of my stomach. My mind is racing with every scenario I can imagine. I picture them in bed together; laughing in restaurants; him giving her presents – the thoughts are driving me insane. Who is this faceless woman who has stolen my husband? I thought we were happy? I know we don't get down and dirty anymore, but when you reach your fifties it doesn't matter; there are more pressing issues like watching *Britain's Got Talent*, *Come Dine with Me* and David Attenborough's *How the Earth was Made*. We were cosy together and settled. I jump out of bed and strip off the sheets. As I do this, an envelope flies off the bed, it looks like it was under my pillow. I slowly open the envelope to find a letter inside from Tom, it reads:

> *Cathy,*
>
> *I've tried my best to stay with you but I just can't do it anymore. There are lots of reasons why I'm leaving you, too many to tell you in one letter. When I married you, you were fun to be around, you dressed nicely and made me want you sexually, but over the last ten years I haven't felt anything for you.*
>
> *You seem to think it's alright to wear black leggings all the time. You even wore them for my Uncle's funeral which really upset me.*
>
> *It annoys the shit out of me when you refer to the President of the United States as Barack Hussein from Obama.*
>
> *Another annoying habit you have is, for thirty eight years, every time the clocks go back you always say 'but it's not that time really, it's an hour later'. Cathy, it's not. THAT'S THE TIME!*
>
> *Oh yeah, the other annoyance: every time we go into a restaurant and they bring a bowl of water so you can wash your fingers you say, 'Oh I didn't order soup'. IT'S NOT FUNNY, but you spend anything up to five minutes laughing at your joke.*
>
> *Vegans DO NOT eat bacon and yet you still served it to my Mother for years.*

Four years ago you bought me an Indiana Jones DVD twice, first for my birthday and then again, at Christmas. That's how little you care about me.

All the time you refer to the dog as your baby. I was your baby once.

All you ever do, Cathy, is watch the TV (although you refer to it as the telly.) You play songs from the 70s because you believe you are still young – that's why I told you Donny Osmond was dead. Did it stop you? NO, you played them more and wailed throughout the songs. Cathy, you're a nutter, just like your Mother.

I sit on the bed and stare at the letter. I have no words to describe how I feel because I don't know how I feel. I start to feel really angry so I open the window and throw out the bed sheets. They scatter on the ground like a rainbow patchwork of misery. I walk down the stairs and pour myself more wine, then make my way into the garden and try to smell the warm night air, but I can't get my breath. A panic washes over me so I sit on a patio chair trying to regain my composure. I get the letter out of my pocket and read it to Rupert, his little face gazes into mine and his head cocks from side to side as he listens. I curse Tom, but I try not to swear in front of the dog.

When I calm down I look around at the beautifully manicured garden and I start crying again. Rupert sits by my feet and gives me a look of 'I'll never leave you, Mummy.' That makes me worse, and I wonder how he could have left our poor little Rupert. After all, it was his suggestion we should get a dog. He said it would be company for me when he was away, and when the puppy arrived we both cooed over him like he was our little baby- now he's telling me he's jealous of him? How pathetic is that?

I walk back into the kitchen followed by Rupert, my loyal little soldier, and pour myself a brandy.

I stare at my beautiful kitchen, then, from nowhere, a rage comes over me. I ring Tom on his mobile phone again but it's still switched off. I walk up and down the lounge in a rage talking to myself. Then I remember something: Tom left with an overnight bag, therefore his clothes are still in the wardrobe. I run up the stairs and start looking through coat pockets in an effort to find some evidence. I find nothing and that angers me even more so I start throwing his clothes out of the window; they land in a neat pile below. I run downstairs and go straight in the garage. I'm pleased there's a large bottle of mentholated spirit waiting for me. I tip the whole bottle over the sheets and clothes and put a match to them. It only takes a couple of seconds and I have a massive fire. I go into the garage and find bits of wood and old furniture, and the whole lot goes on. I get myself comfy on a patio chair, pour my wine and put a baked potato on the fire to bake. Whilst my potato is cooking I change into a lovely dress I'd bought on the cruise. It has faint dragon flies throughout the print and even though my hair and face looks a mess, the dress looks lovely. I raise a glass to myself in my drunken stupor.

"This isn't a pair of leggings is it, Tom? Kiss my arse." Although the baked potato is black, it tastes delicious. I have it with butter, salt and pepper. I drink more wine then slowly go through the house to see what I can find to keep my bonfire alive. There's so much stuff Tom has left behind that I find it hard to carry it. After I've sorted through the things Tom used to love, I place our video camera on the patio table and look into it. My reflection is terrible but I don't care. My hair is stuck up, I have mascara that's run down my face from crying and my teeth are as black as coal from eating the potato; I actually look like a mad, homeless fifty-four year old woman. I start by picking his guitar up. I talk into the camera.

"Tom, this is the stuff you left behind, so I'm assuming you don't want it. Here we have a nearly new Gibson studio, hardly been played and has no home anymore because the owner can't be bothered to take it with him, he has a new love interest so it has to go. Remember, Tom, a guitar is forever not just for Christmas."

I smash the guitar with a hammer and throw it on the fire. At one time I wouldn't dream of breaking anything, but tonight I feel like something has possessed me. The flames are now quite high and I need to take my cardigan off to cool myself down. Next on are his old records, they melt quickly like poppadums being thrown in hot cooking oil. I look at the camera.

"All your Northern soul records gone, Tom, wave goodbye to them … aww go on."

Next is the wedding album, it shrivels into black dust and I'm joyous as I see Tom's face melting. I think the seven pairs of shoes and trainers are a mistake because the plumes of smoke are reaching a new high and the whole of the back garden is covered in thick black smoke. I look at the camera again.

"There you go, are you happy now?"

I knock back the wine and dance a little jig, then walk back to the camera and put my face right up to the lens.

"Goodnight, shithead."

I laugh and plonk myself down on the patio chair. The heat from the bonfire is intense and I feel myself nodding off. After a few minutes I can hear sirens in the distance and they appear to be getting closer. All of a sudden the back gate opens and I wake up with a start. Four burly fire-fighters run into the garden. Am I dreaming? Is there really a gang of handsome men in my garden? I smile as they pass me one by one. *This could be my lucky night*, I think to myself. Then Tom appears in the garden. What does he want? He always spoils my fun and pisses on my parade. Tom's face is red with anger.

The fire brigade give him a lecture about burning things in the garden and they quote the law to him. Tom nods and apologises.

"My wife's not been very well lately. She's not her usual self."

I stand up half staggering, half dancing and slurring.

"I haven't been myself because you have left me for another woman … well I say woman, what I should really say is a slut."

The firemen smirk and put their heads down. Tom tries to get me back in the house but I won't go, so he gets annoyed.

"For God's sake, Cathy, go inside."

I flatly refuse to move even though my body is swaying, I stand defiant. The fireman looks at Tom.

"I hope we won't be visiting the property again."

Tom shakes their hands and bows his head. Then it dawns on me that a neighbour must have reported the fire. I shout at the top of my voice.

"So, we have a spy in our mist, do we?"

I stagger towards the left side of the fence and look over. It's obvious that Linda and Ian are out, so I smile like an evil witch who's just found Sleeping Beauty. I then stagger to the right of the fence and see George cowering and listening to the conversation. When he sees me he looks over the fence and smiles.

"Hello Cathy, how are you?"

I don't even answer him. I just point my finger at him. He

tries to say something but I don't give him chance. I put my face in his and shout.

"Fuck off!"

George is terrified and runs into the house. Tom looks like he's going to collapse because in our entire married life, I've never behaved so badly. Once again, he tries to get me into the house.

"Cathy, please stop shouting and swearing," he whispers.

"I'll say what I want, Tom, it's my mouth," I laugh hysterically.

"Well nobody else would admit to having it," Tom says, shaking his head in despair.

"Very fucking funny … not," I laugh.

****

It's well past midnight and Tom is drinking a brandy. I'm lying on the sofa with Rupert. Tom speaks quietly to me.

"Cathy, I think you need to see a doctor."

"Why? Have you given me a venereal disease?" I say, laughing.

Tom shakes his head in disgust - *disgust*! - it's me that should be disgusted. I smile at him.

"Who is she?"

Tom sips on his brandy then wipes his lips with a hankie.

"Cathy there isn't anyone else. I don't know why you have this crazy notion that I'm with someone else, I'm not. The marriage just wasn't working."

I sit up and look him straight in the face.

"Not only are you a coward and a liar, you haven't even the guts to come clean, have you?"

Tom gets up to go, so I lie back down on the sofa.

"Close the door after you."

Tom stops and tries to kiss my head but I slap his hand away.

"Tom, fuck off," I say, looking at him.

****

I wake up and see the rain lashing against the window and wonder if last night was a dream. When I walk into the kitchen and see all the documents on the kitchen table, it's clear it's not. I can see a large brandy glass on the side with bits of cauliflower in it. I stare at the glass until the memory of the night before comes back to me. With not an ice cube in sight, I'd put frozen cauliflower into the drink to cool it. Things were so much more dignified a few days ago, when I thought I was in a bubble of marital bliss. The effect of the drink has worn off and I spend all day constantly ringing Tom, leaving hateful messages for him to call me at once. There are also messages of me sobbing down the phone and pleading to know what went wrong. It's the not knowing that is sending me mad. If I knew, I could deal with it, couldn't I?

As the days go by, the severity of the situation sinks in and I find out that Tom has re-mortgaged the house and is behind on the mortgage payments. They are also coming to repossess my car. My emotions are all over the place and I go from cursing to numb – there's no in-between. It only takes two minutes to realise that Tom must have forged my name on the mortgage documents, so he could re-mortgage the house. Or maybe *she*'d done it. Maybe she pretended to be me. That thought is more than I can stand and I sprint to the fridge in search of alcohol, but there's nothing in. I rummage through cupboards until I find some cooking sherry. I gulp out of the bottle but it tastes of Christmas cake which makes me cry. I sit and cry for the world, for all the starving children, the poor abused children, the tortured animals and the cat I had as a child that got run over. Only panic stops me from crying when I realise I need to sort out the night's supply of alcohol. I log on to the internet shopping site and dart straight to the alcohol section. I order twelve bottles of wine, two bottles of gin and two bottles of tonic water. It's the only time I don't think about Tom. At the end of the internet shopping I'm asked for a username. It is hard to think of one, I am too maudlin about the woman who has stolen my husband. Three hours later the supermarket van pulls onto the drive. I feel sorry for the older gentleman who struggles with all the bottles; as he approaches the door he shouts, "Fur coat no knickers." Oh my God, I didn't think he'd shout out my username loudly. I quickly point to the hall and run back inside to safety.

At 9.51pm I'm so drunk I can't watch the telly. I want to watch the end of a programme so I cover one eye with my hand which makes everything normal again and for a minute or two. It feels like I am waiting for Tom to walk through the door. By 10.14pm I'm singing Gloria Gaynor's *I will survive.* The music is so loud it vibrates my chest and I haven't danced like this since the 70s. By 11.04pm, I'm sobbing in a heap to Freda Payne's *Band of Gold.* As I listen to the words all I think about is Tom, my Tom, and I twiddle with my wedding ring as if I'm affirming that he's still mine. I even play Bing Crosby's *White Christmas* despite the fact it's only June. I remember Pop coming into my bedroom when I was a child, carrying a stocking which consisted of a small present, a Satsuma and some nuts. This makes me howl and sob.

"What lovely parents I've got. They would never leave me like he's done," I say out loud.

****

I wake up the following morning and realise I've found my way to bed even though it has no sheets on it. Then the whole ritual of the day starts again. I don't see a soul and the phone doesn't ring – I check the receiver several times to make sure it's working. The rest of the week is a total blur and the day they come for the car, I don't even answer the door. The documents are in the glove compartment and the keys are in the ignition. Rupert shows his loyalty to me by barking at the men who have come to take it away. The only feeling I have is utter despair. I try to phone Tom again but it seems his mobile has now been disconnected. I don't know what to do with myself. I walk into the kitchen and try to decide wine or tea? The wine wins every time. This is the only decision I can make at the moment because my brain is so numb. I keep getting flashbacks of our first meeting, our wedding day, the day I gave birth and the day he left. This doesn't happen to me, it happens to other people. I decide to ring Tom's place of work only to be told he's been moved to another branch. The receptionist, who was once so chatty with me, can't wait to get me off the phone. Does everyone from his workplace know? Am I the only person that didn't know?

****

It's Saturday evening, day ten, and I have to tell our daughter, Louise, that her father has gone AWOL. Should I tell her he's gone off with a trollop, a husband stealer, a whore? Or should I save that until I become really bitter? Or should I keep quiet because he might come back? Maybe he'll come back and beg for forgiveness... but would I really have him back after what he's done, after plotting behind my back and re-mortgaging the house? Where's the money gone? Has he set up home with that vixen? Or has he taken her away on a romantic holiday? My thoughts are driving me insane. I look out of the window and stare at the sycamore tree in the front garden and I remember how small it was when we bought the house. My eyes scan the lounge area, where I fix my eyes on all the beautiful things we've bought together over the years. Paintings costing hundreds of pounds, plush sofas with silk scatter cushions, lamps and scented candles and a luxurious rug from the Middle East. I love sitting in this room with my glass of wine watching terrible telly programmes, but now it looks so cold and uninviting. The telly is on in the background and some middle-aged woman is murdering a song by Petula Clarke.

"Mum, I'm home," Louise shouts from the kitchen and promptly tips all her dirty washing on the kitchen floor while I pour us both a glass of wine. After twenty minutes my little girl cries with temper and in her twenty-seven years on this earth I have never heard her swear like that. I don't even know some of the swear words, but I am determined to remember them for the day I see that little weasel. Louise has always had a strained relationship with her father and it comes as no surprise to her.

"I love my dad because he's my dad, but I don't like him as a person. You're better off without him, Mum. He's a bully and a control freak."

I nod. Yes, Freak. I like that name 'Freak.' When we finish the bottle of wine I tell her we are going to lose the house. She roars with laughter – it's a mixture of hysteria and wine.

"I hate this house, always have."

That makes me roar with laughter too, and the two of us laugh and laugh until we can't breathe. We stay up until the early hours and put the world to rights. In the morning, I busy myself doing her washing because it makes me feel normal again, normal and needed.

****

Sunday night comes too soon and Louise heads back to the hospital where she works. She hugs me at the door.

"I'll ring you in the week, Mum, and you know where I am if you need me."

That comment makes me cry and feel all maudlin again, so, when I see her car turn the corner at the end of the road, I head back to the wine, snivelling as I go. That night I decide to ring everyone we know. I go from trying to be light-hearted to begging them for his phone number. Our mutual friends have clearly taken sides and they're not even answering their phones anymore. I then do something I bitterly regret – I ring his mother. I only get to "Polly, do you know Tom's left me?" before Polly comes back at me with a tirade of abuse. I know we've never been close but I was married to her son for thirty-eight years, for God's sake. Can't she show me any compassion? Apparently it's all my fault. I have pushed him into the arms of another woman because, apparently, I'm selfish and, to make matters worse, she tells me what I've always known:

"I've never liked you, Cathy. You're nothing but a gold digger. You haven't worked for years, you've let him keep you."

"I've slaved in this house: cooked, cleaned, ironed and brought up Louise - that's not an easy task, bringing up a child," I scream back at her. Her reply is vicious.

"Most women bring up the children, Cathy, and do all that. You're nothing special. I brought up four children and they've all done very well for themselves."

Does she know about the house and the car going? I try and tell her but again she comes at me.

"Do you blame him? The poor man's given up. You've destroyed him!" and with that, she slams the phone down on me. I sit on the sofa and stare into space. Why does everyone but Louise and Rupert hate me? What's gone wrong? It was only a month ago we were on the cruise - we held hands, laughed and chatted to other couples. Tom said it was now 'our time', a time to enjoy life, and all along he knew he was planning to leave me. Maybe it was a farewell cruise - it would have been nice to have known. I feel such a fool and in the end I fling myself on the sofa and cry like a baby. I try to ring my best friend who is visiting relatives in Australia, but I've no idea what time it is over there and the phone just rings out.

As the weeks go by, I get credit card statements in the post that show that the Freak and the slag have dined at expensive restaurants, gone to the theatre and shagged in expensive beds all over the country. It appears they are working their way through the good hotel and food guide. Then the penny drops, if the Freak had the slag with him when he travelled, the slag must work with him. Tom never had any imagination, so of course it was his secretary – it's the oldest cliché in the book. A breakthrough! I decide to turn detective and within minutes I find out it is his secretary. I go to the company website and look at the staff profiles and there, underneath Tom, literally underneath him is the bitch. Not hard to find, was it, Freak? I ring his new office and pretend to be someone from a sister company. The young inexperienced receptionist gives me her name.

"They're out today for lunch and won't be returning to the office." She says it like they are a couple who have been married for thirty-eight years. Her name is Francis Smith. I instantly drop the 'r' and with my mouth twitching, I start shouting out "Fanny Smith… what a name." I stare at the computer not knowing whether to laugh or cry. Then I become bitter and pretend not to care.

I think they will make a lovely couple because the Freak is

called 'Thomas Horace Wilbur' (after both his grandfathers.) "So that's a good match," I say out loud. I stare at her on the company website, she's not what I imagined. She's small with crooked teeth, slim in a boyish kind of way, has mousey hair which has been badly streaked and she's dressed up in a suit that looks like it's come from one of the many high street shops. I howl with laughter at the sight of her; she looks like an awkward politician, a lonely woman with loads of cats – a piss-smelling spinster. I knock back my wine and imagine her private parts must smell like cheesy wotsits and she *must* have genital warts, I can just tell. I copy and paste her picture and print it out, don't ask me why but I thought it was a good way of torturing myself even more. I sit with my G&T and stare at the picture, studying every mark on her face. At one point I'm actually talking to her.

"What have you been doing today, shagging my husband?"

She seems to roll her eyes at me.

"You can roll your eyes all you want, you little slut. Couldn't you get a man yourself, so you had to steal one?" I come back at her. Then I stand up in front of her, "Cheers, fucking cheers. I didn't want him anyway."

Then half an hour later I'm crying my eyes out, because what does Fanny Smith have that I haven't got? This situation is becoming unbearable to live with, I can't seem to be able to pull myself together and it's only a matter of days before the bailiffs will be arriving.

****

It's Monday, bank holiday morning, and although I've got a massive hangover I still manage to clear the garage of the Freak's tools, mountain bike, golf clubs, vintage wine (which would be wasted on me), a generator and anything else I can get my hands on.

The drive is full of things, and the leaflets I'd put through people's letter boxes have definitely done the trick because a small crowd's arrived. I hang up a banner in front of the house and it reads:

> **Thomas Burton-Whittaker has left me for his secretary. Our house is soon to be repossessed, so I'm selling off goods this Monday (5th.) Please come along and grab yourself a bargain. All proceeds will go on wine and gin.**
>
> **You've all been such lovely neighbours over the years (apart from George next door.) Thank you.**
>
>

From Cathy, a slightly bitter and scorned wife. x
>

"I won't be a minute, then you can all dive in," I shout to the crowd.

I pin up another poster. It's Fanny's picture and underneath I've written:

> **Lost dog.**
>
> **Likes to sniff shit.**
>
> **Answers to the name Fanny Smith.**
>
> **Last seen fucking Thomas Burton-Whittaker.**

The neighbours think everything is hilarious but they are definitely on my side. Some close neighbours are really kind and offer to help me move if I need it.

****

It's 4pm, everything has gone from the garage sale and I'm £1,660 better off than I was this morning. Clare from across the road is going to buy the sofas and her husband is removing the luxury kitchen and bathrooms and re-fitting them in their house. I don't mind eating takeaways and peeing in a bucket for a few days; my dignity has gone, it went when Tom walked out the door.

****

At 8pm, after a long bath, I pour myself a large G&T and I suddenly feel much better and in control of my own life. Let the new life commence, here I come. Cathy Burton-Whittaker is now Cathy Mathews. At least Pop will be pleased I'm carrying on the family name.

CHAPTER 2

I slowly open one eye and look around the room. As I look towards the ceiling I see Donny Osmond smiling back at me. I stare at his face.

"He told me you were dead, Donny. What a hateful swine he is." Donny agrees with me and for a moment, he looks like he's looking at me in a pitiful way. I walk to the bathroom in my pyjamas and turn on the shower. I look at my naked body in the mirror and I don't like what I see. My breasts have dropped to where my waist once was and I don't have a waist anymore, it's barrel-like. My belly looks like the hangover on a cliff and the inside of my legs resemble baby back ribs, as they go in and out in all the right places. No wonder Tom had gone off me.

I walk into the bedroom and look in the wardrobe. My Wonder Woman outfit is neatly folded at the bottom of the wardrobe. A memory flashes through my mind as I remember the night I wore it in the seventies and all the male attention I got that night. I lift it up and I can't believe how tiny it is. I put on the top and it stretches to breaking point, my fat is spilling out of it and the top doesn't even go down to my belly button. I have back fat all the way down my back and my arms are huge and white. Getting on the skirt was a struggle to say the least and I only manage to get it slightly past my thighs when it splits.

I walk into the kitchen to find Mum making tea. She's just about to pour me a cup when we hear a piercing scream coming from upstairs. We both run up the stairs only to find Pop hopping about on one leg.

"Joan, get it off me," he screams.

Mum makes him stand still while I watch in horror. Then in a flash she rips off a plaster and stands looking at it. Pop looks at the patch too.

"What the hell is that?" he asks.

My face goes bright red as I realise what it is.

"It's just one of my HRT patches, Pop. It must have come off when I was in the shower."

Pop doesn't look happy at all and quickly ushers me and Mum out of the bedroom.

****

After everyone has settled down we sit around the table for breakfast. Pop looks ashen.

"I need to go to the doctors. That patch might have been pumping chemicals into me. I might be contaminated," he says woefully.

Mum nods. "Yeah, things might start dropping off. You know what they did to those poor babies in the sixties, they lost limbs, the poor little buggers."

I sigh heavily.

"It's not those types of chemicals, Pop. You'll be fine."

As usual Mum makes it worse.

"You could end up with a pair of tits."

Pop looks scared so I try and intervene.

"Mum, that's not going to happen."

Mum shrugs her shoulders.

"Look at your Uncle Edward, he's on steroids and he's got tits like Dolly Parton."

"That's because he's twenty six stone," I say, exasperated.

Mum puts her teacher head on and I know a lecture is coming.

"They didn't have all that rubbish in my day. No, we just had to get on with it, tough as old boots we were."

Pop picks up the paper but he's not happy. Mum doesn't look up and continues to rummage through her handbag.

"That's what probably put all that weight on you, Cathy."

Pop stands up and starts making breakfast. He can't help but have his say.

"That's probably why he left you for another woman."

My jaw drops, I cannot believe what my own mother and father have just said. I turn to Pop. "Thanks for that, it's very brutal, I must say."

"Where are my glasses?" Mum pipes up, not having heard what Pop has said.

"There, on your head," I say, looking at her.

She shakes her head.

"Not those, my old ones. I don't want to wear these new ones out."

She looks confused and I realise just how old my parents have got. She looks at me.

"I'm getting very forgetful these days. The doctor has told me to write things down so I don't forget. Your Pop's just the same with his memory and he doesn't listen to a word I say." She looks at Pop with annoyance. "I don't want any breakfast, I'll just have a few biscuits."

Pop ignores her and carries on cooking. I look around the

kitchen and nothing has changed in thirty-eight years, not even the wall paper, which is wipe clean and supposed to look like tiles. There's still a Formica cupboard with china cups hanging init. The large kitchen table is covered in a chenille cover to protect the wood, the teapot has a multi-coloured cosy on which hurts my eyes when I look at it and although the house is very clean, it's extremely tired-looking, just like me. I thought coming home to the bosom of my parents' house would comfort me, but in truth, it's made me feel stressed and depressed. I'd also forgotten how they bicker and how outspoken they both are. Pop puts three breakfasts of bacon and eggs on the table. Mum looks at the breakfast in disgust.

"I knew you weren't listening to me, Stanley. You've forgot the toast."

Pop ignores her and eats his food. I didn't think for one minute I would eat the breakfast but I did; I even ate half of Mum's. Who'd have thought I would be back home at fifty-four, menopausal and pot-less? Mum stands up and looks out of the window.

"Oh Cathy, I love putting food out for the birds. Look at that little robin redbreast. He's been there for hours, bless him, he must be starving."

I stand up and walk towards the window. After a few seconds I turn to Mum.

"That's not a robin redbreast, it's a red pepper."

"Is it?" Mum asks, wiping her glasses.

Pop shakes his head with annoyance and carries on reading his paper. I knew this was going to be a long day.

"I've never liked him, he was full of his own self-importance," Pop chirps up suddenly from out of nowhere.

This is the last thing I wanted - a full blown debate about my now estranged husband. Mum joins in.

"He walked in the best room like he owned the house and kicked the budgie on to the fire."

Pop shakes his head and looks sad as he remembers the incident. It's clear he can't let it go as he almost shouts, "Poor little bugger was only flying around for a bit of exercise and whoosh, kicked on the fire in his prime."

We've been having this conversation for over thirty years, even when I was with Tom, and the outcome is always the same. I feel it my duty to defend the day they met Tom. Don't ask me why this is because I have no idea.

"He didn't kill Joey on purpose," I feel compelled to say.

Pop shoots me a look that could kill and Mum takes a hankie out of her handbag and wipes her nose. I watch her, knowing exactly what's coming next.

"Talking of fire, have you talked to your brother recently?"

"No, and I don't want to, he's a waste of space." I say, shaking my head.

"It's not his fault he's an arsonist, the midwife made him like that." Mum starts to snivel again.

I shake my head in disbelief. I'd heard it a million times before but Mum has to tell the story one more time.

"He was blue when he came out, so the midwife put him on a shovel and held him near the fire to warm him up."

I can't stop myself from saying "She should have thrown him on it."

Mum stares at me.

"That's a terrible thing to say."

"How long did he get?" I ask, now driven purely by curiosity.

"His solicitor told him he'd get three years, but the judge knew him so he only got eighteen months." Mum smiles with pride. "It's good to know people in high places."

I start to giggle as the whole scenario is complete madness. For my own amusement, I continue the conversation.

"What was he convicted of this time?"

Pop puts his paper on the table and doesn't see the irony of what he says next.

"He's a son of a bitch and your mother thinks it's my fault."

Mum flies off the handle.

"I didn't say it was your fault, I said I blame you."

Pop looks at me and says, "He pinched a car that was a cut and shut and then crashed it into a tree."

Mum's in a world of her own as she says, "Thank God it was a BMW at the front, it was the air bags that saved him from being hurt. The air bags lifted him through the sun roof and when the police got there he was sat on the top of the car, bless him." She stands up and gets a picture out of the sideboard. "They printed a lovely picture of him in the Evening Standard. I went down for a copy."

I look at a picture of a forty-nine year old man-child grinning from ear to ear like he's a film star, on top of a car that's broken in two. Mum takes the photo off me and kisses it before she puts it back on the sideboard. Pop shakes his head and sighs.

I stand up and look through the kitchen window, wondering how long I can stick it out in this mad house. Then I notice something in the garden: a big blue plastic object.

"Mum, what's that in the garden?"

"Oh Cathy, I can't believe I didn't tell you," Mum screams with joy, "We've got a swimming pool."

I can't believe my ears.

"You and Pop have a pool?"

"Well it's a blow up one and it didn't cost much," Mum say, modestly. "We'll go in it later with a glass of eggnog."

I go outside to take a closer look at it. Maybe I could lie in it later and dream I'm back in the Caribbean with Tom. That temporarily puts a smile on my face.

****

I can't believe three hours have passed and Mum is still brewing up and telling me all the gossip.

"Cathy, you should have seen Doris's face when we got the pool, green with jealousy so she was."

The stress is getting too much and I need to get out of the house.

"Mum, would you give me a lift into town? I think I'll get some wine for tonight, I don't fancy eggnog, and I need to get some dog food."

Mum bends down and strokes the dog.

"Dog food? I don't think so. This little man will eat only the best whilst he lives here. Won't you little man?" Rupert rolls over so she can tickle his belly.

We both get in the car and Mum seems to love the fact that

I need her again. Off we go in her battered old Skoda. As we drive up the High Street, Mum suddenly screeches to a halt and, as I'm thrown forwards, she puts out her arm across my body to save me going through the car window.

"Mum, what the hell happened then?"

Mum starts looking at the foot peddle.

"I never know if I'm on the speedometer or the brake."

The car kangaroos towards the supermarket.

The supermarket shop is a nightmare, with Mum talking to everyone she knows; she even speaks to people she doesn't know. I'm shocked as she asks shoppers about their shopping and lifts things out of their trolleys.

"I've been wondering what they taste like, are they nice?" She then gets into a full blown conversation about anything from the price of bread to politics.

I'm worried about the politics conversation when Mum makes a reference that Ronald Regan was the UK Prime Minister and boasts about having a signed picture of Nancy Regan. In truth she does, but it is a picture she bought at a car boot sale a good twenty years ago. I finally walk off when she refers to Ronald Regan disgracing England with his affair with Monica Lewinski and says that Margaret Thatcher had warned him to end the affair. She then went on to explain that Winston Churchill had sacked both Margaret Thatcher and Ronald Regan for conspiracy. It's also a conversation too many when Mum asks an elderly woman about her Tena Ladies.

"Oh, do they work? You're never the same when you have kiddies, are you? I only have to cough and I piss myself."

I walk up the aisle away from Mum and look at products I have no intention of buying.

As we get to the checkout, Mum notices that the woman in front of us has a packet of biscuits for cheese on the conveyer belt.

"Oh, Cathy, we need some biscuits."

Then, to my horror, she picks up the biscuits and puts them with her shopping. On the way out, Mum stops and turns to me.

"Cathy, they're very ignorant and lazy in that shop, they throw all the shopping down and they never ask if you need any help. Last week I was struggling and couldn't pack the bags quick enough. Your Pop went mad and went into the shop to complain."

"Why, where was Pop?" I asked, confused.

"He was sat in the car, waiting for me."

I stare at Mum and I can feel my heart palpating. I think to myself, *please get me home so I can open my wine.* We get back in the car and all I can hear are my bottles clinking together in the boot. Mum pulls out the throttle in the car, hangs her handbag on it and off we go back home.

I've always loved driving up Mum and Pop's street; 1930s semis on both sides of the road with most of the houses framed by trees. It's a very pretty road, one that you would expect to see on an advert. The semis are very well kept with beautiful gardens and hanging baskets and every Sunday, from as far back as I can remember, the men of the houses mow the lawn and wash their cars on the driveway.

****

The evening is so warm and I can't wait to get in the

oversized paddling pool. I arrive in the kitchen in my swimming costume; I thought that black would be slimming and, with white stripes down each side, a bit cosmopolitan. Mum is mixing a large jug of eggnog and lemonade when she spots me walking into the garden. She stares at me.

"Cathy, you look like free Willy in that costume."

As if my confidence isn't already lower than a snake's belly! I neck the first glass of wine within 2 seconds flat. Pop comes in from his allotment and goes for a shower, mumbling to himself as he walks in the house. Rupert runs behind him. I stroll to the pool, slowly walk up a small step ladder and, as I get to the top, I turn around and try lower myself in. However, I can't because my hips have become wedged inside the ladder. Mum sees what's happened, runs to the pool and starts splashing water over my thighs. The neighbour, Doris, comes out of her house with a drink. I look like I'm suspended in mid-air as she stares at me.

"Hello, Cathy, you gave me a fright then. I didn't know you were visiting. Oh how strange – you're levitating! You shouldn't dabble with all that nonsense, Cathy, it's the occult."

Mum runs inside shouting for Pop to come and help. I feel so humiliated and nervously talk to Doris.

"Your garden looks nice."

Doris smiles.

"I've been at it all day, my back's killing me."

Out of embarrassment I decide to go for it, so I jump off the ladder and land in the pool with an almighty splash. Large amounts of water escape over the sides like a mini-tsunami. I'm coughing and spluttering, then, all of a sudden, the pool bursts its banks and hundreds of litres of water gush out, taking me with it. Within seconds I've smashed through the battered old fence and into Doris's garden. The water gushes over Doris and sends her sliding across the sodden grass. All the flowers Doris has planted have been ripped out of the ground by the force of the water. The only thing that stops me is a small bush. Mum runs into the garden, followed by Pop.

"Cathy, get off that peony bush! The devil lives underneath them." Mum screams, then turns to Doris. "The only way you can get the devil out from under the bush, is to tie it to a dog's tail and let the dog run off. Thank God we've got the dog, Cathy."

Pop goes back inside the house for his bath and again, he's mumbling to himself.

"Would someone please order me an ambulance, I think I've broke me hip," Doris says with a groan.

****

This morning I decide to open both eyes at the same time. I know exactly where I am, I'm in my old bedroom at my parents' house. But this morning the bed covers feel really tight and as I turn to the side, I can see that Mum has put three teddies in bed with me. There's a glass of milk on the bedside cabinet and I have a French plait in my hair. Then I remember last night; the crying, maudlin and Mum hugging me like I was six years of age again. I can still hear her voice ringing in my ears.

"I told you it would all end in tears, Cathy. You should have listened to me."

I fluff up my pillows and sit up. The bed still has a pink candlewick bedspread on it and old-fashioned nylon sheets that crackle when you turn over. The wallpaper is still the same too, it's psychedelic with swirls of bright yellow and orange flowers. The wall that has a window in it looks very depressing; Pop put the paper on upside down and all the flowers look like they have died. Pop told me and Mum that it was supposed to look like that as it was the natural order of life, you live and then you die, and we never questioned him. The large glitter ball that hangs from the ceiling is not a good thing to look at, especially when you come home aged fifteen after knocking back four cherry Bs in an hour - it makes the room spin much faster. The picture of the *Partridge Family* has seen better days and there are several dart holes all over David Cassidy's head. My brother Steven swore blind it wasn't him that threw the darts but he was the only one in the house that had a dart board. One day I threw a dart at him, hoping that it would stick in the door and frighten him. It didn't. It stuck in the back of his head instead and he screamed the house down. Mum accused me of trying to murder my younger brother and I was devastated. That's the only time I have ever really felt any pity for Steven. I walk across the landing and into his room. He's still got wallpaper with clown faces on it and I shudder as I look at them. As a youngster, I found them very scary and to be honest, I still do. The wallpaper is still the same in the bathroom too; it has hundreds of birds every square metre and as you glance past the shower, the birds look like they are diving into the sink to kill themselves. Again, Pop said he'd done it on purpose because it looked like they were taking a bath in the sink.

I walk into the kitchen in my pyjamas and find Mum is reading a magazine. I look through the window and see that the garden is full of mole hills and is still sodden from the burst pool.

"How do you get rid of moles?" I turn and ask Mum.

"Get a good concealer from the chemist," Mum answers without looking up.

Pop walks into the lounge smelling of aftershave and wearing one of his best shirts. "I'm off to the allotment," he says, looking at Mum.

Mum folds her arms.

"Allotment at this time? You're going to the pub aren't you? It's getting earlier and earlier with you."

'I'll go where I bleedin' well want to. Stop nagging me.' Pop laughs as he leaves the house.

I pour two cups of tea and sit at the table. All of a sudden, Mum screams.

"Would you look at that?" She lifts up the magazine and there's a picture of a really fat woman. The accompanying headline reads: **I married a fat feeder.** Mum reads the article out loud.

> **On the day the builders knocked down the front room wall, the humiliation was terrible. My kind neighbour could see how utterly devastated I was and covered the whole of my face and body with a blanket. The neighbours gathered to watch as the fire brigade lifted me out of the room on a hydraulic winch. Some sniggered. A special re-enforced stretcher had been sent from America for me to lie on. My huge forty stone body heaved back and forth as ten fireman helped to rescue me.**

"That makes me look like twiggy," I smile.

"Hardly," she smirks.

"I'm not forty stone, am I?" I ask, flabbergasted.

"Not yet you're not," she replies, pouring more tea. "*She* wasn't born that big though, was she?!" Then she screeches as she remembers the plans for the day, "Go and get dressed, "We're going to see a clairvoyant this morning."

I'm speechless.

"A clairvoyant? You're seventy-two years old. Why would you want to go to a clairvoyant?"

"It's not for me," Mum laughs. "It's for you. I want to know if you're going to meet someone and I can get my house back. Not that I'm pushing you out or anything."

I slowly walk up the stairs to get dressed and the last thing I want it to visit a clairvoyant, I have no desire to know what lies ahead for me.

****

Mum pulls up at the traffic lights and smiles.

"I remember when me and your Gran went to see one. She had to stop the car, then she screamed at me to get out."

"Why did she want you to get out?"

"Not me," Mum says, solemnly. "We had two ghosts in the back. They thought they were coming home with us."

I can feel a headache coming on. At this point, Jamie Oliver comes on the radio and I turn to Mum enthusiastically.

"I love Jamie Oliver's recipes, maybe I could cook one night?"

"No, he's not as good as Keith Floyd," she says, shaking her head. He's a proper chef."

"He's a proper pisshead." I laugh.

Mum thinks for a minute, then says "He's a posh drunk: sophisticated. Something your father isn't."

I can't help myself and quietly say, "You do know he's dead, don't you?"

"No he isn't," Mum screams. "Cathy, you've got a very spiteful streak in you and a nasty tongue. I watch him every

Saturday morning on the telly."

"Honestly, Mum," I laugh. "He's dead. They're all repeats."

Mum is furious and starts to drive faster. I turn to look out of the window, silently wishing I hadn't said anything. It's clear we're lost now but Mum insists she knows where she is going. I take the satnav out of my handbag; it's the only thing I took from the house apart from my personal belongings. Mum stops the car and points at it accusingly.

"I'm not having that on in the car. Her voice grates on my nerves."

I ignore her, meanly thinking I know the feeling. I enter the address and stick the satnav on the window. Mum pulls her face but drives up the road without further comment. We've only been driving a matter of minutes when she taps the screen and it goes blank. This really annoys me.

"Mum, don't touch the screen."

"She's getting on my nerves," she says, pulling over, "and she has no idea where she's going. I've lived here all my life and I know where I am."

We pull into a petrol station and I get out of the car to fill it up. When I've paid and returned, the satnav is upside down on the window screen and it's been turned off. I feel so agitated.

"You've been messing with this, haven't you?"

"I haven't touched it," Mum says, shaking her head.

I turn the satnav back on and we carry on up the road. It suddenly gives directions, which irritates Mum. She leans into it and says "Not you again, keep your opinions to yourself."

I become angry.

"Mum, it's not a human being in there."

"Exactly, it's all guess work with her." Mum shouts and tries to take the satnav off the window, while I try and wrestle it off her. I bang it back on the window screen and all of sudden a man starts giving directions in an Irish voice. We look at each other in surprise. Then it says "I said turn left, you fecking eejit." Mum is flabbergasted. Then the man says "Take the motorway it's fast as fuck." Mum pulls over and looks at me.

"He's not very professional, that man at Sap Nap headquarters, is he?" She leans into the satnav. "Shut it with your bleedin' foul feckin' mouth."

We arrive outside a big old Victorian house. A lady answers the door; she looks like she's a throw-back from the 1920s and she's knocking on 70 if she's a day. She invites us both in and escorts us to the best room.

"I won't be long," she says, smiling so that we can see the lipstick on her teeth. She leaves the room.

"It stinks of old mothballs in here," Mum says, sniffing the air.

I put my finger over my lips for mum to be quiet. The lady comes back in and smiles at us through her yellow teeth. She has re-applied the red lipstick and now looks like the joker out of the Batman movies.

"Right, would you like a reading separately or together?"

I say separately, but Mum disagrees.

"Together. We've no secrets."

So, off we go, into an equally cluttered middle room. This room is filled with heavy furniture and there are hundreds of books on the shelves, all of which are covered in dust. Old newspapers are in piles everywhere and although the furniture would have been grand in its time, it is now broken and battered. Huge heavy brocade curtains hang from the large window and most of them are yellow and bleached from the nicotine and sunlight. The clairvoyant introduces herself as Elvina Andrae De-Walt. She speaks in a very theatrical way and waves her arms as she speaks.

"Because you've come in together, you might get each other's messages."
I cast a critical eye over Elvina. She's wearing clothes that look like they've come from Victorian times: an off-white ruffled blouse that is tucked into a long purple velvet skirt and a black shawl that matches her fingerless lace gloves.
"Like I've said, because you've come in together, you might get each other's messages," she repeats, flinging her arms in the air. "The Spirits don't point to you, they just give messages through me." She sits, spreading out cards on the table between us.
"I'll start with you," she announces, turning to Mum. "I have a large gentleman here showing me a piece of meat. He wants to give you a hug."
Mum becomes serious before she answers.
"I think it's me brother-in-law."
"Well, he's very fond of you." Elvina smiles.
"He is." Mum nods.
"He's happy on the other side."
"Other side of what?" Mum asks, looking confused.
"He's not dead," I point out to Elvina.
"Well, someone's here," she says shortly, clearly getting annoyed.
"Unless he's died today," Mum frowns. I roll my eyes. Elvina turns to me and points.
"I can see you in a white car."
"We came in a white car," I sigh. I'm not at all impressed.
"Oh God! You are good, Elvina," Mum squeals.

Elvina smiles sadly. She takes Mum's hand and looks like she's going to cry.

"My dear, dear, love, I can see you've had a very big trauma in your life."

Mum snivels and nods her head.

"I've had a very big trauma. It was years ago, though."

Elvina throws her arms in the air.

"I knew it! What happened to you, my child?"

"I got married." Mum says, blowing her nose. Then she points at me, "I had her. I didn't want to get married, but my mother made me."

I stare at Mum. I've never calculated the year I was born and the year my parents got together. I am so shocked that I turn on her.

"You never told me you were pregnant with me when you married Pop!" I feel like a small child that's just been told there's no Father Christmas. Mum is very sheepish.

"I was only seventeen, Cathy. You had to get married in those days – it was a different age."

I feel numb with the revelation. Elvina can feel the awkwardness between me and Mum, so she quickly looks into her crystal ball.

"Cathy, I can see you on a white unicorn going towards a church," she states, causing Mum to gasp. This is the last straw for me and I sigh heavily, which makes Elvina annoyed with me. She bangs on the desk. "Are you a non-believer, Cathy?"

"It's not my cup of tea," I explain, nodding, "that's all ... why don't you prove me wrong?"

Elvina is furious but Mum pipes up.

"Oh Elvina, our Cathy's has had a terrible time just lately," she explains, placatingly. "Her husband has just left her for another woman."

I can't believe Mum has just told Elvina that my husband

has left me. I want to get up and walk out as the whole thing is a farce. Elvina knows I'm losing interest and suddenly becomes chirpy, taking my palm.

"Oh Cathy, I can see that you have three children - one girl and two boys."

I look pointedly at Elvina.

"No Elvina, I have one child, a daughter who is now twenty-seven. I can't have any more children because of my age."

Elvina ignores me and shuffles the cards. She seems embarrassed and focuses on Mum. "Right, Joan, I have an important message for you. I think your husband will pass over suddenly, without warning."

I can't believe what she's just said. Elvina leans in to Mum.

"Is there's something you want to ask me?"

Mum gasps and whispers "Will I be found innocent?"

Elvina stares at Mum then turns over another card.

"Joan, I can see a trickle of extra money coming into your household."

"Oh, that'll be my widow's pension," Mum smiles.

That's me done, so I stand up and put my coat on.

"Come on, Mum, were going."

Mum stands up and puts her coat on but Elvina jumps up and holds her hand out.

"That's fifty pounds please... with the special discount."

Mum gets the money out of her purse but just before she hands it over, I snatch it away and peel one twenty pound note from the fifty.

"I think it was worth ten pounds each. I'm sure you'll agree Elvina." She is shocked but takes the money anyway and Mum and I leave the house

"Come back anytime for friendly advice," Elvina shouts after us.

As we begin to drive home, Mum looks at me.

"You should have given Elvi Crème de- menth all of the money. She was good, wasn't she?"

"No, Mum. Actually she wasn't good, she was crap."

Mum shrugs her shoulders, sniffles and says "Well she gave me some good news."

****

When we get home, Mum decides to be nice to Pop considering he hasn't got long left on this earth, so she makes him his favourite tea of liver and onions with chips and peas. Even Rupert gets some. It looks revolting and it starts me reminiscing about my old life of fine dining: fillet steak, lobster, French cheeses and good wine. Now the Freak's buying these things for Fanny with the money he took out of the equity on *our* house. A rage comes over me and I have to walk into the garden to try and calm down. Mum can see I'm deep in thought, so she comes over to me and hugs me.

"Don't worry, pet. It'll all work out in the end. And when you're Pop goes, maybe we could buy a little red sports car between us? Oh, and we can go on holiday together."

The phone rings so Mum runs in to answer it. I walk further down the garden and sit on a rusty Victorian bench. After a minute, Mum finds me and sits next to me. There really isn't anywhere to hide in this house. I remember how big the house used to look when Steve and I were little, but now it just looks like what it is - a small, three-bedroomed semi-detached house with a beautiful garden, situated on a tree lined road. Mum taps my hand.

"We can go to bingo tonight, if you want?"

I decide to go to bed early and stare back at Donny.

CHAPTER 3

This morning, Mum drops a bombshell.

"Pop's in court."

"Why?" I ask, unable to believe what I'm hearing.

'Drink driving." Her answer is sharp. "I'm sick of him. I hope the judge throws the book at him today and locks him up."

Pop walks in carrying a suitcase.

"They're not going to lock him up. It's his first offence."

"We might be lucky." Mum smiles and pushes past me, walking towards her car. I offer to drive but she's having none of it, so I throw Pop's suitcase in the back while Mum gets in the front and revs the engine to death. Black smoke billows out of the exhaust. Pop sits in the passenger seat and looks like a little lamb going the slaughter.

"Pop, don't worry. They'll just slap your wrists, that's all," I say, trying to make him feel better.

Mum looks in the rear-view mirror so she can see me, then starts mouthing a conversation with me so that Pop can't hear. I fear that we'll all be killed at any moment.

"Mum, watch the road," I can feel my heart beating fast.

"Shut up, Cathy," Mum tuts. "I'll have you know I'm a very good driver."

There's tension in the car and I'll be glad when we arrive at the court. As we pull up at the lights, Pop points to a row of terraced houses that are for sale.

"Years ago I could have bought all of them for five

hundred pounds," he says with a true sense of nostalgia.

I look at the cottages and they're very quaint.

"Why didn't you buy them?"

"Because I didn't have five hundred pounds." With that, he looks at me like I'm stupid.

"You've never had any ambition Stanley," Mum sighs, shaking her head in disgust. "Not like me. I could have been someone."

The journey to the Magistrate's court is a long one because Mum goes the long way round and they're both bickering.

"You've never had any money because you've pissed it all up the wall," she snaps. "I should have married Walter."

Pop nods. "I wish you had."

We arrive at the Court and are greeted by the Usher, who shows Pop what court he's in. At 10am on the dot, the Usher calls us into Court. As we all file in, the three Magistrates stare at us: a man in the middle and women on either side of him. One of them has a kind face and seems young but the others are old and couldn't muster a smile if their life depended on it. The duty solicitor asks Pop to step into the witness box. Pop dodders over and sits inside.

"Who is representing you today, Mr Mathews?" the solicitor asks,

Pop puts on his theatrical voice and swings into action.

"I, your good lord, is representing myself."

The Magistrates can't quite believe what they're seeing as Mum takes out a small flask, some biscuits and her knitting.

She nudges me.

"Isn't that a lovely colour? I've started knitting for the Americans."

"Why are you knitting for the Americans?" I whisper, bemused.

"Because they're all dying from starvation and they've got no clothes or blankets."

"The Americans? Dying of starvation? That'll be a first. I think you mean the Africans."

Mum ignores me and carries on knitting. "Can you state your name please?" The Magistrates asks Pop.

Pop looks confused.

"You know my name, you've just said it."

"Can you state it for the record, sir?" the male Magistrate sighs.

Pop frowns. "I haven't got a record."

The Magistrates all make notes, then the male Magistrate asks, "You need to state your name for the record … our record."

Pop huffs and puffs before shouting, "Stanley Mathews. Like the great footballer Stanley Mathews who played football until he was fifty years of age. He was and still is the greatest footballer of all time and…"

"Thank you for that, Mr Mathews," the male Magistrate smirks. "I appreciate your love for the great footballer, but we need to continue."

"I wish he had Stanley Mathews' money instead of his name," Mum shouts.

Mum and Pop are about to start bickering when the Magistrate bangs a small hammer on the desk.

"Let us carry on with the matter in hand."

"Lock him up and throw away the key," Mum pipes up.

The male Magistrate tries to compose himself and carries on the questioning while the younger female Magistrate sniggers.

"On the eleventh of May, twenty fifteen," he begins, "you were travelling along Corporation Street in South Yorkshire when officer 3442 asked you to step out of the car because he had a suspicion that you had been drinking."

Pop salutes the Magistrates like he's in the army and says "Correct."

The Magistrate continues the questioning.

"The officer found you to be over the limit. In your defence, you said you hadn't eaten and had only consumed two pints of lager, which would have resulted in the alcohol going through your blood stream quicker than usual. Have you anything to add to that, Mr Mathews?"

Pop points to Mum.

"She doesn't do me any breakfast anymore. In fact, she doesn't do any cooking anymore. She's a lazy mew."

Mum jumps up and stabs Pop in the arm with one of her knitting needles.

"Wait until I get you home, Stanley."

All the Magistrates start to laugh, they can't help it. All of a sudden, Pop's hearing aid starts making a high pitched sound. Pop panics.

"Hang on. I think I've tuned into Cavalier Taxis," he fiddles around with his hearing aid but he can't turn it down. Mum leans forward and slaps Pop on the arm.

"Turn it off. I'll tell you what they say."

The bench look at each other and smile. The charges continue.

"You were taken to the station and found to be over the legal limit. Your reading was 60mg. How do you plead?"

Mum jumps up: "Guilty as charged."

Pop can't hear a thing and is looking round the room. He turns to Mum.

"What did he say?"

This is Mum's moment of glory and she really goes for it.

"He said you're a disgrace to your family and a good-for-nothing fecking eejit."

"Mrs Mathews, sit down and be quiet," says the male Magistrate, who is now red in the face. "Don't you use that tone with me, young man," Shouts Mum.

I try and tug on Mum's coat so that she sits down, but she won't.

"This is a serious offence and one I can't deal with lightly." The Magistrate in the middle booms at her sternly.

"Glad to hear it," Mum shouts.

Pop looks at Mum and shrugs his shoulders. Mum becomes stern and leans into Pop.

"He said you can only go out three times a week and on Thursdays you *have* to take me to bingo... oh, and Cathy, now her husband has left her for another woman."

All three magistrates look at me and I can feel my face going bright red. I feel powerless to the whole situation and I want the floor to swallow me up. "Are you clear on the charges, Mr Mathews?" asks the Magistrate.

"He's clear alright, he watched Colombo for years – he knows the system," Mum puts her hands on her hips as she makes her point. Then, as the Magistrates start laughing, she decides to sit back down.

"Are there any mitigating circumstances that you want to put before the court?" the young Magistrate asks. Pop shakes his head. The young Magistrate feels sorry for him and smiles. "Nothing? Maybe something you would change about that particular day?"

Pop thinks for a moment. Then nods his head.

"Yeah, I wish I'd have had a few more pints. I'd rather get hung for a sheep than a lamb."

The female Magistrate raises her eyebrows, urging Pop to be quiet, but he doesn't heed her warning. "And I wish I'd have stayed out longer. The earlier I come home, the more time she has to nag me. She'd drive Jesus to drink, my Joan."

Mum stands up and digs him in the arm.

"Don't blaspheme the bloody lord, you drunken git."

The male Magistrate composes himself and looks at Pop.

"I'm sorry, Mr Mathews, but I'm going to have to ban you from driving."

I lean over and tell Pop what's been said. Pop smiles then looks at the Magistrate, takes his driving license out of his pocket and holds it out in front of him. The Usher takes it off Pop and hands it to the Magistrates.

"It's ok son, you can have it," he says quietly. "I only use the car to go to the pub and back."

"Oh, thank you your Majesty," Mum says, jumping up. "He needs to be off the road."

"Why are you saying your majesty?" I ask, nudging her.

"Because it's a Magistrate's court, Cathy." Mum looks at me with disgust. "Where do you want to go?" she continues, as we leave the court and get in the car.

Pop points ahead. "The pub."

****

I decide not to get out of bed today, as there doesn't seem any point. I am officially in mourning and long for my old life back. The life that up until recently, seemed so perfect. Maybe I can live in ignorant bliss, turn a blind eye to Tom's indiscretions and just get back to normal? However, deep down I know I can't even consider it. The house is quiet for once. Mum and Pop have gone to market to get all their bargains: cheap chicken pieces that take forever to cook, coffee that tastes of treacle and soil, pies that have no fillings in them and potted beef and shrimp in plastic containers. Their shopping list has never changed throughout my life: a piece of beef or chicken on a Sunday, steak on a Thursday and Mum's homemade curry on a Friday. Monday is bubble and squeak, which in layman's terms is the leftovers from Sunday dinner. Tins of fruit salad with carnation cream come after most meals. I remember sleeping over one Friday night when I was pregnant and I didn't want to be alone at home. Pop came in with a plate full of cow heal and tripe. I was sick at the sight of it and when I'd finally stopped being sick, the two of them sat and chomped on a plate full of tripe covered with salt, pepper and vinegar.

I know I came across as a food snob at the time but Tom and I just didn't eat like that. We were adventurous; we ate out at Jamie Oliver's restaurant and other fine establishments. A treat for Mum and Pop is fish and chips from the chippy on Good Friday. I begin to think about Mum and Pop's life. I wish they'd spend some money on themselves, go out more or go on holiday, but they won't. Then a terrible realisation comes over me - maybe when they both pass over, I will still be here in the house, alone with the crushed velvet curtains with matching knitting basket and the freestanding white Belling cooker. The thought makes me close my eyes and turn over.

****

It's ten past twelve when the doorbell rings. I try to ignore it but whoever it is won't go away. Eventually I go downstairs and open the front door. There in front of me stands Tom, my Tom. He's wearing a striped jumper and a pair of jeans. He never wears jeans, he doesn't like them, he says they are made for poor people who need clothes to be robust and that will last a life time. I'm speechless and stand staring at him; he appears very nervous because his face is twitching and he keeps scratching his balls. Maybe he has a nasty infection off Fanny? Then, without any warning, he leans in and kisses me on the cheek. It's the type of kiss you would give a long lost friend or your mother. I can't remember inviting him in, but there he is bold as brash in my mother and father's lounge. I don't know what to say. Why have I suddenly become mute when only this morning I had so much hatred for him and wanted to read him the riot act and beat him within an inch of his life? He looks at me with great pity.

"Oh, Cathy, I've missed you. I didn't think I would, but I have."

What was I supposed to say to that? I sit down on the sofa and Tom sits opposite me. It takes me two minutes to ask him why.

"Tom, how did you get in so much debt and why did you have an affair?"

At first he can't answer me. Instead, he looks awkward and edgy, like he doesn't have an answer. I calmly ask again. He takes a deep breath and replies.

"Cathy, you know we haven't been getting on for years … have we?"

"That's news to me," I snap, "Is this a sex thing?"

"No, Cathy, it's not a sex thing." He has the cheek to look hurt as he replies.

I jump up and start pacing up and down with my voice slightly raised.

"It must be, otherwise you wouldn't have dipped your LITTLE wick at the first opportunity... that's assuming it is your first fling."

Tom stares at me.

"Cathy, that's not fair."

"What's fair about you leaving me for your mousey little piss-smelling secretary?" I laugh hysterically.

Tom stands up to leave so I immediately push him back down onto the sofa. I'm determined to have my explanation. "Cathy, she was there for me," he says, putting his head down as he speaks, "It just happened, it wasn't planned."

I grin at him.

"Right, let me get this straight. You've only slept with her once?"

Tom gets his rash; the one that starts from his neck and within a minute covers his face. I walk up to him and push my face into his.

"You'd better start talking, Tom, and it better be good."

Tom can't speak, which angers me even more.

"Go on, Tom, admit it! How long were you cheating on me?" I shout at the top of my voice.

Still no answer. I laugh out loud.

"Come on, tell me. This isn't about you pinching an extra hundred pounds in a Monopoly game, or sitting me near the mirror when we play cards so you always win. I could live with that. Why did you get behind on the mortgage? You've got a good business, for Christ's sake. This is about you being a liar and a cheat and you still can't come clean. All you did was leave me a pathetic note stating all the things you thought were wrong about me."

Tom squirms on the sofa. He's never seen me like this and now he's about to get everything. I'm not holding back. I sit next to him and he looks like he's scared to death, which pleases me. I very slowly and gently whisper to him.

"Was it in the office at work?"

He nods his head. I surprise myself because I'm not jealous. Instead, I decide I really need to know the finer details.

"Did you fall and your tongue accidently slipped into her mouth?"

"For God's sake, Cathy," he says, jumping up, "why are you doing this?"

I sit grinning at him and he hasn't a clue how to handle me.

"What did you do with the money?" I ask again.

Tom is sheepish but I won't let it go. When he finally answers, he's practically whispering.

"I got into trouble with credit cards and a loan from the bank, then they piled on the interest so I took out one loan after another and it all got out of hand … I'm sorry."

"You obviously wasn't spending it on me, you little creep." I am livid. "*You* took my money and squandered it. You were showering another woman with presents, no doubt. You were reckless and you stole from me and for that, I will never forgive you."

Tom suddenly clutches his stomach and his face goes white as a sheet. I think he's doing this to divert the questioning away from him, but then his face goes a greeny-colour and he immediately rushes to the downstairs toilet. As he does, his phone rings and it's Fanny. The devil in me takes over. I answer it.

"Hi Fanny, Tom's just in the bathroom at the moment getting showered and dressed." The phone is silent. "How's it going?" I ask.

Fanny is clearly shocked to the core when she replies.

"What a strange thing to ask. Anyway, who are you?"

"It's me, Cathy, Tom's wife." I laugh "Do you remember?"

Fanny immediately puts the phone down on me. I quickly re-dial her number but she doesn't answer. I ring the new office number. She obviously hasn't a clue that I know where the new office premises are. The receptionist puts me straight through and I hear the shrill of her voice again.

"Good afternoon, Frances Smith speaking."

I dive in for the kill. "Don't you dare put the phone down or I will come over and speak to you in the office in front of all your colleagues, and you wouldn't want that, would you?" Fanny is silent. I suddenly become chirpy.

"Tom's come round so I could look at his rash. It flares up every now and then. He got it whilst we were on holiday in Bangkok."

Fanny remains silent but her breathing is laboured. I carry on talking and I find it all very amusing.

"We're very liberal, me and Tom. We're both bisexual and Tom can't say no to sex. I have to keep a check on his penis. I'm the only one that he trusts." She sounds like she's snivelling which makes me worse. "Fanny, don't ever let Tom forget his tablets when you both go away for work or a holiday. He will be ever so poorly if he doesn't have them. He disguises them in a multivitamin jar." I laugh to myself, knowing Tom is hooked on multivitamins. Before I hang up the phone I sarcastically say "You see, being the other woman doesn't make you special Fanny. You're second, the runner up, so I'm afraid you don't get a prize and he will do the same to you." I shout out to Tom. "Tom, your dirty little secret is on the phone. Will you phone her back when you're dressed?"

Tom doesn't reply because he's too busy blowing raspberries out of the arsehole he normally talks from. I come back to Fanny in a chirpy voice.

"He'll call you when we've had some lunch, goodbye."

I quickly delete how many minutes I've been on the phone to her and I scan through his messages. One message is from her to him and it simply reads 'I'm missing your pork dagger, come home ASAP.' He replies 'I will snicker doodle you when I get back home,' followed by a graphic description of what he did to her with a chocolate Snickers bar. At this point I actually thank the Lord that I am allergic to peanuts. Tom comes out of the bathroom looking ashen.

"I'm sorry about that, Cathy."

"Why are you saying sorry?" I smile. "I always knew you were a shit house."

Before Tom can answer me, his mobile rings again.

"I'll take this in the car, if you don't mind," he whispers to me. "It's business." As he walks through the door I hear him say "No, she's not like that. No nothing's happened."

Tom is ages in the car and when he finally comes back in, he stares at me for what seems like hours.

"You've changed since I met you, Cathy."

"Yes I have," I laugh. "I've got fat."

"No, Cathy, you're still gorgeous to me."

"Then why did you leave me for a woman who looks like a thin Ann Widdecombe?"

"That's the old Cathy, witty and full of fun," Tom laughs out loud.

"What do you want Tom?" I'm becoming bored now.

He fumbles in his jacket pocket and hands me a small wad of cash with a patronising smile.

"I knew you wouldn't have any money and I feel it's my duty to pay maintenance to you. After all, I did abandon you... and my solicitor said it would look better for me in court."

I stand frozen.

"Court?" I say in a squeaky voice.

"Well I presume you wouldn't have me back ... would you?"

A rage comes over me and I run at him, thumping him on

his chest as I do so. After a few minutes I'm exhausted and sit on the sofa sobbing. Tom looks at me with tears in his eyes. He walks over to me and puts his arms around me. I can feel his strong muscles through his cheap striped jumper that I know Fanny has probably bought for him. The flood gates open and as I inhale his aftershave, I cry like a baby with little bubbles and snorts coming out of my nose. Words randomly pop out of my mouth like 'court?', 'why?', 'why her?', 'what's wrong with me?' I make a complete fool of myself and the more I cry, the more Tom hugs me. He makes noises like, 'there, there' and 'oh my sweet Cathy', 'let's get the old sparkle back' and 'I can always come back and we can start again.' We sit and embrace and then Tom begins to caress me. He kisses my neck and starts to fondle my droopy breasts, scooping them up and then letting them fall back on my chest with a slap. That old familiar feeling comes back, I lead Tom upstairs to my old bedroom and in a defiant moment I tear down Donny Osmond's poster and throw it on the floor. I fall backwards onto the bed. Tom doesn't wait to be asked twice and strips off to the waist. He's hungry for me and I wallow in his desire. Tom kisses me passionately and I know at that moment that I've neglected him sexually. All he ever wanted was to be loved by me. As he playfully kisses me, he laughs and says, "Maybe you could be my mistress, Cathy?"

I stare at Tom's face. Has he really just said that to me? Tom realises what he's said and squeezes me tight.

"Cathy, don't go all righteous on me. You're like a cuddly pair of old slippers, that's what I love about you."

Every inch of my body freezes as I stare at this man, a man I don't know, have never known. Tom's an adulterer and now he wants sad old Cathy to be his mistress and get to the bottom of the queue. A rage comes over me like I've never known and everything I want to say comes flooding out. Tom can't get ready fast enough and all he keeps saying is "You've taken it all wrong, Cathy, you always do." The swear words come and I even remember a few words Louise had used. However, the word that has the most impact is when I call him an arse-wipe. His face is a picture because the worst thing I've ever called him before is a vain pig and a monster. Tom runs out of the bedroom and towards the stairs, his legs wobbly with shock. He can't navigate the stairs though, and halfway down he loses his footing and rolls down every stair until he hits the hall floor. As he's lying in the hallway, groaning, Mum and Pop come through the door with bags of shopping. Mum drops the bags on the floor and starts to hit Tom with an umbrella she's bought from the Donkey Sanctuary. Pop picks up Rupert, who isn't at all interested in what's going on, and walks into the lounge with him.

"You don't want to witness all that, do you, Richard?" I can hear Pop saying to the dog.

Tom manages to get out of the door but Mum is just as fast and chases him up the path, trying to hit him with a frozen chicken in a carrier bag.

"God, you mad cow, you're trying to kill me," screams Tom.

"You deserve to die. You leave all your wet dirty towels all over the bathroom floor," Mum screams like a warrior.

****

Mum pours us both a large glass of sherry and we sit in the kitchen to calm down. I swig the sherry, look at Mum and for a split second, I have a moment with her; an understanding of life and men. Then we both fall into fits of laughter whilst Pop is in the lounge watching the wrestling on TV. After three glasses of sherry I pour my heart out to Mum and for once, she doesn't interrupt me. I explain that I think I've neglected him and how we never have sex anymore, so I really feel it's partly my fault he's had the affair. When I finish talking, she gets hold of my hands.

"Cathy, you're not to be blaming yourself. Men are men, they're wired up wrong, their dicks rule their heads."

I laugh hysterically because in fifty-four years, I have never heard my mother say the word 'dick', and the fact that she had a straight face made it funnier. It's as if we've both found a new friend in each other.

"Mum, why did I let him in and why did I try and seduce him after all he's done?" I ask quietly, hugging her. "Why don't I hate him?"

"Oh, Cathy," she sighs, stroking my hair. "It takes years to really hate them. Look at me and ya Pop. It's taken me over fifty years … give it time love."

When we run out of sherry, I open the chilled wine. Mum beams.

"I could get used to this Shirley Valentine stuff." I smile at her, feeling glad to be near her and back in the safety of our old house. Another glass of wine inside Mum and her tongue starts loosen. "Your father was really kinky years ago."

"Mum, please, not now," I shake my head and plead, but it falls on deaf ears.

"He used to get in bed and say, 'Joan can I get on?' Then, years later when he became really adventurous, he would say, 'can I get under?' – disgusting it was... and now, Cathy, I have the devastating news from Cream-del-monte that he will be taken any day. So there's hope for us all. Remember, God moves in mysterious ways."

CHAPTER 4

It feels strange waking up with Louise next to me in bed. It feels like it did years ago when I was allowed to have Jane stay overnight. We sit talking for a while then Mum brings a letter in to me: a large brown envelope – that can only mean it's official. When I read the letter I discover that it's from Tom's solicitor and it has a few extra things added to the list of what makes me such a terrible wife:

- The marriage has broken down irretrievably;

- Unreasonable behaviour;

- Physical violence (from me to him);

- Verbal abuse;

- Insults and threats (from both me and Mum);

Furthermore, he quoted "There was Violence and abusive behaviour within the marriage. My wife comes from a violent family and I feel it is learnt behaviour."

I laugh.

"That's the battering Mum gave him, Louise."

Louise chuckles. I look at Mum.

"There's no mention of adultery or desertion?"

Louise takes the letter off me and laughs.

"The cheek of him. I'll tell you what, Mum, it's put me off marriage altogether. I knew he was a difficult man, but this is all lies and it's all been done very quickly."

"That's because I'm a bad wife." I laugh "It's only taken

three months for the divorce to come through and your father paid for it."

Mum and I look at each other with a smile. She sits on the bed, deep in thought.

"You can't get divorced if you're a Catholic," she informs me. "Catholics have to stay together through anger, hatred and misery – just like the good lord intended."

"Some people are madly in love and lust and can't keep their hands of each other." Louise laughs.

Pop walks in the bedroom and looks at us all. He shakes his head as he says, "Getting married for sex is like buying a Jumbo jet for the free peanuts."

"What a lovely thing to say." Mum says, smiling at him.

"Grandad, how much does it cost to get married?"

"I don't know, I'm still paying," Pop grunts.

"Oh, ignore him, the silly ole fool," Mum cackles.

****

It's late afternoon. Louise and I sit on the sofa, talk about her work as a midwife. Mum is making a stew and her first ever attempt at dumplings. After about an hour, I walk into the kitchen to make coffee for us all. Mum is standing at the work top and there's flour everywhere.

"Can I help, Mum?"

"No it's fine, it's all under control." Mum shakes her head.

"Mum, why are the dumplings shaped like fingers?" I enquire.

"Don't be interfering Cathy." Mum becomes annoyed. "Or me and you will fall out. Besides, that's what it says on the packet."

I pick up the packet and it reads 'Roll dumplings with flowered fingers'. I can't be bothered getting into an argument with Mum so I go back into the lounge and sit with Louise.

The meal is a complete disaster. The dumplings look like fat pigs' trotters and the meat in the stew is really chewy. I feel sorry for Mum but she won't accept any help from anyone, especially Pop. At 8pm, I offer to buy fish and chips for everyone but Mum won't agree.

"Cathy you're very extravagant and you need to pull your belt in now you're on your own."

Pop stops watching the news and turns to me.

"The food hasn't gone to waste. Little Ronald has eaten all the meat."

I look at Rupert and feel sorry for him. Not only is he in a new home, his name gets changed every other day. Surely things are going to improve soon.

And improve they do! Jane comes back from Australia and wants to know the whole sorry story about my break up. Jane has never liked Tom and always lets everyone know how she feels. The first day she met him her words were "What the hell … he's too big for his own boots." I laughed it off, explaining that it was his private education in an all boys' school that sometimes makes him come across as arrogant. When we got engaged, she was really pissed off and Tom accused her of being jealous. The day we got married Jane said nothing. There wasn't really any point because it was obvious to everyone that the wedding was going ahead. Not everyone approved of Tom and his family. Auntie Val flatly refused to come to the wedding. Mum knew the reason, but Auntie Val told me that she was in bed with an old war wound. Funny, since she'd never been in the war. The morning I put on my wedding dress, Mum cried with happiness. Pop looked me straight in the eye and said, "Cathy, you don't have to go ahead with this if you don't want to." I was horrified by what he had said but laughed it off. On the way to the church I had serious doubts about going through with the wedding and at one point, I nearly told the driver to turn around. It wasn't Tom I was thinking about when I made the decision to let it all go ahead, it was all the guests who had made a huge effort to attend. So I sipped on a glass of Champagne and put it down to wedding day nerves. By the time I got to the church I'd got carried away with the whole wedding thing and happily walked down the aisle, linking my arm through Pop's.

Jane had the time of her life, mainly because she ended up copping off with Tom's friend and at the end of the evening, in her inebriated state, she shouted "What an effing good piss up has been had by all." It was true that Tom's parents were rich compared to mine. Polly and Gerrard made our wedding into the social event of the year. Polly completely took over, insisting on only the very best for her son; she also insisted on paying for everything. This hurt Mum and Pop and I felt really bad about how Tom's parents were behaving. The only way I could handle the situation was to tell Mum and Pop that, in their world and circles, it was a family tradition that the first son's marriage was paid for by his parents. In reality I knew Polly's game. Polly thought she was royalty and she wanted to have everything perfect. Everyone knew she was doing it to impress her friends and make herself feel good. Tom and I had never been brought into the equation. All my Mum wanted to do was to buy her only daughter her wedding dress and Pop wanted to get his old MG midget out of the garage and dress it up. When I told Polly, though, she nearly had a nervous breakdown and told me it had already been sorted: I was having a vintage yellow Rolls Royce with a grey roof and my dress, which was being made in Paris, was being picked up the following week by herself and five of her friends. All this feels like a lifetime ago.

I can't wait to see Jane but Mum won't let me use the car and insists on driving me to Jane's house. When Jane opens the door she looks like a sex goddess, beautifully tanned and happy. I feel safe now that my friend of fifty years is back on English soil. Mum insists on coming inside with me and for twenty minutes I can't get a word in edgeways. Mum tells Jane everything about how Tom has treated me and how she'd given him a good hiding for trying to take advantage of me. She chats to Jane like I'm not there, then takes her into the utility room where I can hear her say "Jane, I think our Cathy's an alcoholic and it's all his fault."

"Oh, Joan, I don't think she is. She's just going through a bad patch. It'll pass," Jane reassures Mum. When Mum's about to leave, she spots a fruit bowl on Jane's table with painted oranges and lemons on it. She picks it up and admires it.

"Jane, where did you get this lovely bowl from?"

"The pound shop," Jane laughs.

Mum is mesmerized.

"How much was it?"

"A pound, Joan." Jane looks at me and smiles.

"Can I have it?"

"Of course you can." Jane says with a nod.

I'm grateful that Jane knows Mum – it makes situations like this a lot less awkward. Then I suddenly remember a situation years ago, when Mum and Pop met Polly and Gerrard. Polly was bragging about all her worldly goods and antiques. She laughed hysterically and over-the-top when she said "People, people, everything in this house is for sale, take your pick." Ten minutes later, Mum found a Kenwood chef mixer that cost over a hundred pounds, so she stashed it in a carrier bag and put two pound coins into Polly's hand. This amused Polly and her friends, as she thought Mum was having a laugh with her by thinking it was some type of up-market jumble sale. So when Polly took the two pound coin and put it in her pocket, it was a done deal for Mum. At the end of the evening Mum refused to give the mixer back, which resulted in Polly being red-faced and embarrassed. For a good twenty-five years, Polly would ask me through gritted teeth "Is *my* mixer still working?" and I would smile sweetly at her and say nothing. Mum finally leaves and Jane uncorks a bottle of wine before opening her laptop, which is loaded with holiday pictures and scenery from Australia. Thirty per cent of the pictures are of scenery and the beach whilst the other seventy per cent are of Jane with various men in night clubs, sunbathing and doing what we both do best – drinking.

****

It's 2am and Jane and I are talking over how I feel about Tom leaving me for another woman. Jane puts Tom down at every opportunity and I agree with her and add my own bit, but some things I say are made up and I do it because I want to make myself feel better. At 3.10am, I'm crying my eyes out in Jane's spare bedroom and Jane is shouting at me from her bed.

"Cathy, shut up! We need to get some sleep. He's not worth it."

I slide back to being four years old again; arguing with Jane in-between blowing my runny nose.

"It's all right for you, you're footloose and fancy-free, not a care in the world. I've lost everything and he's labelled me as a bad wife."

"So bloody what," Jane shouts back, "He's a prick."

Eventually I shut up because I know Jane can't function without sleep. When I wake up in the morning I look like an albino frog. My eyes are puffy from crying and my hair is stuck up. The lipstick I kept re-applying last night whilst telling myself I was very attractive, is now smeared all over my face. When I walk into the kitchen, Jane laughs.

"Would you look at the state of you and the price of fish." She hands me a cup of coffee. "We'd better get you sorted out for tonight."

"Jane, I'm not up for going out." I shake my head, "Honestly, it's the last thing on my mind."

"Oh yes you are." Jane says with a laugh. She plugs in the electric rollers and turns on the shower. "Right, Cathy, you're going in ... brace yourself."

****

We walk through the doors of the Fox and Vixen and I catch a glimpse of myself in the entrance mirror. I look like Tony Blackburn. My hair became frizzy earlier, so Jane has styled it in an old fashioned bob. This, combined with the fact that she has made me wear her leather boots, has turned me into a throwback of Purdy from the Avengers. I have an awful feeling that people will laugh at me and start pointing their fingers in disgust. We are shown to a table at the side of the room and, after only a minute or two, Jane is chatting to a man half her age. I wish I'd never agreed to come on a speed dating night and I can't believe how nervous I feel when a six foot bald man walks towards me. He looks like a bouncer and for a second I think he's going to throw me out for looking so ridiculous. When he sits down facing me, I can see he's full of tattoos and looks like a walking ink pad. I am so stunned that I just sit and stare at him. He points to his head, which has a tattoo of a barcode on it.

"This is my old army number."

I look at the other side of his head which has a line of numbers. I point at them and say "What's that, your therapist's number?"

He doesn't reply. I stare at him until the bell rings. The next man to come over is half my age, painfully thin, and is wearing round glasses that are too big for his head. He bends over and shakes my hand – it's so weak that it feels more like a tickle than a handshake. Not like Tom - he has a firm, strong handshake. After a minute he tells me his name is Quentin and that he thinks he's gay. He confesses the only reason he's come speed dating is because his Mum bought him the five pound ticket. I spend all of five minutes counselling him, telling him he must be true to himself and find real happiness. That was easy for me to say. The third man is elderly; I'd say nearly as old as Pop. He sits down and immediately starts talking about his dead wife. At one point he asks me if I am psychic and passes me a pile of rings and chains to see if I can pick up a message from her. I spend five minutes telling him how sorry I am that he's a widower. He looks very sad and lonely as he leaves the table. It makes me wonder what it's all about: we get married, have a family, work, and then we die. What an awful way of looking at things.

The fourth man is Doug and again, he's a lot older than me. He sits down, burps and says "Howdy partner, do you want to have some fun?" I look over to where Jane is sitting and stare at her while she takes a man's number off him. I am so bored, it's painful. Doug tries to make me laugh.

"What do you call a man with a spade in his head?"

"Doug," I reply to the old joke.

He laughs his head off even though it was his joke. Then,

for the second half… "What do you call a man with no spade in his head?"

I can't be bothered answering and the tension in his face makes him look like he's ready to burst. When I still don't reply, he jumps up and shouts, "Douglas!" whilst bursting into a fit of laughter. I thank God when the bell rings. I am now losing the will to live and desperately want to go home. Then, to my horror, a John Travolta lookalike swaggers towards me, smiling from ear to ear. He's dressed in a cream suit, black shirt and his hair is gelled in a quiff. His arse hasn't even touched the chair when he starts with his cheesy talk.

"Do you know what my shirt is made of?"

I shake my head.

"Boyfriend material," he laughs, then he goes straight on to the next gag. "I want to live in your socks so I can be with you every step of the way."

There's no reply from me but that doesn't stop him.

"Is your daddy a baker? Because you've got lovely buns."

This is more than I could take and when Jane looks across at me, my eyes plead with her to rescue me. She runs over and takes the man's hand.

"I think you'll find it's my turn now."

The man is shocked and looks Jane up and down.

"You? But you're a woman."

"Oh yes, so I am," Jane laughs, then leans into him and whispers, "I'm bisexual."

The man's face lights up.

"Oh, I'll hang around then, if that's OK?"

Jane gives him a look that could kill and he walks away from the table. Edging out of his pocket is *The Little Book of Chat-up Lines*. I smile to myself.

"Just give it time." Says Jane, sitting down to face me.

"Jane, I can't do this. It isn't me," I reply wearily.

Jane thinks for a minute.

"OK, just hang on for one more. There's a guy over there and I want his number."

I look across the room to see a man in his thirties, smiling at Jane. There's a small gap until the final man approaches me. He fiddles with his wedding ring and desperately tries to remove it before he sits down. A wave of anger comes over me and I give him a piece of my mind, reminding him what a dangerous game he is playing and how people get hurt because of dickheads like him. He's gobsmacked and can't answer me back. My voice gets louder and louder and people at other tables start looking over. Jane runs over to see what is wrong. I stand up and almost shout at her.

"This little shit is married and probably after sex. He has no idea of the hurt and pain he will cause to his wife or partner." I lean into him. "Have you got children?"

He looks at me with total fear in his eyes.

"Err, yeah, but were not getting on and … she doesn't understand me … and …"

"I don't understand you," I sneer. "Now get out of here before I kick your bollocks to the back of your throat."

The man runs out of the pub and Jane is gobsmacked by my outburst. We decide to leave and go to the pub across the road. Jane goes on about the incident all night and each time she tells the story out loud, she laughs longer. I'm still fed up and I don't want to be part of this game, but I also don't want to be single. I want my old life back, even if it does sound shallow… I don't care.

CHAPTER 5

It's the morning after the speed dating and I'm tired and drained. I can't help but wonder why I went in the first place. Every little thing is irritating me and I feel very unsettled. Mum and Pop have gone to the library because there's a talk on about getting older and keeping fit. When I look out of the kitchen window and see the state of their dustbins outside, I'm furious. Not one thing is being recycled – it is all a huge dumping ground for plastics, bottles, old jumpers and tins. Out of pure boredom I put on the marigold gloves and go outside to sort the rubbish out. I must have been outside for ages when I hear Mum and Pop talking in the kitchen. Pop speaks first.

"Joan, look at our Cathy looking through the bins."

"She must be hungry," Mum says, concerned.

"I'm not looking for food." I shout to them both, "I'm recycling all this rubbish into the correct bins." I walk into the kitchen, look at them both and say "You can get fined a thousand pounds for not using the correct bins, didn't you know?"

"I'm not sorting through rubbish at my age!" Mum looks horrified, "And the rates we pay – it's a disgrace. It shouldn't be called Yorkshire council, it should be Dick Emery council."

"What are you on about woman?" asks Pop as he looks across at her, "Dick Emery? He was a comedian."

"That's exactly what I'm saying. The council are a load of comedians," Mum cackles.

Pop can't leave it.

"It's Dick Turpin. He robbed from the poor."

"And that's what the council are doing to us." Mum nods.

I look at mum and feel utterly drained. Pop has some lunch and decides to take Rupert for a walk. The little dog has become Pop's new best friend and both of them get a lot of pleasure from wandering around the allotments, with Pop talking to his friends and Rupert shitting on the residents' vegetables. Rupert also sleeps at the end of Pop's bed, which is something he was never allowed to do before. Mum's packing up a parcel to send to Africa. It's filled with little cardigans, hats and gloves. I don't know what to do with myself and I feel like I'm in no man's land. I can't go out because I've nowhere to go and Mum wants me to go to the market with her to do a bit of shopping, but I really can't be bothered. I sit on the back step and I long for a cigarette. I gave up smoking ten years ago and at the time I thought it was the hardest thing I'd ever have to do. Sitting here today, on my mother's door step, I realise it wasn't - being dumped at fifty-four is far worse. Mum comes to the step and taps me on the shoulder.

"Cathy, don't sit on the step, lovey, you'll get chin cough."

I suddenly become really pissed off with Mum and fly off the handle.

"Mum, what are all these stupid sayings like *chin cough*? What is 'chin cough?' And what is 'I'm sat here like piffy on a rock bun?'"

"I don't know," she shrugs.

"And what were the other ones you used to say to me and Steven?" I stand up, "'Stop crying or you'll get something to cry for' and 'eat all your carrots or else you'll go blind.' You've never seen a rabbit with a pair of glasses on, have you?"

Mum is in shock at my outburst. I walk out of the kitchen and go to lie down on my bed. Why is my life so shit? And more to the point, when will it ever end? I look through my old drawer and find a picture of David Cassidy. I regret tearing down the poster of Donny Osmond in a moment of madness, so I take the blu-tack and replace Donny with David Cassidy. I lie on the bed, staring at the poster. I never expected my life to be like this when I was fifteen years of age and madly in love with both David and Donny. I remember asking Mum whether you could marry two people at the same time. She was horrified and said "No, Cathy, you can't, you'll be done for buggery." I told everyone at school that they couldn't commit an act of buggery. That was until the teacher came over to me and told me never to mention *that word* again. So I never mentioned Donny or David after that.

I fall into a disturbed sleep. In my dream I can hear women cackling, like Mum does when she finds something funny. Then a gargoyle starts to chase me and I have nowhere to run. Fanny and the Freak get in a lift and I can see them kissing and exchanging bars of chocolate with each other. Then the gargoyle catches up with me and I can see his angry face- the closer he gets the more I can smell honeysuckle perfume on him. I wake with a start with Mum bending over me.

"I've brought you a cup of tea, Cathy."

I jump out of bed in a daze and as I do so, I bang my toe on the bedside cabinet. I'm hopping on one foot and cursing as I go. Mum jumps forward and immediately smacks the table.

"Naughty table for hurting Cathy."

I look at Mum and burst out laughing. Mum looks at me like I've lost the plot. I pat the bed for her to sit next to me.

"I'm sorry for being so horrible to you. It's not your fault,

Mum."

"It's all right, Cathy." She gives me a hug, "You're going through a rough patch, that's all. You've got to have someone to take it out on. Besides, it takes my mind off things and stops me picking on your dad."

"Thank you Mum," I sit up and sip on the tea. "I'll clean the house through for you, give you a rest."

Mum is annoyed.

"There's nothing wrong with the house, Cathy. "What are you trying to say?"

I sigh heavily. "Ok I'll cook us all a meal, my treat. Maybe a pasta dish or a chili?"

"We don't eat any of that foreign muck, Cathy." Mum says as she walks to the door, "Pop had a Vesta curry when you and Steven were little; it made him ill for three weeks."

****

I decide to go to Jane's for the evening so she can help me plan my life and get me back on track. Jane is in an expert in break-ups, having eleven under her belt, so there isn't much she doesn't know. We sip a glass of wine on the sofa and I want Jane to tell me all about the misery of splitting up in the hope that it will make me feel better. Jane doesn't talk about her break-ups though and this disappoints me. She's told me in the past but I never really listened because I was wallowing in domestic bliss. Now I want all the gory details, but instead she tells me about the guy she met at speed dating; apparently he's a Danish gymnast and works for a traveling circus. She said he was flipping her around the bedroom like a rubber ball, at one point even jumping off the wardrobe and landing in the exact spot to enter her. Am I impressed? No. It's Thursday evening and I want pizza and rosé wine like the good old days when me and Tom were a couple. Jane brings out all the pictures of the two of us as we are growing up, but nothing can put a smile on my face. I am clearly becoming a miserable old bag. After becoming extremely drunk, Jane and I start with a deep and meaningful conversation. Jane holds no punches when she says her piece.

"Listen Cathy, he's a shit. Do you remember when you lived together and he got fed up, so he told his mother to ring you up and tell you it was all over?"

"You're right, what type of man does that?" I nod.

"A shit like Tom." Jane opens another bottle of wine. I know she is right, so what can I say? Jane carries on. "I remember when he didn't bring you flowers on the day you gave birth to Louise and his mother told him to buy you some." This sets Jane off into a rant and there is no stopping her. "All that shit with Lisa, his shag buddy… we don't know if they carried on sleeping with one another do we?" Jane is right. This has crossed my mind on more than one occasion. Jane is still angry. "He had plenty of opportunity Cathy, he was away on business all week."

"The thing I can't get over is why I had to lose the house and the car? Why didn't he just leave me?" I cringe as I say this.

Jane shrugs her shoulders. "Who knows what goes through his head and what he's been up to?"

It makes me think long and hard.. Jane's made a very good point about Lisa and Tom. I can feel myself getting angrier and angrier as I recall what has happened between us. I'm in such a temper that I ring Polly to give her a piece of my mind; I know that she'll tell Tom whatever I say and that's exactly what I want right now. Jane encourages me to do it so I dial her number; she doesn't answer and it clicks onto the answer phone. I put the receiver down. Jane tells me to ring back and leave a message, that way she can play it to Tom. I smile and re-dial the number. When it clicks onto answer phone, I'm ready and all fired up.

"Hello Polly, are you out spending Gerrard's money? Because let's face it, you've never had a job, have you? You had the nerve to tell me that you brought up the children but in reality you had a nanny. Where is Gerrard, Polly, do you know? Is Tom a chip off the old block? I only ask as I've heard through the grapevine that Gerrard has had numerous affairs. You've probably turned a blind eye to those though, as you're so greedy and materialistic."

Jane is jumping up and down and whispering "Go Cathy, go Cathy! Tell her!"

"You've not done that good a job at raising Tom, have you?" I carry on. "For him to disrespect his wife, like he did me? To be so bad with money that we lose everything? His private education and university was a complete waste of money for you and Gerrard, wasn't it?" I put the receiver down and feel happy for a minute … then I regret ringing her altogether.

"Don't worry about it, Cathy." Jane squeezes my hand. "She'll get over it and besides, it's about time she knew about Gerrard's little affairs."

I know Jane's right but it is so out of character for me. I've never been spiteful and I've never wanted to hurt anyone. All I wanted to do is get back at Tom.

****

Jane and I are now very drunk and dancing around the house like a couple of teenagers.

"You're too good for him, Cathy," Jane shouts at the top of

her voice. "He was batting above his average when he met you. Fucking Mummy's boy!"

I laugh out loud and we finally fall onto the sofa, completely out of breath.

"We'll go and live together in a hippie commune and breast feed babies for money," I turn to Jane and slur. "Then we can have dogs, cats, chickens, goats and horses."

"Who needs a man, Cathy?" Jane agrees.

"Well, we certainly don't, Jane," I shake my head and garble, 'and we won't have to shave our legs and armpits anymore, so that's a bonus."

Jane stands up but wobbles as she does so.

"Right, Cathy, you're going on an internet dating site and YOU ARE going to have a one night-stand."

"I *will* have a one-night stand!" I smile and reaffirm what Jane has just said.

We spend the best part of three hours looking at beefy men on the internet and we both agree that some of them are probably male models that have just been hired to lure women into signing up with the agency. In the end, we can't see the pictures because we're so drunk and everything is just a blur to us. Also, we can't get up the stairs for fear of falling back down. We both sit back in the lounge and I know I'll have the hangover from hell in the morning.

****

Jane and I wake up and we're huddled together on the sofa, still in our clothes from the night before. There are post-it notes all over the walls saying 'I AM going to get laid,' 'I AM going to have a one-night stand,' 'I AM going to become a cougar,' 'I WANT to be a slut and a whore,' and 'I'm going to shag someone for money.' I think the last two comments were a post-it or two too far. Still, we had a laugh last night and it did cheer me up! However, I am still bothered about the message I put on Polly's house phone and I tell Jane I'm worried she might go to the police.

"What's she going to do - report you for telling the truth?" she laughs. I nod but I'm still not convinced. I'm not bothered about what Tom thinks, I just wish I hadn't come down to that level.

After four cups of coffee, Mum collects me from Jane's house. The minute she gets there, she starts snooping around and looking in Jane's cupboards. She notices a packet of biscuits from Harrods.

"Jane, have you been to Harrods?" she looks accusingly at Jane.

"No, my sister bought them for me," Jane laughs.

Mum inspects the biscuits with a smile on her face.

"I'd love to go to Harrods," she says dreamily, "its proper posh. Joan Collins shops in Harrods; so does the Queen, God bless her."

"You can have them if you want, Joan."

Mum's face lights up but she's not content with just having the biscuits.

"Was it just the biscuits you got, Jane, or did she buy you anything else?"

Jane laughs and takes some Earl Grey tea out of the cupboard along with some chocolates. Mum sits at Jane's table and stares at the chocolates, before very slowly opening them and putting one in her mouth. When she finishes it, she looks at Jane and says "Oh Jane, they're gorgeous – nice and crunchy." She then puts another three in her mouth. Jane quietly giggles. I go to take one of the chocolates and Mum slaps my hand.

"Stop it, Cathy. You're trying to lose weight."

I look at the box and lean forward to read it. On the box it says 'Chocolate covered Giant Ants and Grasshoppers'. I gasp. Mum reads the box and starts heaving like she is going to be sick, so Jane grabs some water and gives it to her. Mum gulps on the water whilst trying to get her breath, and I rub her back to reassure her. Jane picks up the box and studies it.

"I had no idea they were chocolate ants. My sister told me they were quite expensive." Jane smiles ruefully at Mum. "I'll throw them away Joan."

"No, don't throw them away! I'll put them in a dish and Pop can eat them. He won't know anything different if I don't tell him." Mum looks ashen. "Come on, Cathy. We need to get off."

As we walk into the hallway, Mum stops and looks at a post-it note which reads, 'I'm going to become a slag.' I look at Jane and she giggles.

"My dad used to work with slag," Mum smiles. "He'd come home as black as the ace of spades."

Jane can't contain herself and screams with laughter. Mum's face is serious as she carries on explaining.

"He did, Jane. He worked in a furnace. It had to be at a low temperature to stop it forming scum. Many men did awful jobs like that; you had to if you needed money."

We leave Jane in a heap on the stairs, laughing her head off. As we kangaroo up the road, I can feel myself becoming very nauseous from last night's booze. So, when we get home,

Mum insists on making me a full English breakfast – 'a piss pot breakfast' in her words. I'm on my third cup of coffee and I've just finished my breakfast when Mum turns the radio on. *Lucille* by Kenny Rogers comes on and Mum sings at the top of her voice.

"With four hundred children and a dog in the field."

I immediately interrupt her. "Hungry!"

Mum stops singing.

"You shouldn't be hungry after that big breakfast."

"The lyrics, Mum." I can feel my stomach churning in irritation. "It's 'four hungry children and a crop in the field'."

"It's not, Cathy, don't be so argumentative." Mum's annoyed with me.

"Mum, how can anyone have four hundred children?" I know I shouldn't make things worse but I can't help it.

"She may be a foster mother," Mum snaps back at me. We are interrupted by a ringing sound. Saved by the phone! Mum picks up her very large, dated mobile and paces round the kitchen as she speaks.

"Oh no! Oh no! Have you ordered me and your Pop a pass? Right, we'll be there on Monday, son. Can you hold out until then? Is there anything else you need, poppet? OK and some Haribo Tangfastic sweets and chocolate. Oh, our Cathy's here, do you want to speak to her?"

Before Mum can pass over the phone to me I've escaped into the lounge.   Apparently Steven has been beaten up because he's stolen a pair of trainers from another inmate whilst they were taking a shower. As he hasn't been brave enough to admit it, the man's given him a good hiding. Mum thinks it's disgusting that the prison has allowed this to happen, so she's going to visit him on Monday with some supplies to cheer him up. These consist of Haribo sweets, crisps, yogurts, chocolate bars, fruit loop juices and a bag load of penny chews. Pop never goes into the prison because he feels embarrassed and ashamed that his only son is banged up for petty crimes. Meanwhile, Mum seems to think that she's visiting him on a naval ship in the middle of the ocean and sort of hero worships him.

I never knew we were a dysfunctional family when I was growing up, but as the years went by I began to realise that other families weren't like us, and that Steven and I were nothing like each other either. Mum mollycoddled both of us and kept us young, living in a fairy-tale world. I clashed with her even then, but she could never see any wrong in Steven. I remember when he was about eight years of age and the police brought him home for playing on a dangerous building site. Mum's reaction was, "Thanks for giving him a lift home officer, it's getting dark now." The policeman just stared at her for ages until she suddenly ran inside, got her purse, and offered him a fifty pence tip.

I knew I wanted bigger and better things when I was younger but Steven's only ambition was to work on the go-karts at Belle Vue in Manchester. He got a girl pregnant when he was twenty-five and Mum completely blamed the girl for trapping her little boy. Shirley was summoned to the house so that Mum could give her a piece of her mind. Shirley sat in the kitchen, chewing gum; she would drag it out of her mouth, swing it around her finger then push it back in through her bright red lips.

"You're common as muck," Mum screamed at her, "anyone who chews gum is no lady." Shirley laughed, which made Mum worse and her voice reached fever pitch. "You won't take him away from me. I gave birth to him and he's suckled at my breast." Shirley jumped out of her chair and screamed back "He's suckled at mine as well, how do you think I got in this mess?" Mum nearly fainted from the shock of this outburst. The row exploded and to make matters worse, Steven sided with Mum instead of his girlfriend. Mum and Shirley eventually became friends of a sort, but this was mostly for the sake of the baby. Mum supported her with things that she needed. When Shirley went into labour, she insisted her own mother was there as well as Steven – a good job too, because Steven turned up blind drunk and tried to get Shirley off of the delivery bed so that he could get some sleep on it. The midwives decided to make a bed up for him in the bathroom and he snored throughout the whole delivery. When he woke up, Shirley's Mum belted him with her handbag and Mum raced to the hospital to intervene. Mum said Steven was only drunk because he was nervous and a huge row erupted on the ward.

When everything had calmed down, Shirley's Mum pulled the little plastic cot towards her and Mum snatched it back towards herself. This went on for a good few minutes and the poor baby must have thought it was on some sort of ride. When the baby got to six months old it had bright ginger hair and dark brown eyes. Mum spent days looking through Steven's hair to see if she could find any ginger speckles. She also looked at old family photos to see if anyone had brown eyes; we all had blue eyes. In the end mum paid for a DNA test and it turned out that Steven wasn't the father after all. Pop was relieved, as he reckoned Steven couldn't even look after himself let alone a baby. However, I know deep down Mum was more than a little disappointed.

CHAPTER 6

After receiving a nasty letter from Tom's solicitor, I decide to sign the divorce papers. I know it sounds stupid, but the reason I hadn't signed them already was because it was so final. I may have been able to forgive the affair in time, but I could never forgive him for getting in a financial mess and losing me our home. Therefore you'd think I'd have signed them out of bitterness and sent them in the return post. However, I'd been in denial and had pushed everything to the back of my mind, most days pretending it was all a dream. This letter forced me to take control and start a new chapter in my sad little life.

Mum and Jane have been nagging me for days to get my life back in order, so I reluctantly agree to go on another date. Time to move on. Time to let another man see my saggy tits and my bottom that looks like two giant crumpets, not to mention the bingo wings that look like they belong to a jumbo jet. When I eventually feel I can get down and dirty with him, I will go to bed with all my make-up on and lie there rigid, hoping my HRT patch doesn't come off in the night, or, God forbid, I doze off and fart. Then, just before he wakes, I will go and brush my teeth and spray myself with Miss Dior- even my private bits. I will then lie down like a sex goddess, until he awakens and ravishes me again.

Jane and I spend hours drinking wine and searching the internet for men I might like to date. Some look like mass murderers, some look simple- for want of a nicer word, and when we look at others, we can't tell what sex they are.

"Jane, I can't do this! I'd rather be single." I say, looking at Jane.

"Single and living with your parents who are in their

seventies?" Jane shouts, horrified, "I don't think so." I have to admit that it's not a nice thought. Jane starts to write my profile and smiles at me. "Cathy, I'm gonna make you look like a mixture of Jane Fonda and Beyoncé."

"Jane, please." I plead with her "I don't look anything like Jane Fonda or Beyoncé. I'm more a mixture of Dawn French and Cathy Burke."

However, nothing is stopping Jane and her fingers fly over the keyboard. After a minute, she smiles at me.

"All done."

I lean over to look at what she has written but she moves the computer away from me. As she does so, she presses the 'send' button and the words disappear off the screen. We stare at each other until I can finally get my parched mouth to form the words, "Jane what have you done?"

Jane logs onto the website and I already have over ten hits.

"Oh Cathy, that's done the trick!" she squeals. I slowly read the profile Jane has written for me.

'Meet Cathy, who was once a boring, married woman who had nothing to look forward to in her life, a woman that used to watch DVDs and drink wine in the evening. That's until her low-life husband met a woman at work and left her! Cathy has been celibate for a while (well, quite a while – even when she was married) but not anymore. Cathy is now a woman living on the edge and she needs someone to open her ever-wilting flower again (with a little help from Mr KY Jelly of course.)

Cathy has re-discovered single life and now she's ready to party. She can twerk and moves like a panther in the bedroom. Oh no, Cathy doesn't shop at the local supermarket anymore, her favourite store is Anne Summers.'

Jane starts to giggle.

"I'm sorry, it was a joke. I wanted to make you laugh. I never meant to send it." She walks to the fridge and pours us both a large glass of wine. I instantly down mine.

"Jane, how could you? You've made me look like a real slapper. Take it off now."

Jane tries to retrieve the profile but instead a message comes up.

Your data/profile is now live. One of our staff will contact you next week to discuss any changes you want to make to your profile. Good luck & happy dating.

After a few hours, Jane and I are very drunk and start to see the funny side of things. The daredevil in us makes us take things one step further and we start to look at the men who have sent me messages. Man No.1 is called Neal, aged 24yrs. He suggests I buy a webcam the very next day so that we can skype each other and have sex sessions over the net. I can't believe the cheek – he could be my son! Jane and I howl with laughter.

The second man is a real bighead and his profile reads.

'Tickets for sale to go on a hot date with me: *£155 for dinner and £600 if you want me to stay the whole night.'*

Another man even gets my name wrong and his message starts –

'Hi Courtney, I'm Ian and 45yrs of age. I would scramble to you like a rat chewing on a meaty chicken bone.'

And they continue:

'I wear a special aftershave called sex panther and it's

illegal in eight countries. Do you wanna smell it??????'

****

'Because I'm a climber, I love rocks and buildings. Sometimes when I walk past a buildings I stop and hug it, then I get the urge to mount it. Would you like to join me in my journey?'

****

'I like the gym, jogging, hiking and biking.'

****

After a while, I agree to go on a date with a man called Roger; he's 58yrs old, a bank manager and single. He appears normal and as Jane says, I've got to break the ice and get out there.

"Look at him as a dummy run," she says. I instantly begin to worry about the whole dating thing.

****

It's the day of my date. Mum and Jane sit me in my bedroom and try to transform me into the beauty I'm not. Once again, the heated rollers come out and Mum is trying to spread preparation H cream under my eyes.

"Cathy, sit still."

I move away to look at the tube.

"Mum, that's for haemorrhoids."

Mum pushes my hand away.

"I know what it's for, Cathy. It shrinks piles and it will shrink the bags under your eyes too, trust me." Famous last words because when I look in the mirror, I look like a well-oiled mackerel who's been dead for a week and whose eyes are beginning to sink into its head. Mum and Jane are whipping up their talents and my bedroom looks like a scene from a makeover show: clothes bags, shoes and lots of make-up. Mum tries to put eyeliner under the lids of my eyes and the pain is excruciating.

"Mum, you're hurting me," I scream. "What are you doing?" Mum gets cross but carries on anyway. My eyes start to water and I scream out. "Mum, stop!"

Jane looks at Mum then takes the eye pencil off her.

"Oh no, Joan," she gasps. "You've been using a biro. No wonder it's hurting."

"Oh, so I have," Mum grins, looking at the pen. "Now, where's the eye pencil?"

As I'm about to leave, Mum and Jane look at me.

"Cathy, relax… and have a good time." Jane says with a smile.

Mum takes a hankie out of her pocket, spits on it and wipes the side of my face. I squirm to get away from her.

"Mum, that's disgusting. You always used to do that to me and Steven when we were young."

Mum nods. "And it didn't do you two any harm, did it?"

I'm about to get in the taxi when Mum shouts "Cathy, I hope you've got clean knickers on in case you get run over… and if you haven't got clean ones on, you don't live here."

Jane laughs and shouts "And you may get laid." Thankfully the words go right over Mum's head.

****

I arrive at the restaurant and one of the staff takes my coat.

I can feel the butterflies in my stomach and I think I'll throw up at any moment. I am shown to the bar and my date has already arrived. This is a good sign as it shows that he's punctual. Roger has a kind face and is smartly dressed in a grey suit and shiny black shoes. He orders us both a large G&T, which I'm grateful for. We chat about the weather and the price of holidays, then Roger tells me he's a widower. I express my sympathy and we move on with the conversation.

The evening has started well, and he's ordered chateaubriand, which impresses me. We both joke about what would have happened if I'd been a vegetarian. After two G&Ts, a glass of champagne and a bottle of wine, we're both very relaxed and laughing at silly things. Dessert is crème brulee, which is delicious, and for a moment it feels like I'm out with Tom. Roger makes me laugh by telling me that when he gets all maudlin, he eats cakes and asks whether I know that 'desserts' is 'stressed' spelt backwards. The night is going well and I actually feel like an attractive woman again. Roger starts flirting with me and, although I don't fancy him, I flirt back.

"I'm willing to lie for you about how we met." Roger laughs out loud.

I screw my face up and think it's a really odd thing to say; I wasn't asking him to lie and besides, we might not see each other again. I decide not to be so uptight and smile at Roger.

"You smell nice, what have you got on?" I ask.

"I've got a hard on, but I didn't know you could smell it?" Roger laughs.

The wine from my mouth goes all over our table as well as the table to the side of us. I try to apologise as I wipe my mouth but Roger looks really put out as he dries his shirt with a napkin. After an awkward silence we ask for the bill. I take my credit card out of my purse and pray it won't be declined.

"It's fine. I'll get this Cathy, but I'm impressed you offered to pay half." Roger smiles.

I'm not impressed - I've never paid in a restaurant. EVER. I become all maudlin and start to think about the Freak and the Fluff having a meal together, holding hands and being in love. How could she have taken my Tom away from me? Seriously, we've been together for a long time and… I have to stop these thoughts and pull myself together.

When we get outside, Roger puts his arm through mine.

"Do you want to come back to mine for a coffee?"

"That's a bit forward." I laugh.

"I'm a liar," Roger whispers to me, "I don't like coffee."

I look away and the atmosphere is awful. It takes me five minutes to tell him I'm going home and then he looks really annoyed. I thank him for the beautiful meal but he refuses to speak to me. I can't wait to get away from him. By some amazing miracle, a taxi pulls up beside me and the driver shouts "Taxi for Jones." I nod my head and sprint to the car. I don't even look at Roger when I get into it but I can feel his eyes boring into me. I can't wait to get home to be alone with my David Cassidy poster.

****

Pop is waiting up for me and I feel like a teenager again. He puts the kettle on and asks me how the date went.

I sit down at the table and sigh.

"It was okay, but I don't think this internet dating is for me." With this, I kick off my shoes and cuddle Rupert.

"Little Ralph has a girlfriend, haven't you son?" Pop

laughs. The dog wags his tale from all the attention he's getting as Pop and I sit down on the sofa.

"It's a funny thing this dating game, Cathy. In my day you would ask a girl out, take her for a dance on a Saturday afternoon, buy her some flowers and you still might not get a kiss for weeks."

I look at Pop and I can just imagine him when he was young; a real cheeky chappie. I know Mum and Pop were good-looking in their younger days because I've seen photos of them both, but I've never pictured them young and in love. Pop smiles at me.

"The thing is, Cathy, these days girls just drop their knickers. In my day you had to pray for them to come off. Hope the elastic would break and you'd get a little glimpse."

I laugh. I can't believe what he's saying. I've never had a conversation with him like this. Before I leave the room I say "You and Mum have stayed together all these years, what's your secret?"

Pop laughs and says, "The secret is that your mother is always right, she never makes mistakes and she's the boss."

I say goodnight to Pop and go to my room… and what I find there is unbelievable. Mum and Jane are sat in my bed watching back-to-back *Cagney and Lacey* whilst eating pink and white fluffy marshmallows. Mum screams with joy when I walk in.

"Oh, pet, how did you get on? Are you seeing him again?"

"Was he fit?" Jane jumps up. "What was his body like? How much money does he earn?"

I ignore them and put my pyjamas on. The scene looks ridiculous: three grown women sitting in a row in bed as one tells the other two the story of her first date as a singleton.

Mum is shocked when I tell her about Roger's behaviour and she threatens to punch him. I can't see how that's possible when she doesn't even know where he lives.

"You're not giving up and falling at the first hurdle, Cathy," says Jane.

I surrender and tell them I won't give up. Mum goes to her own room while Jane and I settle down for the night, just like when we were kids.

****

The next morning, Mum practically begs me to go to the prison to visit Steven, so in the end I give in. What happened to that pep talk Mum had with me about saying no and meaning it? Mum has a great way of manipulating people- sometimes you can't even remember saying yes.

When we arrive at the prison, Pop stays in the car and I help Mum in with the bags of goodies for Steven. We are searched at reception, which in itself is degrading, then our passes are taken off us before we are shown to a sparse canteen. Steven is already sitting down and his face lights up as he sees the goody bags. Mum kisses him.

"There you go son: Haribo sweets; fruit loops; some games I got you from the charity shop- dominoes and snakes and ladders; and a bag of penny chews."

Steven searches through the bags then looks at me.

"Hi, sis, I believe that fat pig left you."

I am furious and snap at Steven.

"Tom didn't have an ounce of fat on him. He worked hard and brought plenty of money into the house, which is something I could never imagine you doing."

"Oh, yes, Mr and Mrs Perfect," Steven sneers. "He still left you though, didn't he?"

I come back at Steven like a wild animal.

"You've never done a day's work in your life. You're nothing but a petty criminal and a no-hoper."

"Stop it you two," Mum almost screams. Steven looks defeated and starts to munch on his sweets. There are times when I look at Steven and wonder if he's all there - he certainly acts like there's something mentally wrong with him. I sigh as I don't really want to be here. Mum then notices a door at the side of us which says 'Governor's Office' on a shiny plaque. This reminds her that she needs to have a word with someone about Steven getting a good slap off of one of the inmates. She points to one of the officers standing nearby and beckons him with a commanding finger.

"You there, I need to speak to the boss about my boy." Then, before the officer can ask the Governor if he has time to speak to Mum, she marches past him and barges into the office without even knocking. I cringe when I hear her shouting at the Governor.

"Why are you allowing my boy to be beaten to within an inch of his life?"

The Governor clears his throat. "He wasn't beaten that badly," he answers.

Mum is furious. "You're meant to be looking after him. That's why I've paid my taxes all these years. I demand you put him in solitary confinement right now, until he's ready to come home."

It is a while before the Governor replies and when he does speak, I can hear he is exasperated.

"Mrs Mathews, do you know how terrible it would be for Steven to be locked away on his own for seven months?"

Mum can't grasp what he's saying and replies, "It's better than him being killed by a bunch of hooligans and criminals."

"Steven stole a pair of trainers whilst one of the inmates was taking a shower and they got into nothing more than a scuffle," says the Governor in a lowered voice, "It happens all the time when men are cooped up together, day in and day out."

Mum goes ballistic. "What you are trying to say – that my son's a thief?"

I hide my head in my hands. Of course he's a thief, otherwise he wouldn't be in prison. After a few minutes I gently lift my head up, only to find another inmate staring at Steven. The man separates his fingers so they look like scissors, points them to his own eyes then points them at Steven. Steven looks scared and very intimidated. He acts childlike, pushing six sweet and sour cola bottles in his mouth, which makes his eyes water. Mum comes out of the side office and looks at Steven.

"Who's made my boy cry?"

I don't know what comes over me but I feel sorry for Steven and I point to the other man across the room. Mum marches over and starts slapping the man all over the room and, as hard as he tries, the prison warden can't pull her off him. Mum and I are frogmarched out of the prison and I feel so humiliated; in the whole of my life I *never* thought I would be thrown out of a prison. Had I really stooped this low?

CHAPTER 7

I'm not asleep, I'm just deep in thought and trying to ignore the fact that today is my fifty- fifth birthday. Mum brought the post in earlier and amongst my birthday cards is my decree absolute. What a joyous day for all, especially for Fanny and the Freak. I stare at the white paper and the words seem to jump off the page at me.

'A court of law's final order officially ending a marriage, enabling either party to remarry.'

Remarry? *Remarry?* I can't stop looking at the form and the more I read it, the more I feel depressed. Nobody would want to marry me – I'm a bad wife who has let herself go and, more to the point, I'm menopausal and fat! I feel like the words on the divorce form are sent to hurt me; another knife stuck in my heart, leaving a gaping wound that will never heal.

I find it hard to get out of bed. I've had a troubled night's sleep with my hot flushes, so the heat coming off my body is awful and I figure I am being prepared for when I go to hell. I get up, put on my slippers and drag myself across the landing to take a shower, finding my pyjamas are wringing wet from the night sweats. Pop is just coming out of his bedroom.

"I hope you've not used all the hot water, Cathy, because I'm not putting the emersion heater on for anyone."

I look down at my body and whisper. "I'm not wet from the shower I…"

I go back to my room and get back in bed. It's 11am when Louise comes in.

"Hi Mum, happy birthday. Gran says you've got to get up and come down." Louise hands me a beautifully wrapped present but when I open it, it looks like a piece of plastic.

"It's a tablet, Mum," Louise laughs, "it will help you with your dating and keeping in touch with the outside world."

"Thank you," I smile at Louise, "but I don't think I'll be going on any more dates. It's not my scene.

Louise picks up the decree absolute and eyes me cautiously.

"So it's finally arrived ... how do you feel, Mum?"

I think for a minute.

"Relieved, but also a bit sad."

Louise hugs me. Then she laughs.

"I met Dad in the week. Fanny has gone really possessive and has accused him of sleeping with other women. She's even took him to the doctors to get him checked out for sexual diseases. She thinks you and Dad are still sleeping with each other and you seem cool about it. She doesn't trust him at all and she's actually made him get engaged, as if that's going to make him stay faithful."

I look stern.

"Your father shouldn't be talking to you like this, especially when it's about his new girlfriend." When Louise looks away, I giggle to myself as I remember the time when I told Fanny he was bisexual and that his multivitamins were for a disease he'd caught. Serves him right. All of a sudden, Mum shouts up the stairs.

"Cathy, have you been using your Pop's razor to shave your public hair? His face is cut to bits."

"Have I hell. Why would I do ...?" I shout back, stunned.

I arrive downstairs and Mum goes into the kitchen to make coffees.

"Mum, Louise has bought me a tablet," I call to her.

"Why, are you ill?" she yells back. "I've got a cracking first aid kit in here. They've never got any money these young ones. Anyway, I suppose it's the thought that counts."

I slump on the sofa and Louise giggles.

"As if I would give you a medical tablet for your birthday."

"Ignore her, love. That's what I try and do, it's much easier."

There's a small parcel on the coffee table addressed to me and when I open it, it's from Steven. He's got his friend on the outside to send me five large bars of chocolate, some dried herbs and a small plant cutting for Mum.

'That's my boy, always caring.' Mum says, smiling as she fills a cup of water and puts the cutting inside it, then plonks it on the window sill.

Mum hands me a carrier bag and a card. I open the card to reveal a picture of a little doll on a swing. Inside it says, *'Happy 45th birthday Cathy, love Mum, Pop and Rhubarb xxx.'*

Not bad- only 10 years out and who's Rhubarb?

"I don't know," Mum replies, looking confused when I ask her.

"You've put it in the card," I say, pointing to the name. "Mum, Pop and Rhubarb."

"Your Pop wrote the card," she cackles. "He can't always remember her name."

"That's because she is a *he* and *his* name is RUPERT!"

Mum looks serious. "Pop's got an awful memory, I'm worried about him." She looks around the lounge with a confused expression. "Cathy, what have I come in here for?" Then she remembers my birthday present and urges me to look at what she's bought me. When I take it out of the paper I can't believe what I see. It's a dress covered in flowers and it smells like mouldy mothballs. This was definitely from a charity shop. Mum insists I try it on so I reluctantly slip it over my pyjamas. The stench is awful and it's miles too big.

"It'll be fine, Cathy." Mum pulls and tugs on the dress. "I'll get me Singer sewing machine out later and do a bit of nipping and tucking." I catch my reflection in the window and I look like a fat Julie Andrews wearing a Von Trap dress. Mum turns to Louise. "Doesn't your mum look lovely in that dress?" Louise nods but she can't help laughing and covers her face.

"You look a right bugger in that," Pop says, looking me up and down as he enters the room. Mum hasn't heard him and tries to hurriedly sew the dress so I can wear it, but I tell her I'll save it for a special occasion instead. Suddenly the letter box closes with a bang and an envelope falls to the floor. Rupert flies into the hallway and grabs it, While Pop stands up and praises him for his bad behaviour.

"Well done, Ronnie, you're a big man."

Rupert wags his tail and follows Pop into the lounge. Pop catches sight of someone running back up the path and when he lifts the net curtains to look, it's Tom. This makes pop furious.

"The cheek of that man," he exclaims as he hands me the half-chewed envelope.

When I open the card my jaw drops. It simply says,

'Happy birthday Cathy, love Tom.'

Mum gets up from her sewing machine and snatches the card off me. She is furious.

"What the hell is that cheeky feck doing sending you a birthday card, after all he's done? Shall I throw it away Cathy?"

I shrug my shoulders; I'm past caring. Mum throws the card in the air and Rupert grabs it and tears it to bits. My well-behaved dog is now acting like a hooligan that needs an ASBO and Mum and Pop think it's funny.

****

As I sit on my bed and put a bit of make-up on, my mind wanders. Years ago, Mum used to shop at Marks and Spencer's and prided herself on being 'classy.' Since she's getting older, she's shops at the flea market, charity shops, and her favourite - the pound shop. Poundland is heaven in her eyes. She comes home with all sorts of tack: a plastic bird that now sits on the fence in the back garden; a novelty squirrel feeder that makes the squirrels look like they have a horse's head when they feed; some DIY mop shoes which are a pair of flip flops with bits of cloths stuck underneath – she only used them once because she stood on the cloths, fell and nearly knocked herself out. Pop was furious and threw them in the bin. The last Christmas I spent here with Tom, she put ice coolers into his whisky that were the shape of false teeth; every time he looked at them he winced. In my G&T was a small ice Titanic on its side and, as much as I love G&T, I couldn't drink it.

I hear Jane peep her horn, so I go into the kitchen to say goodbye to Mum and Louise. To my horror, Mum is chopping onions on my tablet. I scream and she puts her hands up like I've got a gun.

"What?" she shrieks.

"That's my tablet!"

Mum panics, scrapes the onions off it, and then rinses it under the tap.

"Oh, I'm sorry love. I'll get the onion smell out of it."

I snatch the tablet off her and put it on the radiator to dry out. I can't even say goodbye because I'm so annoyed. Louise can't look at me for laughing.

****

Jane knows I'm fed up with the situation at home.

"You could stay with me," she says when I tell her, "but that little shit of a son of mine is coming home in a few days. I'm dreading it."

"Why?" I'm shocked.

"Because," Jane laughs resignedly, "he hasn't paid any rent for six months and he's contributed nothing to the bills. The other housemates are sick of him. I tell you, Cathy, when he gets home I'm going to tip him upside down and take what I think he needs to pay- there'll be no messing with me."

I laugh. I've always liked Jane's son, Josh, but he's so laid back he's horizontal. He totally winds Jane up because he's always partying, even when he can't afford it, and calls himself 'the one and only social butterfly.'

We arrive at the shopping centre and look in the windows of a few shops. One of the shops is Dotty P's.

"I look massive in this window," I say, sizing myself up in my reflection.

"So do I." Jane says, doing the same, smoothing down her

dress and turning from side-to-side. There's seventies music coming from the shop so Jane and I have a little boogie outside, causing a few shoppers to laugh as they pass. We walk further on and see a newly refurbished shop, so we peer in through the window.

"I think it's a pet shop," Jane says. A girl comes out and gives us a leaflet that offers us a 25% discount that's valid for the day Jane and I look confused, which makes the girl laugh.

"They're Garra Rufa fish. They eat the dead skin off your hands and feet, it feels lovely afterwards."

"Now if they were mini piranhas that strip the fat off you, I may have given it a go," I say to Jane, laughing.

She screams with laughter and we thank the shop assistant and walk off.

"Ugh! The thought of them eating the skin off my feet. I can see them gagging now," Jane grins.

We walk into a lovely clothes shop that has tops and dresses in an array of colours. I pick up a top and some leggings, then turn to Jane.

"Jane, there's no way these are a size 18/20, is there? Look how small they are!"

Jane agrees. Suddenly, a shop assistant comes over to us; she is probably a size 00, if that exists.

"Can I help you ladies?" she smiles and chirps.

"These are *never* a size 18/20." I appeal to her.

"They are, madam." The assistant looks at the labels and smiles.

I pick up a size 12 and measure it to the size 18/20 and they are exactly the same size. I have a sarcastic grin on my face as I point to both garments.

The shop assistant shrugs and looks me up and down.

"There's another shop around the corner, they do clothes for fat lasses."

My jaw drops open. The assistant points to the shop entrance.

"The shop is on the left, it's called Pleasantly Plump – they have loads of nice stuff in."

Jane comes back from having a look around but I can't speak because I'm in shock. The shop assistant becomes very nervous and starts to waffle.

"The people who own the shop are really nice. They also own Buddha Belly, and the Indian restaurant on the High Street... they're all fat and... happy."

Jane and I walk out of the shop in disgust.

"Aren't some people cheeky?" Jane tuts and I nod.

The next shop we enter has a lot to choose from. Jane picks up a dress for me to try on but when I come out of the changing room, she pulls a face.

"It's not you, Cathy."

I feel disappointed and possibly a little affronted.

"Jane is it not me, or is it too tight?"

"Both," she says, screwing her face up painfully. "It looks like someone's poured you into it and forgot to say 'when'."

I know she's right but it still makes me feel depressed with the whole situation of buying clothes. I can never get anything I like: they either don't fit me properly or they're too old-fashioned. Suddenly Jane passes me a red and blue dress.

"Cathy, don't look at the size, just try it on."

I try on the dress and it's lovely. The panel along the front is an illusion and I look and feel a lot slimmer.

"Oh, Cathy, that looks really nice," Jane says, taking a quick look at me round the corner. I feel happy with the dress so I take it off and walk out of the fitting room.

"There's a woman in the cubicle next to me and she's massive," I whisper, linking Jane's arm and giggling. "I'm glad I'm not that big. She has a hole in her knickers too!"

"Let me go back and see," Jane laughs and sneaks back into the changing room for a peek, then slowly turns around and looks at me with a sullen face.

"Cathy, there's nobody in there. It's just a mirror on the wall."

I feel around inside my leggings to try and locate the 'hole' and, sure enough, it's on my left cheek.

****

Jane and I are in the pub eating burger and chips. I pick up a load of coleslaw with my fork.

"Oh, I love coleslaw, and it's homemade."

Jane shovels a pile of chips into her mouth and nods. I take a large bite from my burger and sigh.

"I think I'll go back to Weight Watchers. I'm fed up, Jane, and I don't understand why the weight's not coming off."

"I've thought about having liposuction," Jane says, "but I can't afford it.'

"Jane, Bill Gates couldn't afford to pick up the bill if I had it done," I laugh out loud.

Jane is laughing hysterically and turns to me.

"Sometimes when I look in the mirror, I don't see a fat person."

I make an unladylike snorting sound.

"Can I borrow your mirror then?"

Jane gulps wine from her glass and she can hardly speak as she says "I can remember when I was 36 24 36."

"I can," I add, swigging on my wine, "and that was my forearm, neck and thigh."

We are rolling around helplessly and the rest of the pub is wondering what the hell we're both laughing at. A while later, the waitress comes over and asks if we want a dessert. At first we both say no, but then we call her back and say we're going to share one. When she takes the order and walks off, I panic and go after her.

"No, make that one cheesecake and one sticky toffee pudding and make sure they're low fat." I laugh but the waitress doesn't.

After we've eaten our food we can hardly move and eventually we both waddle out of the pub. We walk into a large chemist and try on a few lipsticks. After a while, I look at Jane, grinning.

"Jane, I've forgotten what I came in here for. Honestly, these menopausal patches are pumping fat into me and eating my brain cells at the same time."

Jane roars with laughter. A rep approaches us, looks at our hair, and then hands Jane a free shampoo sample for fine and wispy hair. She looks at me and hand me a sachet for battered and abused hair. As she walks off I turn to Jane, who is still laughing her head off.

"Cheeky cow," I growl.

We both walk over to a demonstration where a young, skinny girl is showing customers a slimming machine. The model lying on the couch is equally as thin but she's wired up with electric pads all over her body. The rep looks at Jane and I and starts to explain how the machine works.

"These are electronic pads that vibrate and break up the fat around the body," she informs us, indicating the key areas on the model's body. "Then any extra body fluids are dispersed and you naturally get rid of it. You can read a book or simply relax in a comfy chair as you lose weight."

I can't help but ask "Can you sleep in them?"

The rep looks stunned by my question and sarcastically replies "Oh no, I wouldn't recommend that madam."

"We're not buying them then," Jane shakes her head at the rep, "and besides, they're far too expensive."

The rep looks hurt, as if Jane has personally insulted her. She strokes the machine like she's in love with it.

"This is a bargain of a life time," she purrs. "You'll not get an offer like this again. It's a small price to pay for getting rid of *excess pounds*." She emphasises these two words as she looks at us, her raised eyebrows suggesting, 'you two really need to buy them'. As Jane and I walk to the car park, each of us carrying a large box containing a machine and electronic pads, we try to maintain an air of philosophical dignity. Jane kisses her box before she puts it in the boot of the car.

"The minute I get in, I'm going to wire myself up and watch TV."

"I don't care what she says, I'm sleeping in mine," I smile, placing my box carefully in the boot. We both laugh and get in the car.

"Well Jane," I sigh, "that's all my birthday money gone and I still haven't got any clothes- well, apart from the dress. Thanks for a lovely day and the lunch though."

****

When I get home, Mum and Louise have made me a birthday tea consisting of sandwiches, sausage rolls, crisps, nibbles and cakes. Mum beams and Louise smiles. I am completely overwhelmed and hug both of them. Then Jane comes through the door and sings at me.

"Hey birthday girl, I've got wine."

"You little sneak, Jane," I laugh, "Is that why you got me out of the house?"

Even Doris from next door comes round and brings me a case with make-up in it, but it's the kind you'd give a teenage girl. Everybody takes a seat and Mum pours the wine. Even Rupert has a seat at the table and he's busy licking a sausage roll that Pop has put on a plate for him. After about ten minutes, Doris takes my hand.

"I feel for you Cathy," she says in her thick Irish accent. "You don't deserve all this shite."

I look at Mum but she looks away. It's obvious she's been telling Doris everything about my personal life and the terrible break-up with Tom. That makes me feel worse because I'm obviously a good case to gossip about, with all the drama that's happened over the last couple of months. I burst into tears. Mum comes over and hands me a tissue.

"Cathy, stop crying," she says, hugging me. "If you cry on your birthday you will cry all year."

I laugh through the tears because I remember Mum used to say it to us when we were young- along with all her other sayings.

Later on, when the drama has ended, everyone has a drink and a laugh. As usual, when it's time for everyone to go home I want the party to carry on.

"Come back everyone. Don't go, it's only early," I shout at the top of my voice as Mum pulls me back indoors to keep me quiet.

Mum points out that it's 12.20am, so I go back inside and pour myself another drink. Mum is annoyed and tries to take the drink from me, but I'm having none of it and wrestle with her.

"Cathy, you're always the last to leave the party," she shouts, putting her hands on her hips. "You never know when to say no, do you?"

I laugh. No-one can piss on my parade today. I clutch my presents and hobble up the stairs to bed. However, once I'm in bed I become all maudlin and start talking to myself and if that wasn't bad enough, I start answering myself too. I cry and my voice sounds like I'm being strangled.

"Why did he leave me and divorce me? I'm not a bad person, am I?" I sip on the wine I've taken to bed and my head is begins to loll from side to side. I look up at David Cassidy. "Are you glad you didn't marry me? I'm a horrible person and I'm a terrible wife *and* I wouldn't have given you any sex. You had a lucky escape." I lie down, still holding my glass of wine and I swear I can hear David Cassidy talking to me in a soothing way.

****

I'm trying to come round from a drunken coma sleep. My mind is awake but my body won't move and I can't open my eyes. When I try to sit up I feel sick and there is no way I can stand up for fear of collapsing. I can hear Mum on the phone in her bedroom but I haven't a clue what's she's talking about.

Am I dreaming, am I awake or am I dead? Mum talks quietly but I can still hear her.

"No, it's my third baby and I need to speak to a midwife." Then I hear Mum blow her nose and carry on the conversation. "Am I dilated? Yes, I'm absolutely over the moon." There's a silence, then Mum talks again. "Yes, I need to speak to Louise... well can you give her a message? It's about her mother." There is a pause and I assume that the other person on the phone is talking. Mum's voice becomes louder as she says "Have you ever seen a horror film and it looks like a blood bath?" I listen and wonder if Mum has the TV on in her room, because what I'm hearing doesn't make any sense. Mum's voice becomes really loud. "No, it's not a blood bath it's more like... a shit bath, so I may need an ambulance. Also, I think she's had a stroke- one side of her face has dropped. It's horrible; she's not been well, you know. Her husband left her for another woman and she's had a baby with the little shit. Can you get Louise to ring me, love?"

I must have dosed off again because I'm suddenly woken from a deep sleep with Mum and Louise standing over me. Mum has her hand over her mouth and is quietly saying "Oh good Jesus, it's horrible..."

I can feel my face pulsating and I feel very uncomfortable. Louise helps me sit up in bed, then slowly takes the electronic pads off my face, chin, chest and arms. She hands me a mirror and in all fairness, I do look like I've had a stroke. Not only that- I'm covered in melted chocolate. It's all down my chest and face, and the large bar of melted honeycomb chocolate is positioned in the crack of my arse so it does look like I've had a severe bout of diarrhoea. Mum sits on the bed looking extremely worried.

"Is she going to live?"

Louise folds her arms and looks at Mum.

"Is she going to live? Not if she carries on like this."

Mum snivels but doesn't say a word. Louise is annoyed and becomes stern with me.

"Mum, I can't believe you wired yourself up when you were extremely drunk. I know you've had a bad time lately, but this has to stop and you need to get a grip on your life."

Mum nods through the whole conversation. I get up and sit on the chair at my old dressing table. I have the hangover from hell and I look terrible. Louise runs the shower then strips the bed. For some reason I go all childlike and whinge like a naughty kid.

"I was trying to lose weight whilst I was asleep. I'm fat and ugly and I can't have a baby anymore. Not that I want one, but the choice has been taken away from me with this awful menopause."

Louise stares at me as she's clearing up all the mess.

"Mum, have you any idea how dangerous it is to go to bed electronically wired up?"

"Not to mention the electric bill, Louise." Mum nods and continues, "I bet it was spinning off its axel."

"Gran," Louise turns on Mum impatiently. "Would you go down and make a pot of tea? I'll sort my mother out and then we'll come down."

Mum nods and leaves the room. Louise looks at me and for a moment I feel like she's the parent and I'm the child.

"Mum, I can't believe Gran. She rang the hospital and said to my student that there was a blood bath, then said 'no, it's a shit bath' *and* she pretended to be pregnant."

I can't take in what Louise is saying because my head is banging and the voices inside me are demanding we go back to bed.

Louise helps me to clean up the dried-on chocolate from my ever expanding arse and then I take a shower, get dressed and go downstairs. Pop, Mum and Louise are all sitting around the table and it looks like a meeting in the House of Commons. My coffee hasn't even touched my lips when the intervention starts. Pop is first.

"Listen, dolly, you need to get yourself sorted out. You'll never find another husband behaving like you do. Look at the state of you."

Mum rubs my hand. She has to have her say.

"You need a direction in your life, love- something to cling onto. I've felt like you, love, honestly, and I looked at religion. I wanted to be a Buddhist but I couldn't stop killing flies and I didn't fancy shaving all my hair off, and they've got no fashion sense."

Pop shakes his head and I can't believe what I'm hearing.

"Religion? Why would I look at religion, Mum? I've just got divorced, I don't need God."

"Mum, we're worried about you," Louise interrupts. "It's only because we care."

I feel like they're all ganging up on me, so I make a quick getaway and go to my room. I ring Jane to come and get me so that we can have a liquid lunch together. I know Mum, Pop and Louise care and worry about me but I don't want to listen to them lecturing me.

****

Jane and I go to an Italian restaurant and they have a

special lunchtime offer on: any pasta or pizza dish and get a free glass of wine. We'll only have one glass of wine then make our way to Jane's house, which is just up the road. The first glass of wine doesn't even touch the sides of our mouths, so I put my hand up and ask the waiter for a bottle as well. Jane stops him and asks for a litre instead. We laugh at each other.

"Sod it," Jane says. "Why not? You only live once, Cathy."

As always I agree with her. Three hours later and the restaurant staff want to close up. We can hardly speak as we ask for the bill and another Sambuca. Once we have paid, they literally push us out of the door. As we stagger down the road we hold onto each other so that we don't fall over. We cross the road to get to Jane's house and a car nearly hits us. I put one finger up and Jane puts up two. The car stops and Tom jumps out.

"What's wrong with her?" He shouts at Jane.

It takes me a minute to focus and we're still holding each other up. Tom gets hold of my arm aggressively.

"Cathy, get in the car."

"Get your dirty hands of my friend, you little creep," Jane slurs, pulling me back towards her.

Tom shakes his head in disgust as he looks at me.

"Cathy, I said get in the car," he demands.

Jane staggers towards Tom

"Don't you tell her what to do," she shouts, "You're nothing to do with her now."

Tom is trying to be calm and I'm so drunk that I can't speak. As Tom tries one last attempt to grab me, Jane goes berserk and pushes him away. She can't pronounce her words properly.

"Tom, go back to whatever hole you crawled out of. We're having a good time."

I nod in agreement and Tom gets in the car to drive off. He's disgusted. Jane leaps onto the front of the car and hangs on to the windscreen wipers. He turns them on and Jane is sliding from side to side on the bonnet of the car. All of a sudden she slides down the bonnet, taking the wipers with her and ending up in a heap in front of the car. I gasp and all my emotions are emphasised because I'm drunk.

I lean into the car and grab Tom's hair.

"You've killed my friend," I wail, "and now I'm going to kill you."

Tom is terrified and gets out of the car to move Jane. As he bends down, I kick him up the arse and he goes flying onto the road. I slap my hands together as if I'm brushing sand off them and although Jane wobbles, she stands up. Tom screeches off up the road and we sit down on a small wall.

****

I wake up on Jane's sofa and I've got mushrooms all down my top where I've been sick. Jane comes down the stairs and puts the kettle on.

"Oh, Cathy, I feel so rough."

"Jane, I think I'm going to die."

I think about the evening before, when Tom saw us both drunk, and then I find I have five voicemail messages from him. It dawns on me that he still has my number and I've not changed it. It was alright for him to move on with his life and now I think it's my turn. Jane gives me a SIM card that she's never used and in an instant, something else has changed in my life. It takes us four hours to come round and by then, Jane has persuaded me to go on another date.

****

My second date is with a university graduate who is sixty years of age. I am unable to remember his name because he is slurring when he tells me. According to him, it's never too late to learn and he thinks I should enrol on a course, live in student accommodation and get laid every night after drinking ten pints of lager in the student bar… just like he's done. He even has the nerve to ask me when I last had sex with anyone. How can I tell a complete stranger that it was over a year ago, with my now ex-husband, and that's probably one of the reasons he left me? My mind freezes and I can't think straight. Why am I talking to someone I don't know? Someone who obviously just wants to get laid? I am just about to stand up to leave when another round of drinks arrive. I sigh and sip my wine because there's no way I am letting it go to waste. The thought of going back to Mum and Pop's seems like a fantastic idea right now. I'd even watch re-runs of *Only Fools and Horses* with Pop. I look at this stranger in front of me and wonder what Tom would think if he could see me now. As I look up from my drink, the man closes one eye and stares at me. I know that look because I've done it a thousand times myself, when I try to focus on something through intoxicated eyes. "I've only just noticed how chubby you are," he says, laughing out loud. "Aww, well, at least there's plenty for me to get hold of. We'll have to be quiet though, so we don't wake up the others at the hostel."

My gulp is so loud that it sounds like I have a huge Adams apple in my throat. I excuse myself and go to the toilet, and that is the last he sees of me.

On the way home in the taxi, I keep thinking about the dates I've been on. What's wrong with these people? Or is it me? Am I no better? Maybe I'm grossly overweight, ugly and a hardened drinker? Then I become all maudlin again, thinking about the Freak and the Fluff and how they are probably sat at home, drinking rose wine and holding hands.

"It won't last you know," I say quite loudly, startling the taxi driver. Oh God, what the hell am I going to do with my life? The taxi driver stares at me.

CHAPTER 8

The minute I sit down in front of the doctor I start crying.
After ten minutes of him gently coaxing me round to find out
what is wrong, I take a deep breath and blurt out, "I've got a
headache."

Luckily for me he doesn't believe it is just a headache and
hands me a glass of water.

"Come on, Cathy, tell me what's really wrong."

I blow my nose and look at Dr Morgan.

"Did you know Tom and I have separated? Well, actually,
we've got divorced. He divorced me for a tart he works with.
Came right out of the blue, doctor. I've lost the house, my car
and my dignity. I know I'm overweight, but that can go, and
I'm not that bad looking, am I, doctor? And…"

Dr Morgan puts his finger to his lips and says "SSSHHH!"
Then he leans back in his chair.

"I know what's happened with you and Tom. I don't want
to sound unprofessional in discussing how I know, but we've
all known each other for several years. We've had dinner
parties at each other's houses, and all I can say is it's a great
shame."

I immediately go into detective mode and lean in to Dr
Morgan.

"Doctor, what did he say? Is he sorry he left me? Was the
Fanny with him?"

Dr Morgan looks confused.

"I think your depressed, Cathy," he states. "I'm going to
prescribe you some antidepressants and refer you to a

counsellor. There's a group of them and they all do different counselling, so you can find one you're comfortable with."

I nod at the doctor because I have no strength to do anything else. I trust Dr Morgan and feel safe when I'm around him and even though I know he's called Craig, it never feels right to call him that in the surgery.

As I drive home I wonder what's been said. Has Tom admitted he's had an affair? Has Dr Morgan met Fanny? The thought makes me feel sick to the pit of my stomach.

****

My first therapy is a 'shaker lifestyle,' which basically means you're shaking off your old life and making room for a new one. The woman who runs the class looks like a fat Susie Orbach, who wrote *Fat is a Feminist Issue*. This brings back a memory for me when, many years ago, a friend told me that Susie Orbach was so hungry one day that she ate her own book. I don't know how true this is because I was given the gossip second-hand, but if it was the case then that was one hell of an appetite.

This hippy therapist is about twenty-five stone and is wearing baggy trousers that look like they belong to Demis Roussos. She has bright red hair, a brown moustache and smells of patchouli oil, sweat and musk. It is also obvious to all that she doesn't like wearing underwear, because her camel toe looks more like an Elephant's foot. She announces her name as 'Constance' and then happily tells us its meaning.

"A girl's name, which is pronounced KAHN-stans, from the Latin and Medieval name Constantia. The meaning of Constance is constant and steadfast. It was introduced to Britain by the Normans and was widely used in the seventeenth century by the Puritans. Both Henry VI's wife and William the Conqueror's daughter bore the name Constance"

This has no relevance to the class and, when she finishes talking, I feel exhausted and can't move a muscle. Constance comes over to me and bends down.

"Cathy you have an orange and black light around you and your aura is lopsided. Do you want me to bless you?"

I can't answer her; I don't have the strength. She begins working with the fresh air above my head.

"That's done the trick," she huffs, five minutes later. "You're now a reddish and blue colour. Be careful because red can make you very angry and you may do things that are out of character."

I laugh to myself because I've been acting that way since Tom left.

Constance chimes in every corner of the room so that no negative spirits can get in. The problem is they are already in and living inside me.

Constance get us all on our feet then bounces around the room, laughing and shaking the energy off her hands. Then she gets us all to do the cha-cha-cha around the room to get rid of negative energies from our exes. I feel uncomfortable bouncing around and screaming Tom's name in an aggressive way, but she insists. Then we all sit on mats and are told to cry. I put my hand up like a school girl and say "I can't cry on demand, I'm not a bloody actress." This annoys Constance.

"If you can't cry on demand, you're not in tune with the universe," she snaps. "Just make noises like you're crying."

I sit on my mat and watch seven women sobbing their hearts out. What the hell am I doing here? Constance stares at me so I make a few noises, but they sound like a baby eating solids and enjoying every mouthful.

All of a sudden, four butch women come into the room

pushing punch bags on wheels. The punch bags are torso-shaped and Constance squeals with delight on seeing them.

"Oh, the punch bags have arrived, ladies."

Constance tells us to line up so that when it's our turn, we can kick the crap out of the punch bags "Get out all your aggression and free yourself," she hollers.

I'm forth in the queue. The first lady slightly punches the bag and says "Go to hell, Ian." We can hardly hear her and the punch wouldn't have moved a pea.

The second lady can't punch the bag because she's sobbing. She turns to Constance.

"I can't do it, I can't hurt him. I still love him."

Constance rolls her eyes then wafts her on.

The third lady is very petite and is wearing a floral dress and sandals that look like they're from a children's shop. Her hair is tied in a little pink bow and she's wearing little lace gloves which look very odd on her. I feel sorry for her because she looks so childlike and vulnerable. Constance smiles her.

"Are you ready Lucy?" she asks quietly. "Come on, show us what you've got," she urges. With this, Lucy steps forward and punches the bag so hard that it falls to the floor. She bends down and grabs it by the chest then repeatedly attacks it, making it lose its balance again. The kicking and head-butting comes next. We can all hear her knuckles crunching with every blow. Constance runs over while we all stare open-mouthed at her. Constance can't get her off the bag and calls for assistance, so the two other ladies run over to help but to no avail. Lucy is on a mad mission and I swear she fights better than any street fighter. A third person runs over to help and by now, Lucy is screaming at the top of her voice.

"Damn you, Paul. How could you shag a melon? How

could you do that to a defenceless piece of fruit? I hate you."

Eventually the punch bag is rescued from Lucy. Her dress is ripped and her gloves are in bits on the floor. The sweat is pouring down her face and her hair is wild. Constance slowly walks away from the bag with a severely wilted Lucy. She sits Lucy down on a chair and kneels in front of her.

"Do you feel better for that Lucy?"

Lucy nods. Constance smiles and says "You really shouldn't be jealous about a melon, should you? It hasn't done anything to you." Lucy stares into space, still frothing at the mouth.

It's my turn and I start to rev myself up for the next brutal battering I'm going to give Tom. I hop from one foot to another and add a bit of snorting for special effects. I start to punch the air in an attempt to impress everybody in the room. The scene is like Sylvester Stallone in *Rocky*. I can feel everyone looking at me, which makes me puff out my chest and dance on the spot. Then someone in the room shouts "Get on with it, you're making a meal of it." The comment throws me and I run at the bag and start bitch-slapping it. The bag responds by swaying to the left. A few people in the room laugh. Constance comes over.

"Is that the best you can do? Come on, kick the shit out of it."

I run at the bag and shoulder it; it feels like I've just hit a brick wall. The bag gently sways. I punch the bag so hard it hurts, causing me to bend over, hug my hand and shout "Ouch!" I can tell I'm a huge disappointment to Constance, who begins to show us all how it's really done. After five minutes, Constance smiles at us all. She's dripping in sweat and has punched the bag so many times and cried out so many names - male and female - that I've lost track. Then at one point she screams, "Why don't I look like Olivia Newton John?" She then seems to come back in to the room and behaves normally again. She claps her hands and smiles at the group.

"Thank you, ladies. I'll see you next week."

I can't wait to get out of the place and literally run out of the door.

****

It takes me ten minutes to start Mum's Skoda and, whilst I'm stationary, Mum phones.

"Cathy, there's a letter at the post office for you. I missed the postman because I was round Doris's house. You have to sign for it."

I quickly turn around and head for the post office. After standing in a queue for ten minutes I finally sign the slip and get the envelope. I sit in the car and take out the contents, which amount to exactly five hundred pounds – my maintenance money. Maintenance for being a fat sad old cow; for not having a husband anymore; or a house; or car. There's a little note inside the envelope which says:

> *Cathy, this is the last five hundred pounds I can give you, seeing as we are now divorced. I feel I've done my bit and now it's time for you to stand on your own two feet. Tom.*

I sit in the car and sigh. Suddenly I look at the back of the envelope and there's an address written on it. It's obvious to me that Fanny has sent me my last maintenance payment/pin money.

Suddenly, I get an urge to drive to the address, just to have a little nosy at what's going on. I get the satnav out of my bag and head towards the address. I can't believe my eyes when I get there. It's a semi-detached house in a nice suburb of East Yorkshire. I duck down as I see Tom make his way out of the property and start mowing the lawn. When has mowing the lawn been a priority to him? When he was married to me he was always at the golf club or working away. We had a gardener for convenience. I can't take my eyes off him. Then, without warning, a rage comes over me just like Constance said it would. I stare at Tom and I want to gut him like a fish. What tips me over the edge is when I see the Fluff bring him out a cup of tea on a saucer. I get out of the car and run towards the house. When the Fluff sees me, she runs inside. Meanwhile, Tom's in shock and freezes, his tea running down his new jeans. I stand with a menacing look on my face, so he tries to take my arm and lead me back to my car, but I'm having none of it. I can see the Fluff looking through the pearly white net curtains.

"Who has net curtains these days?" I shout at Tom. Tom shrugs his shoulders.

A neighbour walks into their garden and starts to prune a small shrub that is attached to Tom and Fanny's property; his head is stretching to see what is going on. Tom puts his arm on my shoulder and takes me inside their house. I don't want to go in but another part of me does. We walk into a very neat kitchen; it's not as nice as the one we had, and it's a bit dark considering the size of the room. Ours was more modern, bright and airy. Fanny is nowhere to be seen which, for some reason, annoys me. Tom points to a kitchen chair for me to sit down. I slowly sit and find I have no desire to leave. Something in the pit of my stomach makes me want to stay and I'm too annoyed to cry. Tom says nothing but is nervously walking up and down the kitchen and it's ages before Fanny shows her ugly face. She walks in and leans against the kitchen sink. She can't look at me so she stares at the wall in front of her. *What a coward*, I think. I stare at her in her dowdy trousers and jumper. I have to admit I don't look my best. How can I? I've just been to a therapy lesson to help me move on with my life and now I'm sat in Fanny's kitchen. How's that for moving on? Finally, Fanny looks at me and, in a bitter voice, she spits "What do you want Cathy?" I can't answer her. What did I want? I stare back at her and think what a cheek she's has to ask me anything.

I start to think about the conversation I had with Tom in my parents' lounge. He'd told me it started as a one night stand with Fanny and that she listens to him and understands him, whereas I don't. So why am I sat in their kitchen? Tom looks at me and sighs.

"Cathy, you can't stay. We're going out. Is it about me stopping the money?"

"No, you're right, we're divorced." I shake my head, "I need to get on with my life and support myself."

Tom looks shocked at what I say. Fanny stands, staring at the wall. The mood is very intense and my stomach starts to churn. In my head I want to get up and run back to my car. Another sick side of me wants to have a good look around the house and compare how she washes her towels and her choice of bedding, but I'm frozen to the kitchen chair. After another long silence, Fanny looks at Tom and in a gentle voice says "Tom, please sort this out."

I wonder what on earth she's going on about. Very quickly, the kitchen door opens and a boy of about twelve years of age comes into the kitchen. He smiles at me and I smile back, not knowing who he is. Fanny panics.

"Simon, go to your room, we're speaking."

The young boy sighs heavily and pulls a face.

"I need Dad to help me with my homework," he says in a

whiny voice. "I want to go out and play football with my friends."

Fanny takes hold of the boy's arm and walks out of the kitchen with him.

"We're going out," she shouts back at Tom in a cocky manner.

I'm riveted to the spot; surely it can't be Tom's child. No… never in a million years, he just calls him 'Dad'. He couldn't have kept that from me… he wouldn't. I feel my heart is beating out of my chest, I'm feeling faint and I flush from cold to hot. I'm stunned beyond belief. My head tells me to go, get some fresh air, but my heart tells me to stay. Tom sits down at the table and sighs heavily.

****

I close the door of Mum's Skoda and put the key in the ignition. I stare at the house *my* Tom shares with Fanny and the boy – Tom's son. I have no idea how to analyse this information in my brain. How to process the thoughts I have. Tom confessed he'd been having an affair with Fanny for thirteen years (thirteen, unlucky for some… yeah, me.) He admitted that when he found out Fanny was pregnant he made a commitment to support her and the child. Louise was only fourteen at the time and was going through a difficult phase at school, she also suffered from low self-esteem. He said he made the decision to stay with me until Louise was settled with her life and had been to college and university.

He also explained that he does still love me, but that the boy is getting older now and he feels he needs to be a full-time dad to him. *What a noble man*, I think with such bitterness. He also admitted that he hardly ever went to golf and most of the time he was supposedly working away he was playing happy families with Fanny and his son. Tucking him up and reading him stories. I feel bitter inside as I remember Polly's comment when I gave birth to Louise, it was cutting and cruel: "Oh, I was hoping for a boy. We really wanted to carry on the family name." Thinking about her words now, I could cry my eyes out. No wonder he was in a financial mess, keeping two families for thirteen years. Meanwhile, I've bared the brunt of it all by not having a son. On the other hand, if I'd had a son and Fanny had a girl, he would want his little girl, so either way I wouldn't have won.

Why has this happened to me? Should I be grateful that he stayed for the sake of Louise? Was our marriage a sham? Obviously it was. How many other people know about this? Do his mum and dad know? Does the precious Lisa know? Is Lisa jealous? My thoughts are driving me mad. He also admitted he'd had a week long holiday with them every year for the past twelve years. Oh yes, I remember the so-called trips to Brussels for a whole week. In reality, he's just admitted he was really in Spain, Greece and Italy with his other family. Even Disneyland on one occasion. He never took Louise to Disneyland. That really hurts me and I make a decision there and then that I will never tell Louise. Italy was our haunt: special and romantic. I bang my head on the steering wheel and cry. I'm glad I didn't cry in front of Tom, quite the opposite – at one point he even accused me of being cold… cold about his other life. I wasn't cold, I was numb!

Mum rings the mobile to see where I am and I ask her if I can go to Jane's and come back later. Mum senses there's something wrong but she doesn't ask about it.

CHAPTER 9

Carrying a huge secret is extremely stressful and I spend most days in a world of my own. I know I'll have to tell people about Tom's second family, but for now I can't even get my own head around it, let alone speak about it to anyone else. How could he have kept a long-term affair from me? The birth of a baby? The bills he's had to pay for two houses over thirteen years? What makes me really angry is that I never knew about her, but she knew about me. How deceitful is that?

Even Jane is speechless when I tell her. Jane takes a deep breath.

"The lying, cheating little shit," she shouts. "I swear, Cathy, if he was in front of me now I'd kill him." I hear her draw breath.

"Thirteen fucking years! That's a biggie and a hell of a long time, Cathy."

I have to agree with her. Trying to cope with such a mixture of feelings is unbearable and I wonder what will come out next. All those years he was sleeping with me *and* another woman; the thought makes me feel physically ill, not to mention any other indiscretions he may have had. I feel like we've broken up all over again and it hurts even more than the first time. I'm so angry I can't even cry.

****

I know I have to find a job now that my maintenance has stopped. 'Maintenance' – it sounds so peculiar. I feel the word should be linked to a child not a fifty-five year old menopausal woman. I walk into the kitchen to find Pop's local newspaper. Both my parents read the paper from cover to cover. Mum always starts with the obituaries.

'Oh, Stan," she shouts out to Dad. "Bernard Heaton has died... oh, so has Irene Baxter. What a shame, she was only seventy-eight years old and she died in her sleep. Pity she wasn't prepared for it, the good Lord just took her. It's the family I feel sorry for."

Pop completely ignores Mum. Mum remembers something, gasps and holds onto her cardigan.

"Oh, she was a *bad un,* was Irene Baxter – a thief, a liar and a whore! I hope she got to heaven half an hour before the devil found out she'd gone." Mum then makes the sign of the cross on her body, something she always does when she's been calling someone.

When Pop reads the paper, he goes to the page where the police have named and shamed local thugs for breaking into garden sheds and nicking lawnmowers. He then reads out every name and laughs at their sentences. Mum doesn't listen to him.

The only activity they do together is look at the prices of houses in their area.

"Joan, we could have bought that house for £100," Pop will point to one and say. "Now it's £150,000. It's disgraceful."

Mum points to shops that were once thriving on the High Street.

"Stan, that would have made a fantastic haberdashery shop... I might open it."

Pop looks at Mum like she's gone mad. Then everything is ruined as they start to bicker again.

It's not often Pop has a go at Mum, but today he seems really fed up with her. He puts his hands on his hips and says

"When I drew my pension and looked at myself on my ID, I saw a grey haired, thin, miserable old man looking back at me."

"I know, Stan," Mum says, nodding. "I see that every day." This makes Pop furious.

Most of the time, Pop can't win with Mum's sharp tongue, but today he comes back at her again.

"I thought retirement would be glorious, peaceful and we'd have money to spend. What have I got, though? A stinking pension worth nothing, that's what."

"You've earned your pension, but what you should have done is gone to the social and dropped your pants, then you'd have got disability allowance as well," Mum adds quickly.

Pop walks round the kitchen saying, "Blah, blah, blah." Then announces "I'm going to the pub."

"Go on, go and see your cronies and get drunk," Mum snaps.

"Well, there's no alcohol in heaven," Pop laughs. "So I'm getting my fill now."

Mum shakes her head and starts talking to herself, cursing Pops actions as she does so. She tells herself he's selfish and then answers herself with "Yeah, I know he is." I need to get away from Mum and Pop, so I go to my room like I did when I was a child, and think about my next move. I lie on the bed, wishing I'd gone with Jane and kept her company. She's had to go to Brighton today because in the morning the bailiffs are arriving to throw her son and his friends out for living in squalor. Jane is furious with Josh and she will probably belt him around the head when she sees him. A three year degree has come to nothing; he partied all through university and he's still partying now.

I think about Tom's deceit and how I was living in ignorant bliss. What an idiot I've been. I know I'm not the same person. How could I be after everything that's happened? I feel really annoyed that I have let myself go and for not having any interests of my own.

****

When Pop comes home from the pub, I decide to tell my parents about the Freak's other life. I'm leaving Tom to tell Louise though - why should I do his dirty work? I have no idea how Louise will act: normally she's very calm, being the professional that she is, but this is something very different. 'A biggie,' as Jane would say.

I walk down the stairs and Mum and Pop are at it again. Mum is banging about in the kitchen and Pop is sat at the kitchen table.

"I'm sick of you, Stanley." Mum points a wooden spoon at Pop. "You're a very selfish, difficult man. If you don't change your ways I'm divorcing you… are you listening to me Stanley?"

Pop is sipping out of a can of beer and Mum has no idea that his hearing aid has been turned off. I ask Mum to sit down at the table and I sit opposite them both. I proceed to tell them about Tom's other family and, to my surprise, Mum says nothing and all Pop says is "I knew he was a man of bad character when he killed the budgie."

"Poor Joey," Mum adds, nodding her head solemnly.

Not poor *me*. Or poor *Louise*. Pop shakes his head for a few minutes then starts reading the paper again. Mum and I go into the lounge

"Can you believe all this, Mum?"

"He's probably become religious as well."

"There you go again, talking about religion," I sigh heavily and frown as I answer her. "What's religion got to do with it?"

Mum gets her knitting out and puckers up her breast.

"I saw a programme where a man married five women. Oh, the jealousy was awful. I felt sorry for the kids involved. Maybe he's married to more than one woman? He'll have to join a religious group, otherwise he'll be charged with soggily."

I stare at Mum drop-jawed, and there isn't a word in the world that could describe how I feel. Then Mum smiles and says "The man on the telly had a beard."

After a few G&Ts, I become desperately sad and start to cry. I can't help it, I'm just so emotional and mentally exhausted. Mum kneels down in front of me and puts her hand on my knee.

"Cathy, cheer up, the worst is yet to come." I can't speak so Mum speaks for me. "All that gin's no good for you, that's why they call it mother's ruin. I got pregnant with you on gin and look at what's happened to you."

****

I decide to take Rupert for a long walk so that I can clear my head. We walk along fields and I think about my life and how it's turned out. I don't regret giving birth to Louise for one minute and I think she has the best of me and Tom in her. What I do regret is not being vigilant and taking more notice of everything. I even wish I'd hired a private detective. Then again, why would I suspect the man I married would cheat on me? Was it my fault or was it both of our faults? I really don't know.

When I get home, Mum is on the phone and wafts her hand at me, motioning me to move on and not listen in on the conversation. I go into the kitchen and take off the dog's lead. Mum is deep in conversation with her sister. When Mum is on the phone to Ireland, her accent often becomes deep Irish and half the time I can't understand what she's saying. However, today I can hear every word.

"Oh, Val it's been awful. Our poor Cathy, she's been through the mill and back again and then back *again*. What a monster he turned out to be… well, we know, don't we? We know he's a murderer and now it seems he's also a deadly jelly fish." Mum is silent for a few seconds, then she almost shouts. "Yes, Val, his eyes were too close together and he had a big nose."

Mum is only quiet to draw breath and then she's off again. "Well, I suppose you're right Val, she's got the luck of the Irish, she's got rid of hers… when will ye be coming over the pond then?"

Mum always refers to 'over the pond' since she saw an episode of *The Golden Girls* on TV. It's hardly over the pond from Ireland to Yorkshire.

"Oh, Val!" She suddenly shrieks. "We can't have Christmas early. A turkey never voted for an early Christmas." She cackles and puts the phone down, then immediately calls someone else. "Oh, Doris, yes there's been an upgrade - the filthy feck was living a double life… do you remember *Dallas*? Well that's what it's been like here. Tom is JR and he's having an affair with Pam, Bobby's wife… I think it was Pam but it could have been Kristin, and come to think of it, our Cathy is a dead ringer for Sue Ellen." Then Mum whispers "She drinks too much as well … I might get a sign saying Fort Knox for when me sister comes over."

I know at times I'm as bad as Mum but I can't help myself.

"It's South Fork," I shout into the hall. "Not Fort Knox."

She ignores me and hums the *Dallas* theme tune while she's dialling her next number. The person obviously isn't in so Mum leaves a message. She draws breath then says, "Hello… its Joan here… Joan Mathews… wanting to… give you valuable… gossip about Cathy… that's Cathy Mathews now… but she was once a shot gun wedding barrel type of name… I can't remember it though… goodbye."

"Mum, do you have to gossip about my private life?" I'm standing in the doorway by now.

"I'm not gossiping." Mum shakes her hands. "It will get out eventually."

I'm furious but I end up pleading with her.

"Mum, you promised. It was a secret."

"Cathy, it's not a secret after three people know about it," Mum says, laughing it off, then counts off on her fingers: "That's me, Pop and our Val."

****

The following day I meet Louise for lunch and she is furious about how her father has conducted himself.

"Honestly, Mum, I want nothing more to do with him. He's lied to both of us for years. Did he think it would never come out?" I can't answer her because I still can't get my own head around it.

"It's not the child's fault," Louise sighs. "It's all Dad's doing. He should have come clean at the beginning and just left."

"Louise, your dad stayed because you were only fourteen years of age," I reply, shaking my head, "and it was a difficult time for you at school. The new baby wouldn't have known any different. You were older and you needed him."

"Mum, I can't believe you're defending him," she says, slamming her knife and fork down on her plate. "We've all been living a lie and that tart knew exactly what she was doing by getting pregnant. All she could see was a businessman: nice house, nice car and she was on the payroll... Jesus."

I can feel myself welling up, which upsets Louise.

"I wasn't sticking up for him," I quietly say. "I was only telling you what he told me."

"I'm sorry, Mum." Louise squeezes my hand, "I know you are. We're well shot of him. And as for his other family- let them get on with it."

I sip my wine and know I need to pull myself together and get on with life, even if it does feel like I'll be climbing Kilimanjaro. I stare at Louise and I can see she's not herself; she looks tired and drawn and she's lost a lot of weight. Tom really has messed up everyone's life and, for the first time ever, I hope Karma pays him back.

****

Jane makes me go online and go on another date. Her words are "The only way to get over one, is to get under one." I don't quite know what she means but I am sick of staying in and torturing myself about the Freak and his other family. They're on my mind morning, noon and night and it's giving me a headache. I bet Fanny's laughing at me and thinking she's won- and in a way, she has. I wish I could move on and stop thinking about them. "I don't think I've much chance of finding love again," I say repeatedly. However, I don't think I found it in the first place, I was just blinded by his charms.

****

My third date is a bitter and twisted man named Peter

who, from the minute he sits down, talks about his wife and their bitter divorce. Apparently, she found out he was saving money for a rainy day and when she had her day in court she screamed in front of the judge: "Rainy day, rainy day? It's pissed down in our house for over thirty shitting years and that money NEVER made an appearance."

The Judge gave her half of Peter's savings and he can't and won't get over it. He also tells me that he's had over fifty affairs but, to be honest, looking at him, I can't quite believe him. The meal is awful slop and its stone cold. When I decline the offer of going back to his brother's house for a shag, he goes bonkers and starts shouting.

"You're a fat bitch anyway, I wouldn't touch you with a barge pole. You're nothing but a prick teaser."

Prick teaser? Me? I'm wearing a baggy jumper, leggings and boots. I am hardly a prick teaser. Off I go, back home in the back of a taxi, and I've been in them so many times now that I'm on first name terms with the drivers. Marvin, my favourite taxi driver, looks in his rear view mirror at me and chirpily asks. "How's your date gone?"

"Don't even ask." I roll my eyes, "I got the low-down on his divorce and the bitter break-up he'd had. Then he calls me a prick teaser."

Marvin laughed until he could laugh no more. 'You're an attractive woman and if I wasn't already married I'd take you out.' I smile and feel instantly uplifted.

****

The minute I get home, I go online and change my profile for the third time.

Fifty-five year old woman seeks genuine companion to share her life with. Enjoys going to the cinema, eating out and going for walks in the park with her little dog.

It's short, sweet and to the point and even though it is boring, I'm still getting around twenty hits every day, mostly from sex-starved men. One guy has the cheek to email me and say "You're not bad looking. A bit plain but okay. However, you're a bit on the big size for me. If you lose some weight though, I may be inclined to give you a go." When I read it, I feel like begging to meet up with him until he agrees, then I would knock his teeth down his throat. This dating game is something else and the rules have drastically changed, it's just a world of shallow, self-obsessed men. I even have an offer of a date from a lesbian, which makes me smile. She actually says I am gorgeous. I send her an email back thanking her and explaining, "I'm not a lesbian, but I'll keep your number, in case I ever change my mind." Jane finds everything I do hilarious and says it's the best laugh she's had in years.

****

Mum and Pop are good to me. They never take any money off me – they let me save it to buy wine. It can't go on though, so today I need to register for work at the local job centre because I'm officially broke. I'm petrified because I have never set foot in a job centre before. Years ago, when I was sixteen, I went to a careers office just for advice. It was nothing formal, just a little chat with a woman who looked like she should have retired years ago. She gave me some advice so I would never be out of work in my life. She said if I always wore lipstick, smart clothes and conducted myself in a ladylike manner, I would never be out of work. She also added that if I don't know something, I should act like I do anyway because then I will come across as confident.

The first job she thought would be good for me was a sewing machinist and she knew of a factory nearby that was looking for trainee machinists. How could I take that? I couldn't even sew a button onto a blouse? The second option was to go and work at Woolworths, "There's one in every town," she chirped, but I turned my nose up at that, which got the woman quite annoyed with me. The third job she suggested was a typist and, in her own words, you had to be one of the elite to be a typist. Then hopefully I could climb my up the job ladder and become a secretary. We sat staring at each other for what seemed like ages before she snapped at me: "Well?"

"I'd like to be one of Pan's People," I quietly said.

"Pan's People?" she shrieked at the top of her voice. "Pan's People? What the hell is that, a company that makes cookware?"

I was shocked that she didn't know who they were and I felt it my duty to put her right."

"They're dancers on the TV, *Top of the Pops* actually to be exact."

She went completely over the top and started tutting very loudly, making a spectacle of herself. I left the office with nothing more than a leaflet on how to write a letter correctly.

Mum shared my desire to be a Pan's Person and one night she quietly told me that when she was young, she wanted to show her knickers to the boys in Paris. So she thought ambition to be a Pan's Person was a sign that I was following in her footsteps.

It seemed I was more academic than everyone thought and, at twenty-six years of age, I graduated from Northumberland University with a degree in History. That was the day I met Tom. After several groups of students had their pictures taken outside the fantastic building in their caps and gowns, we all retired to the local pub and, after drinking my own body weight in cider, we had our very first snog. We moved in together three weeks later and partied on a daily basis until our loans and overdrafts ran dry. Then we tearfully left each other and went back to our parents' to put our degrees to good use. I didn't apply for any jobs because I was still on a high from university and I missed Tom terribly. I'd only been home a couple of days when I found a picture of Steven in my cap and gown. Mum had framed it and put it on the lounge wall. I couldn't believe what I was seeing and the fact that Mum had gone along with it was crazy. Steven didn't have one CSE, let alone a degree.

When I asked Mum she swore blind that she thought Steven had also done a degree and Pop just said "He's an idiot." It was six weeks until I saw Tom again and I'd lost loads of weight because I'd been pining for him. He took one look at me, walked over and snogged the face off me. From then on we were inseparable. We went to parents to tell them we wanted to move in together. Mum wasn't happy and made us promise we would buy bunk beds and not sleep in the same bed. That was the night of the tragedy, when Tom accidently kicked the budgie into the fire. Tom was trying to make me laugh by marching into Mum and Pop's like he was in the army. His steps were exaggerated and when he went into the lounge, the budgie swooped down to the ground but landed on Tom's shoe, so when Tom kicked out his leg the poor thing was kicked onto the fire and crackled away whilst everyone watched in horror.

It was a while before Mum and Pop would let Tom back in the house so we tried to get ourselves a flat, but the rents were too high and neither of us had a job. Polly and Gerrard said we could live in their annex on one condition: we got married. In truth, she didn't want her affluent friends to see her precious son was living over the brush. I also knew that deep down she thought Tom could do better than me, so we got engaged. We lived in the annex for a year until we decided to buy a house together. Again, Polly interfered and told us to buy the best we could and aim high so we didn't have to move when we had children. They put the deposit down for us and we went house-hunting. Tom's degree was in business management and marketing, so it came as no surprise to everyone when he set up his own business and it became very successful within the first two years. Export and import was booming and we reaped the rewards of his hard work and knowledge. Tom's parents had funded a lot of the project and, when he offered to pay them back years later, they declined to take the money. I never knew how much the investment was and Tom didn't discuss money or the business with me. All I had to do was keep the house nice and get things ready for our new baby. Now, at fifty-five years of age, I'm heading for the job centre to sign on.

I walk into a building that looks like a concrete jungle. Inside, they have plastic chairs that are bolted to the floor. Perspex shields divide the staff from the public and the smell is something else - a mixture of cigarette smoke, sweat and alcohol. There are a few decent people in here who are looking for jobs on a machine and the place is packed. I take a ticket out of a machine and find that I'm number eleven in the queue.

My appointment should have been 10am and it's now 11.45am. Every time I ask someone how much longer it will be, they simply shake their head and say "We're doing our best." Every ten minutes, I spray my top with perfume, stick my head into my blouse and take a deep breath. Even that doesn't kill off the bad smells around me though.

When I finally sit in front of an advisor, she tells me I haven't filled in the form correctly and asks me to stand aside and finish it off. "No," I say to her through gritted teeth, "I will finish the form here and, if you don't mind, you can then check that it's all okay."

She looks at me and says "We're not meant to do that, but on this occasion I will allow it."

When the form is complete, she tells me that Jobseekers Allowance is paid at the rate of up to £73.10 per week. I'm glad I'm sitting down because if I hadn't been, my legs would have gone from under me. £73.20 - I used to spend that in less than an hour at Waitrose!

As she does a job search for me, I tell her that I've got a degree in History

"You've not used your degree for anything useful?" she smiles at me sarcastically.

"Obviously not," I reply. "I chose to have a child instead."

"Well that won't get you a job now, will it?" she says patronisingly. "That's unless you want to look after children in a nursery or school?"

I'm furious. How *dare* she speak to me like that?

"We have a lot of jobs for cleaners," she says, tapping her computer. "There's one here in a nursing home."

I feel as though I may faint any minute.

"I can't work in a nursing home," I say with a slight shudder. "The smell would be too much for me and I'm not that nice with old people. I have elderly parents and I know what they're like."

After a long silence, she passes me a signing on card.

"Beggars can't be choosers you know," she helpfully informs me. "Eventually you will have to take something."

****

I can't wait to get back into the fresh air.

On the way home I curse the Freak and Fanny. How dare they take my life away from me?

When I get in, I tell Mum all about what has happened and she listens intently. Mum can't believe the government are going to give me money.

"They're giving you money for nothing?"

"It isn't for nothing," I sigh. "I have to do a fortnightly job search."

"Seventy-three pounds a week," she says, raising a sceptical eyebrow. "That's good. Me and your Pop could manage off that. Can we apply?"

I don't even answer. I'm too angry. I want to cry, scream and throw myself on the floor like a petulant child. I'm so frustrated. How could any intelligent women get a degree and never use it? How could I let a man keep me all these years and trust in him so much? I remember, when Louise started her degree, she was sitting in the lounge and announced "I'm never going to rely on any man. I'm going to be completely independent and have my own money." I remember laughing at the time, thinking she was talking like a Suffragette and that when she finally found someone she would take care of the house and have babies. How things have changed and now I'm afraid I've been left behind because of my own stupidity.

CHAPTER 10

The night flushes are as bad as ever and I can't cope with the other symptoms. My hair is falling out and I have visions of me bumping into the freak and the Fluff and I'll be completely bald. My mood swings are terrible; is that the menopause or my situation? Either way I have to do something about it. I'm on my last one hundred pounds courtesy of the government and I desperately need to get a job. The Jobseekers Allowance does help but it's nowhere near what I need. It's only fair that I give Mum money for petrol when I use her car and every week I try to buy some of their favourite foods - like tripe and cow heal – on that night that I go to Jane's. I am sitting in the garden having a coffee with Mum. I want a bit of moral support so that I can try to understand the whole menopause thing, so I ask her again how she coped. Her reply isn't what I expect.

"Cathy, I've told you - I just got on with it. There was none of this nonsense when I was younger."

I become frustrated and say "You must have had some symptoms, certain things that changed?" Mum thinks for a minute.

"My pubic hair fell out and what was left went grey."

We are silent for a good five minutes. Where do you go in your mind when you've just had an answer like that? I decide to go back to bed and feel sorry for myself. After all, I wasn't getting any sympathy from Mum.

****

Mum had been trying to help when she found an advert in the Sunday papers for a menopausal magnet – I suppose it's her way of showing she cares - and today it's arrived. Rupert grabs the jiffy bag and throws it around the room. This amuses Mum and, much to my annoyance, she gives him a little treat when she takes it off him. Then she hands me the parcel and I read the included leaflet.

Eliminates symptoms; it's discreet and sits comfortably inside your underwear. This is a drug-free product for the relief of hot flushes, heart palpitations, mood swings, anxiety, weight gain, fatigue and irritability. This magnet helps to balance the mind and body and helps you to keep in tune with the movement of the Earth.

"Irritability?" Mum laughs "Shall I get one for your Pop?"

I laugh but I'm intrigued by this new object. Could this be the answer to my problems? It's certainly worth a try and nobody will suspect I have a magnet in my knickers. I put it in them and hope for the best.

The list Mum gives me for the supermarket is as long as my arm. I walk in the store and I'm met by an array of bargains. As I walk through the barrier, my body involuntarily moves towards the metal on it and I look like I'm trying to do the limbo. I quickly look around and hope nobody has seen me. Then I head over to the fishmonger.

"What can I do you for?" he asks pleasantly.

I laugh and say "I'll have three pieces of salmon, please."

The fishmonger wraps up the fish and is humming a tune. He hands me the fish and says "Just remember, if it swims it slims."

"Do you think I'm fat?" I stammer in surprise.

The fishmonger is horrified and quickly tries to apologise.

"No, I didn't mean that, you're lovely, honestly."

I don't know why I've reacted in this way and suddenly

there's a moment of awkwardness. The fishmonger is becoming nervous. We stare at each other for a moment and then I try to walk away, but my pelvis is stuck to the metal counter. I feel so embarrassed. I start to stretch and wiggle my body. The fishmonger joins in as though we are at an exercise class.

"My wife does Pilates," he chirps.

I smile, then with all my strength I pull myself away from the counter. The fishmonger stares at me wobbling away up the aisle. As I approach the bread counter, my body picks up speed and once again my pelvis is thrust out in front of me. I literally run towards the bread slicing machine. I try grabbing things to slow myself down, but a loaf of bread is hardly going to save me. The baker sees me approaching and has a look of horror on his face. Just as I'm about to have a nasty encounter with the bread slicer, the baker grabs hold of me.

"Woe, woe, steady on, love." He sits me on a chair covered in flour. "Bloody hell, are you planning on killing yourself?"

I shake my head but I can't talk because my breathing is laboured. The baker bends down to look at me.

"Surely nothing's that bad. Besides, the machine wouldn't kill you... it would cut you up a bit, though."

I'm in a daze and wonder what just happened. I want to go home, but I can't go back without the shopping. Eventually I regain my composure and thank the baker for his concern. I head towards the aisle that sells household goods and, as I turn around from picking up a salad bowl and some new pot towels, my hip moves towards the cutlery. Two large knives attach themselves to my pelvis. I struggle to prise them off. A young shop assistant stares at me, then talks into his walkie-talkie.

"I need help in aisle 12, there's an evil entity trying to stab a woman." The young man approaches me with caution. "Excuse me, madam, those knives are extremely dangerous."

I don't even answer him. I need to get out of the shop as soon as I can. The knives drop to the floor and the shop assistant can't take his eyes off me as he gently picks them up and puts them back on the shelf.

I get to the checkout and my face is blood red.

"Are you having a hot flush?" The cashier smiles and almost shouts. I smile back and keep my head down as I unload the shopping onto the conveyer belt. The cashier stops scanning the shopping and starts to demonstrate how her hot flushes come up her body. She points at her chest.

"Oh, it's bloody terrible. It comes from my chest, to my neck, then my face." She touches all the parts of her body. I stare at her in the hope she'll continue scanning the shopping again, which she eventually does. An old lady joins the queue and listens to the conversation.

"Oh, I remember those hot sweats," she suddenly squeals. "I had really high blood pressure. I collapsed one day and was rushed to hospital. I've never been the same since."

The cashier stops scanning the shopping again.

"My auntie Beryl ended up in a mental hospital."

"Oh, love, how long was she there for?" asks the old lady.

The cashier thinks for a moment and replies. "Till she died."

The old lady pulls a sad face, which makes the cashier even worse.

"I had a terrible discharge, awful it was," she almost shouts.

The old lady ignores her, turns off her hearing aid and walks towards the café. I wish I had a hearing aid that I could switch off. It would help me when Mum and Pop start bickering. I pay for the food and I'm really anxious now. As I walk away from the cashier, the magnet slips down my leggings and gets trapped at my ankle. My left leg suddenly attaches itself to the supermarket trolley and I hop of out the store, across the car park and get in the car. Once inside, I sigh heavily; even an innocent trip to the supermarket has left me completely stressed. I remove the magnet from the bottom of my leggings and put it in my handbag. I had no idea the magnet would be so strong. When I tell Mum of my experience at the supermarket, she doesn't seem shocked at all. Instead, she simply looks at me and says "It's a magnet Cathy, that's what they do."

****

Jane and I take ages getting ready and we're playing all the songs we loved from the seventies. We sing at the top of our voices to the Bee Gees and then the songs from *Grease* and *Saturday Night Fever* come on as well. This delays our trip out by two hours.

When we finally get to the pub, we order a bottle of wine. My feet are already hurting from dancing before we went out, so we sit and eye up the local talent. It takes us all of three minutes because there isn't any. I feel too old to be sat in a pub listening to pop music. Then a song comes on and the words are ridiculous. The young lad is singing: *"I'll take a grenade for you, walk under a train for you, but you won't do the same for me."* We both laugh and Jane says, "Dead right we won't!" At 11.30pm, we decide to go to a club. Regal is a newly refurbished nightclub and when we queue up to get in, the bouncer says to us both "OAPs get in free tonight."

Jane and I laugh because we think he's joking, only to hear

him say it to two old men behind us that look like they're in their seventies. The wine is so expensive that we decide to have what all the younger girls are having; a pint of lager and a jägerbomb dropped into it. They go down a treat and at three drinks for a fiver, it isn't breaking the bank. After a few pints of rocket fuel, Jane and I take to the dance floor and strut our stuff. Some people laugh, but we don't care. The two old men, who were behind us when we came in, ask if they can buy us a drink.

"I think we'll have a double G&T, thanks mate," Jane shouts.

The men look at each other, then one of them says "Think again, we were thinking you're more half a lager girls."

Jane and I are in shock. Then the other man speaks

"We're pensioners you know?"

"No shit," Jane laughs.

"And I'm on the dole," I shout above the music. I feel very liberated by saying this.

"You can tell," says one of the men as he looks at me.

What was that supposed to mean? I think to myself. The men walk off, which makes us both giggle.

At one point we are sat at a table and we notice a man in his forties staring at us. The devil in me comes out and, mixed with the demon drink, I lift my blouse up so he can see my tits. Jane is laughing so much that she nearly wets herself.

"Cathy, your bra's got a hole in it and your nipple is sticking out."

I laugh and when I look again, the man is gone. Then suddenly the Freak and Fanny come into to my mind and a rage comes over me. I suddenly turn to Jane and say "Can you believe he had a secret for thirteen years?"

Jane shakes her head, downs her drink and wipes her mouth with the back of her hand.

"Makes you wonder if you can trust any of them," she slurs. "That's why I'm happy on my own."

I down my drink too and agree with her.

"I'll never marry again, he's put me right of men."

Jane grabs my arm and leads me to the dance floor. We both dance around our handbags to Tina Turner and Jane begins twerking and passes wind at the same time. I find it all hilarious and fall to my knees laughing.

"Oh God, Jane, this is the life - having fun, fun, fun, fun."

****

In the kebab shop, Jane starts giggling.

"God, that club was full of old swingers wasn't it?"

"Including us," I laugh.

Jane suddenly becomes serious and decides she wants to make a drunken confession.

"Cathy, if I tell you something, you won't tell anyone else, will you?"

"My lips are crossed," I slur as I wobble towards her and put my finger to my lips.

Jane then tells me that when we were both younger she fancied Hughie Green from *Opportunity Knocks*. I'm so shocked that I don't know whether to laugh or cry, but it certainly sobers me up a bit.

"Hughie Green?" I whisper. "He was an old man, even

back then."

Jane nods her head and slurs "I know, it's true though."

"When I was little," I say, wanting to join in with the confessing, "I loved Charlie Drake. You know, with his funny laugh."

Jane howls in hysterics.

"He was so small that they used to pick him up and sit him on the bar."

I can't catch my breath, I'm laughing that much.

Once outside the kebab shop, Jane asks me to hold her kebab. She then tries to pole dance on a sign that says 'heavy load.' A few cars beep their horns and some are just laughing out of their car windows. Jane then slides down the pole and falls to the floor in a heap. A car pulls up beside us, so we immediately get inside and Jane gives the driver her address.

The man turns to us in the back and says "I'm not a taxi driver; I'm waiting for my daughter to come out of the club." We both pull a face, then Jane says, "Please take us home, we've had a lot to drink and our legs have run out of petrol."

I look down at my feet and whinge "I've only got one shoe on… please take us home, it's only round the corner." The man's daughter gets in the car and looks at us in disgust. A few minutes later, the driver agrees to take us home – it's far easier for him than listening to me and Jane beg. Also, we're too drunk to get out of the car.

****

When I wake up in the morning, I'm fully clothed and in bed with Jane. She has her arm around me and there's half a kebab on the quilt cover. I slowly sit up but Jane doesn't move. My head is banging and I feel really sick. I look in my purse and I've spent thirty-five pounds out of my Jobseekers Allowance on booze, despite only getting it from the post office yesterday morning. The first half of the night I can remember but the last bit is a blur that comes back to me in flashes that aren't very nice. I can't remember how much I drank and I know it's totally irresponsible for a woman of any age, let alone fifty-five, to act how we both did. I remember looking at myself in the toilet mirror in the club and the person I saw looking back at me was someone else; someone that had aged dramatically, who was alone and who had pain and stress written all over her face. She was fat and acting like she was eighteen again. Mutton springs to mind.

I have an appointment this morning so I get dressed and ring for a taxi. I can't afford one but it's better than waiting for a bus. In the taxi I look at my phone and there's loads of selfies of us pulling funny faces; there's even one of Jane's knickers and she's taken one of me kissing a man on the cheek. At the time it all seemed like fun but now I feel a bit ashamed.

When I arrive at the building it's packed with young couples with buggies and screaming toddlers. There are also a few unkempt men and I wonder if I should go and sit with them because, after all, I smell of booze and my clothes are creased and smelly. I book myself in at the reception area, then sit down and wait. I'm looking around when I see a young girl with four small children. She's arguing with the woman behind the desk and she's begging to be re-housed on an estate called Birch Hall, which by anybody's account is an extremely rough estate. She won't let the woman get a word in edgeways and when she finally shuts up, the woman behind the desk tells her that she can have a house on that estate because nobody wants to live there. The young girl seems extremely happy. Another poor soul is asking for a flat but he can't string a sentence together, he's so drunk. There's also a young family that are trying to explain about repairs that need doing.

"We've not been able to have a bath for a month because of the plumbing and now my girlfriend is pregnant again and it's the council's fault."

I can't help but put my head down and laugh to myself. What is this world I am now living in? Of course I knew this world existed, but to see it first hand is something else.

It takes the local council five minutes to tell me that I can't have a house, flat, bungalow or cardboard box because I don't qualify as homeless. I'd foolishly told them I'd gone back to my parents' house and, when they asked me how many bedrooms they had, I'd told them three. The man was a little sympathetic when he saw my face and quietly told me that if I could get a letter from my parents to say they were kicking me out, then potentially that would make me homeless. I would then be given a small place to live.

****

On the way home I see a ray of light to my current situation and I know deep down Mum wants her house back, although she would never say that, and I need my own space. The word homelessness keeps ringing in my ears and it takes me back to a memory of a homeless woman that used to hang around the shops when we were kids. Her name was Sally and all the kids in the neighbourhood used to chant 'Dirty Sally, dirty Sally dirty Sally." I always felt sorry for her and used to bring her biscuits from home. One day, she went into the supermarket, sat on a mountain of sugar and peed on it. The manager threw her out and shouted "You're barred," so for spite, she pinched a supermarket trolley and put all her belongings in it. I remember one winter, when Mum saw her sat in a doorway and she went over to her and gave her two pounds to get something to eat.

"For the grace of God, I complained I had no shoes until I met a man with no feet." Mum had said. At the time I couldn't understand why she would have seen a man with no feet.

As we walked into the store, Sally shouted to Mum "'Eff off, you Irish cow." Mum was horrified and made a sign of the cross on her chest.

****

When I get home I explain to my parents that I need a letter from them both to say they are asking me to leave. Mum goes ballistic.

"Me? Joan Mathews? Kicking out her first born?" she shrieks. "I don't think so. What the hell would everyone think of me?"

Mum can't grasp that it's only a letter for me, so that I can get a flat. I can't reason with her and when I try to explain, she shouts above my voice.

"Bejesus, who would throw their own child out on the streets? To get raped and pillaged? Not to mention how cold you'd be. Can you imagine the news headlines? 'Cruel mother makes child live in the gutter'? Oh no, Cathy, I won't do it."

I walk into the kitchen and pour a glass of wine. I know I shouldn't because I'm still hung over from last night, but I just can't handle the stress. I'm looking out of the window when I hear Mum talking. At first I think she's talking to Pop, but when I really listen I realise that she's on the phone.

"Yes, that's the correct address, and you need to make a note: I'm not kicking my own child out of this house. All the gossip in the office can stop now."

Mum puts the phone down and I stare at her.

"Who have you just phoned?"

Mum puckers up her breasts before she speaks.

"I've told them lot at the council that you're not to be made homeless. I told them that you aren't yourself and you're not thinking straight. Nobody is going to think badly of me, and besides, what would God say?"

****

Within days, I get a letter from the job centre. It's telling me to go in for an interview and if I don't attend, my money will be stopped. I storm in armed with an endless list of jobs I've applied for.

The woman behind the desk is very patronising as she looks at the list and sighs heavily.

"It's probably your age, Ms Mathews, as well as your lack of experience." She looks as if the world is going to come to an end when she looks at my half page CV. "Ms Mathews, you can't continue to stay on Jobseekers Allowance. The government are clamping down so we need to get you into work… and it's good for your own self-esteem of course."

Before she can speak, I tell her that I'm not looking after children at fifty-five years of age and I'm definitely not going to clean for anyone- let alone anyone in a nursing home. My reaction surprises her, so she leans back in her chair and raises her eyebrows.

All the way home, I keep wondering how other people manage when they have nothing. Why was I finding it so hard to cope? Had I been completely spoilt all my life?

I find out that Louise has put one hundred pounds into my bank account so I can buy something nice and, although it is a lovely thing to do, I feel very sad that my daughter is helping me out because the Freak cheated on me. Mum makes us all a coffee and we sit in the lounge with Pop.

"What are you smiling at?" she asks, looking across at him.

"I'm smiling because I can't hear you."

"Oh Cathy," Mum squeals with delight. "Your Pop has got a new hearing aid. It's that small you don't know it's there."

"How wonderful, I'm very pleased for him."

Mum's deep in thought as she says, "I wish I had a hearing aid," then she jumps up and squeals. "Oh Cathy, did I tell you? Cheryl who owns the cheese shop is pregnant again and it's a different dad to the other kids."

I look at Mum and have no expression on my face. That doesn't stop her though, and she shouts, "We were all saying at the bingo that she can't keep her Cheddar Gorge closed for no one." I don't find it one bit funny and my face is still blank. Mum picks up her knitting and quietly says "She's a whore."

****

A few days later, Pop shows me a job advertisement in the local paper where a mature lady is needed to answer the phone and do general bookkeeping. I whine at Pop like I'm a child.

"Pop, I can't do bookkeeping."

Pop sits next to me and gently places his hand on my shoulder.

"Cathy, you've paid bills," he says encouragingly. "You've shopped for the house. You can do bookkeeping. Come on, give it a go."

Mum appears in the lounge doorway and wipes her hands on her apron.

"Go and give it a go, Cathy. You've nothing to lose and you need to earn some money."

Two days later, I turn up at a small garage that sells second-hand cars. I walk into the showroom and knock on the office door.

"Come in," A man shouts loudly.

When I walk into the office, I see a very large man sat at a desk and he's smoking a huge cigar and talking on his phone. He beckons me in and indicates a chair in front of him for me to sit on. The office looks very dusty and there are papers stacked and scattered everywhere. On the window sill there are empty pizza boxes, kebab boxes and an array of empty cans of coke. I cough several times in the hope that he will put out his cigar but he fails to take the hint. After five minutes of waiting I can feel my stomach churning and I want to stand up and slap his face. Another five minutes go by and my temper is at fever pitch. He takes his ear away from the phone for a second and says "And your name is?"

I screw my face up as I say "I'm Cathy, Cathy Mathews."

He carries on talking on the phone and I find myself wondering if I have ever met such a rude man before in all my life. I'm just about to get up and leave when he takes the phone away from his ear again.

"Cathy, excite me, make me notice you, show me what you're made of."

I can't believe what I'm hearing and I stare at him. He relights his cigar, then, with the phone still in one hand, he picks up the newspaper and starts reading it. I lean over the desk, pick up his lighter and set fire to the newspaper. Then I stand up and walk out of the office. As I leave the building I can hear him screaming and I can see that the sprinkler system has bounced into action. That'll teach him to be so rude and I'm pretty sure he won't forget me in a hurry.

CHAPTER 11

I have regular dreams about the Freak and the Fluff and some of them are really disturbing, like they've won the lottery and I can see them sailing around the world, waving at me. In other dreams, I'm torturing them both and I'm laughing hysterically as I rev up my chain saw. The one I had last night was awful. I'm in the booze aisle at local supermarket and I'm swigging out of different bottles of spirits and putting them back on the shelf. I'm trying to be discreet but I'm not doing a very good job of it. The manager comes running down the aisle after me and when he catches me, he breathalyses me with a giant spirit level and the liquid in the middle won't stop swaying from side to side. The store manager frog-marches me out of the store and, as I pass the dog food aisle, the Fluff is popping out babies like sticky Vicky in Benidorm would pop out ping pong balls. I start screaming "Kill them all, get the shutter down." That's when I woke up with a start.

As I walk towards the kitchen, I hear Mum and Pop talking.

"Have you heard our Cathy screaming in the early hours?" she is asking. "She must have a recurring dream."

"It's that nightmare she has about getting a job," Pop replies.

I walk in the kitchen and sit at the table.

"If you must know, Pop, I'd love a job because then I could move out."

Mum spins round and gives Pop a filthy look.

"You're going nowhere, Cathy, you're good company for me."

Pop stands up and gets the dog's lead.

"Come on, Robin, let's go for a walk." Rupert wags his tail; he doesn't care what names Pop calls him anymore as long as he goes out. I don't know what to do with myself so I head back to my room and lie on the bed. Most days I stay in my bedroom like a moody teenager who doesn't want to be in the same room as her parents. Mum brings food up on little trays that she's bought from the pound shop and I watch back to back *CSI* episodes. Maybe I'm trying to get some tips for the murder I'm about to commit.

****

At 6pm, I take a bath and start getting ready to go out. I haven't got much money but Jane and I intend to get a few drinks paid for by men who can't resist our company. I'm sitting on my bed to kill some time when I see an article on revenge and it makes me laugh.

Wife who donated a kidney to her now estranged husband, wants it back.

Jesus, and I thought my life was a mess. I think about how this woman must feel, giving such a wonderful gift to someone only to have him leave her. If I'd done that for the Freak I would personally take it back. No hospital- just me and him in Fanny's kitchen with some blunt instruments.

Five hours later and Jane and I are hammered again. Jane is arguing with the cloakroom lady, saying that she had a beautiful pink coat when she came in, even though the lady is telling her that she doesn't have a ticket. I want to stick up for Jane but my mouth won't work properly because I'm so drunk. We stagger home holding a bottle of beer each. Jane looks into a photographer's shop window and stares at a picture of three beautiful children huddled together and smiling.

"Aren't they ugly kids?" she says, pointing and screwing up her face.

I haven't got my glasses on, so I have to press my face against the window. When the children come into focus I laugh.

"Jane, they're your sister's kids."

Jane looks again and screams with laughter.

"Oh, so they are."

A little further up the road, I do what I've been doing since I got divorced; I try and get money out of the cash machine and it won't give me any. After three goes, it swipes my card and I end up crying and blaming the Freak, the Fluff and the bank for making my life miserable.

****

I wake up again with a massive hangover. I look at the ceiling and wonder why I feel the need to go back to my teenage years and act like an arsehole. Why haven't I grown out of it? Yes, have a bit of fun... but not to this degree. This isn't *real* fun. It's as if Jane and I want a re-run of our lives – the only difference is we're both fifty-five years of age. I need some structure in my life and I need to get a life too. Not the life I had but a completely new one. Within an hour I'm acting like a child again when I ring Mum.

"Mum, come and get me," I whinge as Jane goes back to bed. When I get home, I receive an email from what seems like a nice man. He has just moved into the area and is looking for friendship.

Why not, I think, *I'm not doing anything else.*

Mum tries to persuade me to wear the dress from the charity shop but I tell her it's too tight for me and that I'll wear it as soon as I've lost weight. Mum starts with one of her lectures.

"No wonder you're putting on weight, Cathy, you never stop boozing. You're just like your Pop. A pisshead."

As I get into bed, I can hear her talking to herself because she hasn't noticed I've left the room.

****

My date appears to be pretty normal. He's called Henry, he works for a university as a science lecturer and he's my age – fifty-five. We meet in a cocktail bar and, apart from the little ponytail at the back of his head, he seems okay. We order a Mojito each and I tell him a bit about myself. Nothing too heavy, only that I'm single and looking to get my life back on track. After a minute, I feel like I'm taking over the conversation, talking about myself too much, so I turn to him and joke "… and over to you." I laugh, but he doesn't. Instead he starts talking about molecules and atoms, and after twenty minutes I realise that every time I nod my head to him, he takes it as a cue to carry on banging on about things I have no idea exist. I'm feeling very bored. The meal of lamb and seasonal vegetables is very nice but the company is hard work and we don't have anything in common. Forty five minutes into the meal and Henry stops talking about work and goes on to tell me about his ex-wife.

Apparently she is a pagan who worships the universe, but he soon found out she was worshiping someone else's husband too. The last he heard of them was that they'd gone to Stonehenge to pray for their souls. I'm not at all interested in any of his boring life, it's worse than mine, and I can feel myself nodding off. When we're having coffee, he talks about the chemicals in coffee and how he's just had a sink plumbed into his lounge so that he can wash his hands in every room. I stare at the wall and the only thoughts in my mind are "Kill me, kill me now."

At the end of the date, I can't get away from him and he starts talking about how the Earth was made. He then grabs my arm and pulls me to one side. At first I think he's going to try and kiss me, but instead, he leans into my ear to whisper, "There are aliens watching us as we speak." I don't know why it frightens me but it does, and I start running towards the taxi rank, screaming.

When I get home I tell my parents about the date.

"What a load of crap," Pop laughs. "There's no life on any other planets. He's a bleedin' nutter, just like the others you've been out with."

Mum stops knitting, clearly deep in thought.

"I don't believe in aliens but I do believe in fairies. I've seen them at the bottom of the garden." She then goes all childlike and starts doing the actions. "They wave at me and say, 'hello Joan.'"

"You're away with the fairies, Joan, always have been." Pop says, shaking his head.

"I'd rather be with the fairies than with you, Stanley," she smiles. Pop just laughs.

****

I meet Louise for lunch and she tells me she's met someone very special. I really am pleased for her. She tells me she didn't want to tell me because she didn't want me to be upset after all that has happened with Tom.

"Louise I'm well over your father. I'm very pleased for you," I assure her, but then laugh just a little too loud when I announce "Not all men are shits."

Louise seems relived and we carry on with our lunch.

Throughout the meal I glance at over at her. She's so pretty, she has a good job and now she has met a man from work. I'm so happy for her. I wonder what the Freak has said about it but I won't ask because I don't want to ruin the lunch. Then an awful thought comes over me and I fast forward Louise's life to her wedding day. A flash photo goes through my mind with the Freak, the Fluff and me all in the same photo shot. I know I would have to face it for Louise's sake, but the thought makes me feel sick and I try to push it to the back of my mind.

We both go back to Mum and Pop's and, to our surprise, they're dancing in the lounge to Mario Lanza. It's such a rare and lovely sight that Louise and I just stare at them until they see us.

Mum cooks a lovely meal of mashed potato, peas, carrots and gravy. Pop asks her about the pie we should have had, but apparently Mum has forgotten to make it. Everyone seems in a really good mood. Mum even gets up and pours some wine that she's bought from the supermarket. At the end of the meal, mum squeals.

"Oh, girls, I've been *vajazzled* today."

Louise spits her drink everywhere and coughs as she tries to get her breath. I haven't a clue what all the fuss is about and I don't know what 'vajazzled' means. When Louise finally calms down, Mum shows us her beautifully painted fingernails with diamonds and pearls on every finger. Louise is speechless and is still giggling. When Mum goes into the kitchen Louise tells me what it really means and I get the giggles too.

"Come on, Rubin," Pop shakes his head in a way that has recently become his custom, and says to the dog, "We'll go for a walk and get out of this madhouse." As usual, Rupert's tail wags enthusiastically as he follows.

****

This morning I'm at a different counselling session. I didn't want to go but I've missed two sessions and thought I should make an effort. The woman is also called Cathy, so that'll be easy to remember. We sit in equal chairs in a cold room. Cathy introduces herself, tells me what counselling she does, then goes straight in for the kill. She asks me what has been happening in my life. Where do I start?

"My marriage has broken down," I begin, settling in my chair for the long haul, "because he had an affair and it turned out it was a thirteen year affair and they have a child together."

I wait for her reaction but there's none. Then she simply reiterates what I have just said.

"So your marriage has broken down because of an affair and they have a child together?"

I stare at her and nod slowly, wondering if she is trying to catch me out. There's a very awkward silence. After a moment, she slightly smiles and says "Do you want to elaborate?"

I raise my eyebrows.

"Elaborate? Don't you think that's bad enough?"

She becomes nervous.

"Has anything else happened?"

"Oh, yes," I reply with measured sarcasm. "The house and car got repossessed and I'm back living with my elderly parents."

She licks her lips and says "So, you also lost the house and car and you're now living with your parents ... that must be tough." This repeat counselling goes on for the best part of an hour, then I pick up my bag and walk out of the room twenty-five pounds lighter. As I get in the car I think to myself that the world has gone completely mad, and that includes me.

The job centre has lined me up for an interview at a fast food restaurant and I can't believe how degraded I feel. There's nothing wrong with working in restaurants when you're a student, or on a part-time basis to get some pin money, but at fifty-five years of age, it's awful. I hope they take one look at me and say "No thank you," but I have a sneaky feeling that they're desperate enough to take me.

The interviews are being held at head office, which is an ultra-modern building full of glass windows. I arrive at reception and the girl takes me to a room which is full of young people, some of which are as young as eighteen. Nobody is older than their mid-twenties. I immediately feel very old and I stick out like a sore thumb. We all have to put our name on a badge, introduce ourselves and tell the group a little bit about who we are. When they come to me I go bright red and stand up. My mind immediately goes blank and apart from saying my name, I'm completely mute.

"Cathy, can you tell us a bit about yourself?" asks one of the trainers, cocking her head to one side.

I clear my throat and when I speak it comes out as a whisper.

"I'm Cathy and I'm divorced and I … err … live with my parents and …"

A few of the group laugh and the trainer doesn't quite know what to say. I feel like I'm in an Alcoholics Anonymous meeting and I'm trying to bare my soul to the group. How must that have sounded, *'I live with my parents'?'* It sounds like it is- sad. During the interview we are asked to form groups and then to deal with various complaints about the food. There's also a mock warming oven so that we can test the temperature of the food with a metal pin. We are shown how to wrap a burger and how to make coffee. At lunch time we all go to the canteen and I sit by the window. A young girl called Josie sits next to me and smiles.

"Do you think you'll like working in a burger bar?" she asks.

"Not really, but it's a job and I need the money," I smile.

"'Me too," she laughs. She eats some of her sandwich and says "I've been trying to get on a reality programme for the past three years. Either that, or I want to do topless modelling, like Katie Price did at the start of her career I want to be famous and earn loads of money."

I nod and look at her. She's about 5ft tall, very chubby and wearing thick glasses and a brace. I whisper to her "I think you'd do very well."

"Cheers for that," Josie's face lights up at my words.

The day flies by and to my amazement, I start to enjoy myself. It's something different and to be honest, I am having a laugh with the youngsters. At the end of the day everyone is told we did really well and we can now get our belongings and go home. The very last cheeseburger is staring at me, pleading with me not to send it to its death with all the cold coffee and dry chips. I take the cheeseburger, slowly unwrap it and bite into it. It tastes delicious and I realise it's been years since I bought a cheeseburger. The trainer looks at me eating and his whole body freezes.

"Cathy, what are you doing? You're not allowed to eat the food on the shop floor."

"Sorry," I say with a mouth full of burger. Surely I won't

get the job now? They won't be able to trust me not to demolish the food.

****

Three days later, I get a letter saying they are offering me the job and they're pleased to have mature staff working in the store. I immediately head off to Jane's. Jane is very sympathetic and advises me to tell them to stuff the job. After all, Tom's paid in more than enough tax to keep me over the years. I agree with her but I know that if I don't go, my money will be stopped.

Three days training later and apparently I'm ready to go on the shop floor. I'm hoping I can get up for a fourth day at 6am. There's only ever been one six in my day and it's not the am one. I put a little slap on my face and head for the restaurant, although how they can call it a restaurant is anyone's guess, it's simply a fast food outlet. When I arrive, the place is buzzing. The griddle staff are cooking beef burgers, hamburgers, and eggs, whilst the orange juice and coffee are well under way.

I look completely stupid in my uniform, which consists of a bright orange shirt and a bright orange and yellow apron and baseball hat. People are shouting orders from every direction and I don't know where I need to be. Everything I learnt at the training HQ has completely floated over my head. Mark, the manager, is twenty years of age and is shouting orders like he's in the army. I go to the till and a more experienced cashier helps me select the orders for a group of teenagers that have just come in. I manage to get the order right so she leaves me on my own. That's when the chaos starts and within a minute the orders are wrong and I'm giving out milkshakes that aren't right. One young girl of about sixteen swigs on her milkshake and starts to wretch. Next thing I know, she's been sick all over the floor. Mark barks at me to clean it up and points to the store cupboard. I have never been good at cleaning my own child's vomit, let alone anyone else's. So when I approach it armed with rubber gloves and a selection of cloths, I too, start heaving. It takes me a good five minutes to calm myself down and as I sit on the wall outside breathing in the fresh air, I can see Mark giving me looks that could kill. I go back to my duties and I've only been back on the till a minute, when Mum and Pop come in. Mum waves at me the minute she arrives.

"Cooey, Cathy, how's it going?"

I want the floor to swallow me up. Pop sits down and starts to read the paper while Mum, rather than taking a place in the queue, walks straight to the front and says "That's my little girl behind the counter." A few people snigger but some are annoyed that she's just jumped the queue. When Mum gets the cashier next to me, she leans over.

"Oh, Cathy, you look really tired," she helpfully informs me. "We're very proud of you. Think about all that dosh you'll have at the end of the month." I can feel myself going bright red, then Mum turns to the cashier in front of her and says "Our Cathy's been through an awful time of it; her husband's left her for another woman. And that's not all - he had a baby with her too…"

"Mum," I interrupt, "go and sit down and I'll bring your drinks over."

Mum walks away from the counter and as she passes other diners, she tells them I'm her daughter.

I give Mum and Pop their drinks and dab my forehead.

"Oh, Mum, it's awful here."

Mum taps my hand.

"I know, love, but just give it time."

"Cathy, get back here and get some work done," Mark bellows across the counter.

Mum is furious and shouts back at him.

"Hey, who do you think you're talking to? She's old enough to be your mother, now drop the attitude. You're not too big to be put over my knee."

Mark goes bright red and I scurry back behind the counter.

****

A week later and I'm getting a bit quicker, but nothing could have prepared me for the smell of the burgers; it seems to seep into every pore, every orifice of my body. Even though I shower twice a day, the smell is still there. Mum tells me she's proud of me every day but Jane finds the whole thing very amusing. In fact, when she sees me in my uniform she has tears running down her face, she thinks it's so funny.

It's my second Saturday, I'm working in the drive through and there, as bold as ever, is the Freak and the Fluff in their car. The little boy is sitting in the back and as they slowly drive through, he smiles at me. I duck down so fast that I hit my head on the counter. The Freak pulls up outside the window and I have to ask him for his order. I quickly pinch my nose with my fingers and say "Hello, sir." Saying the word 'sir' leaves a very bitter taste in my mouth. "What can I get for you today?" I can see the Freak looking for the person who is serving him and Fanny is talking to the little boy. I talk into the mini microphone again. "Can I take your order, please?" The Freak tries to look in the window and I spit back "I'm looking for some straws, sir … carry on with the order, I can assure you I'm still here." The Freak orders food but the double cheeseburgers aren't ready yet.

"What are you doing?" Mark has spotted me and has come to stand over me.

"I've dropped a penny," I smile sweetly at him.

"Leave it!" he yells, furiously. I still won't stand up so Mark apologises to the Freak and says if they would like to come inside, they can have complimentary coffees while they wait. I go into a blind panic as I watch them all file into the restaurant. Oh my God, what am I going to do? I am not about to let them see me in this awful uniform. I can see them sitting down as I peer through the beef burger shelf. I pull my hat over my face and say to Mark "I'll do the toilet check."

Mark isn't happy with me but he's too busy wrapping burgers. I scurry towards the toilet and then I realise Fanny is behind me. I open the door and run inside. There are only three toilets and two are occupied. Fanny uses the toilet then washes her hands. I grab a large mop and with my head still down, I slowly start mopping the floor.

"It's a lovely day isn't it?" Fanny suddenly says. I don't know what to do, so I don't answer her. She says it again and I don't want to ignore her, in case she reports me to Mark and my cover is exposed.

I take a deep breath and say "'Tis a mighty fine day, Ma'am."

The Fluff won't leave the toilet and instead tries to make conversation with me. I still keep my head down.

"Have you worked here long, lovey?" she chirps.

Again, I answer her in a different accent, which turns out to sound a little bit Scottish.

"Not long, Ma'am."

The Fluff laughs.

"My father's from Scotland. "Which part are you from?"

I can't believe what is happening to me and in a quick

attempt to get rid of her, I say "Bonnie, from bonnie Scotland Ma'am."

I cringe after I've answered her. Also, I must have mopped the same bit of floor over and over again. The Fluff picks up her bag and looks inside it. She takes something out and tries to pass it to me. From under my hat, I can see she's giving me a fiver. The bloody Fluff is giving *me* a fiver.

The toilet door opens and Josie walks in.

"Mark say's you need to come out now, there's a big queue."

I grab Josie's glasses off her face and put them on. I can't see a thing because it's like looking through two bottle bottoms. The Fluff is still holding out the fiver so I grab it off her, put it in my pocket and say "Thank you, mammy," which comes out Irish. I sprint from the toilet with my head down, go to the back of the racks and start helping to wrap the burgers.

I can feel someone next to me and I'm trying my best not to look up. Then I hear a voice.

"Can I have my glasses back please, Cathy?"

The rest of the day was a nightmare and I couldn't get the Fluff out of my mind. She's stolen my husband and given me a fiver for him. Jane said it was all he was worth.

****

How I get to the end of the month I will never know, but when I see my wage slip I'm pleasantly surprised. I clear £888 for a month's work and, according to Louise, I've accrued one day's holiday which is marked clearly on my wage slip.

I decide to take the day's holiday the day after I've been paid; that way I can have a lie in and Jane and I can go out for lunch. When I meet Jane in the local pub, I feel really upbeat and proud of myself. I am a worker at last and there is something very rewarding about earning your own money.

"What a crock of shit," Jane sneers. "It's much better to spend someone else's money."

I disagree with Jane on this occasion, though, because I am now a full-time worker and a woman in my own right.

CHAPTER 12

It feels funny getting my P45 through the post. I've never seen a P45 before and I don't have a clue what to do with it. Mark informs me in a nasty voicemail that I can't take holidays when it suits me, they have to be approved. Why have they informed me and written it in my wage slip if they don't want me to act on it? I send him a nasty text back saying "You wouldn't have missed me, there are loads of people who work there. Shove your job where the sun doesn't shine."

I'm back to square one with no direction in my life and I easily slip back into my old ways. I give Mum some money for my keep but she will only take £50 for the whole month, so I calculate that I can have a bottle of wine on most nights and still have money for going out. Funnily enough, I am getting used to being skint all the time.

The job centre sanctioned my money for three weeks, then it was re-instated They decided it was a legitimate sacking and I was indeed no good as a burger flipper, or anything else for that matter, but they did suggest a few courses that I could do to further my skills.

Jane's reaction to this is "Tell them to kiss your arse."

Jane has met a really cute Italian man who doesn't speak very good English, however, he seems to know what Jane's saying and appears a little frightened of her. Jane went to Italy with one of her other friends who's recently got divorced – not a bitter divorce like mine, this one was amicable and her ex-husband even paid for her to go away. Jane thinks how they met is quite romantic and she's gone all soppy on me. I've never seen her like this before. Banito was giving out leaflets to holidaymakers so that they could go into his brother's bar for two free drinks. Jane and Linda went in on a Tuesday evening and didn't come out until Thursday. With only a few days left of their holiday, they both hit the beach to get a tan. Within minutes, Banito turned up and sat holding Jane's hand until the evening, when he had to go to work. When Jane left for the airport she thought she would never see him again, but on arriving back to the UK she found a large bunch of flowers were waiting for her at home. Jane is well and truly loved-up and I'm really pleased for her. Every time we go out, Jane talks about him endlessly. I can't complain, she's spent months and months listening to me calling the Freak and the Fluff.

Jane flies back and forward to Italy at every opportunity and during the weeks she's away, I'm stuck in my room or sitting with Mum and Pop. It's not ideal at my age but I don't know what else to do with myself. The days seem really long and boring and, for the first time in my life, I'm watching the soaps with Mum.

****

The day Banito comes to England, Jane is a bag of nerves.

"I hope you like him," she says, grabbling my arm. I think what she really means is 'I hope you don't slate him like I did when I met Tom.' I'm sure he's nothing like Tom – there's only one of him, I'm positive of that. Banito arrives at 7pm and we all head to the local pub. Banito isn't very tall, he has a slender build, and his hair is in a little bob. He's not someone I think I would go for, but I can see why Jane likes him. Banito and Jane are all loved-up so I don't stay long, just enough time to meet him and give Jane my approval, not that she needs it – it's just something we've always done for each other. The following day, Jane brings him to see Mum and Pop, and I beg Mum to be on her best behaviour. As Jane doesn't have parents, she often turns to my Mum, who loves the fact that Jane treats her like a mother. Banito, with all his charm, brings a small bunch of flowers round for Mum and she is over the moon. Pop shakes his hand then goes to watch the TV with the dog. A little later, we all go into the kitchen and sit round the table. Mum sits staring at Banito and she's smiling all the time. It's only a matter of minutes before Mum speaks.

"So, do you think he's the one, Jane?"

Jane smiles and looks lovingly at Banito.

"Oh, Joan, he's definitely the one."

Mum shakes her head and says, "I am glad, Jane, because, let's face it, you've been round the block a few times haven't you?"

Jane puts her head down. I give Mum a look and try to change the subject.

"Mum, you've always wanted to go to Italy, haven't you?"

Mum nods and says "Jane, who was that man you went out with years ago? He fixed me car… what was him name?"

I jump up and get some wine out of the fridge.

"Right, everyone, come on, let's celebrate Jane and Banito's new found love for each other," I almost shout.

"Was it you he got pregnant, Jane?" Mum asks, sipping on her wine.

"No, it wasn't," Jane sputters, choking on her drink.

"Louise has met someone, we're hoping to meet him soon," I say, trying to change the subject.

"Oh, yes, our little Lou," Mum squeals. She's soon deep in thought again though, then chirps up, almost singing, "I know! He was married, wasn't he, Jane?"

"'He was separated." Jane answers Mum through gritted

teeth. Mum can't leave it and all the time she's talking, Banito keeps smiling. Mum remembers something else.

"His mother was a right scrubber, everyone thought she was on the game. She couldn't have afforded that house if she wasn't."

Banito nods and smiles and it dawns on me that he doesn't understand much English.

"He can't understand what she's saying, can he?" I whisper to Jane.

"Thank God he can't," Jane sighs.

Mum has Banito's full attention as she laughs and says "When I met Stanley, I was a Hello Girl." Mum does all the actions of plugging in the phone cable to connect the call. "Stanley was an engineer for the GPO." Mum goes into hysterics. "I kept telling him that the phone lines weren't working properly so he'd come in the office to see me."

As Pop walks into the kitchen to get a can of beer out of the fridge, he turns to Banito and says "In truth, Joan was cutting people off so that she could have me all to herself."

"It's true, Mum laughs and bangs on the table. "I wanted him to notice me and I hate the bloody public." Then Mum puts on a really posh voice. "But I had a lovely telephone manner, Anita."

"Who's Anita?" I ask Mum and she points to Banito. I knock back my wine.

****

It's days before Christmas and I need some money, so I decide to take some of my jewellery to the jewellers to be melted down. An hour later and I walk out of the shop with £940. Most of the jewellery I had was hideous and some of the necklaces were broken. They were items bought over the years from Dubai and Egypt as an investment and the result has made me more than happy today. I head off to the shops to buy presents for everyone and get the Turkey and some other luxury items. It doesn't feel like Christmas to me; I doubt Christmases will ever be the same again. Perhaps if Louise has children, our house might come alive with laughter, but for now, Christmas day is a posh Sunday dinner.

I'm sitting in the lounge wrapping up a few presents when I see my parents pull up on the drive. They've been to see Steven to give him his Christmas presents. Mum made Pop go in with her this time, because she said it was Christmas and God would never forgive him if he didn't. Pop, being an atheist, said he didn't care what God thought. Mum was furious and gave Pop an alternative: go in or your bags will be packed. Pop was weary and didn't want a fight so he gave in. Mum took a bag of presents as big as a pillow case to Steven. She bought the bag from the pound shop and over the months, she filled it bit by bit. Now they're back and Pop is carrying something into the house. I open the door for them and Pop immediately rolls his eyes. Mum is beaming as she takes her coat and scarf off.

"Oh, Cathy, Steven's made me and your Pop a lovely present for Christmas," Mum clenches her fists in delight and then, in her thick Irish accents, she adds, "Beautiful, it is."

Pop carries the large object into the kitchen, where Mum stands and admires it.

"What is it?" I look and Pop and ask.

Again, Pop rolls his eyes but Mum interrupts.

"It's a wooden BBQ. Steven made it all by himself. He's nearly a fully-fledged carpenter and he's learnt all this from being in prison. More and more people should get themselves in prison, it's a wonderful opportunity. Isn't he clever?"

I really don't know what to say, so I say nothing at all. An hour later and Mum is still singing Steven's praises.

"He's such a bright boy. He takes after me. I've told him he needs to be self-employed when he comes out. With a talent like he has, it would be criminal to work for anyone else."

"It would be criminal if anyone employs him," Pop grins, "the light-fingered little git."

The comment goes right over Mum's head and her praise continues.

"I'm going to try and get him some orders. Do you think Jane would like one?"

I'm speechless. Pop pipes up "I'm freezing, I'm going for a bath."

****

It's Christmas Eve and Jane has gone to Italy to spend time with Banito's family. Meanwhile, nobody in our house is remotely interested in Christmas. Louise has come home in body but not in spirit – she's lovesick. Her boyfriend has to split his time between his two parents who have recently got divorced. If he chooses one then the other will be upset, so he's visiting them both and having two Christmas dinners. I console Louise that things may be better next Christmas, but she looks so sullen.

After we've had tea I decide to get everyone in the mood for Christmas, so I orchestrate a quiz – I found it in a book shop when I was doing my Christmas shopping. The first ten questions are quite easy and every one Louise answers, she gets right. When it's Mum's turn, she messes around and goes to get drinks and peanuts, and she can't give her special eggnog away for love nor money. Finally, we make Mum sit down and join in. Pop asks Mum a question.

"Who painted the Mona Lisa?"

Mum smiles and quickly replies "Bob Hoskins."

"Bloody hell, it wasn't Bob Hoskins!" Pop shouts at Mum.

"It bloody well was," Mum becomes defensive, "he was a drug dealer and made prostitutes work for him."

"Who?" I shout.

"*Bob Hoskins,*" Mum replies in exasperation. I try to calm everyone down and decide to let Mum have another guess at it. She looks confused so Louise tries to help her by mouthing 'Leonardo' to her, but it doesn't help. Mum just smiles and says, "Leonardo de Campo."

"He's that fairy who said he wanted a shit on national TV," Pop says, getting annoyed.

Louise giggles and I shake my head and say, "Pop, he didn't mean to say shit; he meant *sheet*, but his English isn't very good."

Pop looks disgusted.

"I know what I heard, and if he can't speak the language he shouldn't be on the TV."

"I quite fancy him," Mum announces and everyone looks at each other, bemused. The questions flow and when it comes to Mum again, she doesn't want to play.

"Come on, Mum, it's only a bit of fun," I say, squeezing her hand, so Mum agrees.

The next question Louise asks Mum is, "Who landed on the moon in 1969?" Mum looks blank.

"I'll give you a clue Gran," Louise offers. "Adults and

children from all over the world were glued to the TV."

Mum thinks for a minute then answers, "The Clangers ... or was it Wallace and Gromit?"

"Jesus, Joan, no one is this stupid," Pop shouts at her in a fury.

"Pop, it's only a bit of fun," I intervene. "Just leave it."

It's Mum's turn to ask a question and she asks me directly, "Who was the first James Bond?"

"Roger Moore," I reply with a smile.

Pop takes great pleasure in stealing the question and says, "Barry Nelson."

Mum looks shocked and screams, "Who's Barry Nelson, when he's at home?"

Pop sits there and is grinning smugly, so I decide to ask Mum the next question.

"Who invented the light bulb?"

"B&Q." Mum answers quickly.

Louise laughs her head off and I can see Pop getting more and more irritated. I look at Mum. "Okay, that was a hard one, Mum, I'll let you have a go at the next question." I take a deep breath and ask, "What was Gandhi's first name?"

"Goosey," Mum squeals.

Pop goes crackers and walks away from the table.

"Come on, Rodney," he shouts to the dog. "We don't want to sit in here with a load of lunatics."

Mum folds her arms and says "Charming!"

CHAPTER 13

Louise has been in bed for an hour and I watch her gently breathing. I'm so happy she has met someone and I hope they'll be very happy. I get into bed and for the first time in ages, I feel content. I'm just about to fall into a deep sleep, the kind when you jump because you feel like your falling off the Empire State building, when I hear the bedroom door open. I'm too tired to look. Then I feel someone sit on the bed, which forces me to sit up and try to focus. The landing light is on so I can see that it's Mum sitting on the end of the bed.

"Mum, what's wrong? Why aren't you in bed?"

"I've come to read to you," Mum whispers.

It slowly dawns on me what she means, but she's already started reading by then.

'Twas the night before Christmas, when all through the house

Not a creature was stirring, not even a mouse;

"Mum, please don't," I interrupt. However, mum carries on.

'The stockings were hung by the chimney with care,

In hopes that St. Nicholas soon would be there;

"Mum, please, I'm fifty-five," I beg, but Mum ignores me.

'The children were nestled all snug in their beds,

hoping that sugar would soon be tipped over their head.'

"Gran, what's wrong?" Louise says, waking. Mum lifts up her finger for Louise to listen to her and off she goes again.

'The bang on the roof is ... err the driver.'

It's clear to me that Mum has forgotten the words over the years, but she carries on regardless, and by now she's almost shouting.

'Basha, Sasha, Frumpy, Bumpy, Sweaty Betty and Vixen.

Then St. Nicholas comes down the chimney, he likes a drink does our St. Nicholas.'

I've now lost the will to live and reply "Yes, St. Nicholas was Pop for years, we know he likes a drink."

"Don't call your Pop a drunk," Mum frowns. "That's for me to do."

Louise is fast asleep again and I wish I was too.

****

Christmas morning and everything is chaotic. Mum is running all over the place and she's completely forgotten what she's doing. Louise is on the phone to her boyfriend, Pop is watching TV with Rupert on his knee and I'm trying to cook the Christmas dinner. At twelve noon, Auntie Val and Uncle John arrive loaded with presents. Mum and Auntie Val throw their arms around each other and it's a lovely sight to see. I wish I had a sister instead of a jailbird brother. Auntie Val hands Mum a plant.

"Here you go, our Joan. I've got you a placenta."

"Auntie Val," Louise giggles. "It's poinsettia, not a placenta."

Mum doesn't care what it is and puts it on the window sill with her other plants.

The drinks flow and presents are opened. Smellies, hankies, slippers and chocolate are given out. Uncle John goes into the lounge with Pop, neither of them speak because they don't actually like each other. All the ladies are in the kitchen. Louise is trying to be diplomatic with Mum.

"Gran, I have a friend coming over for dinner, he's a doctor at the hospital. He's on call so he can't go and see his family. I hope we can all make him welcome."

Mum smiles at Louise and cackles.

"Oh, a doctor friend, eh? Poor little bugger, having no family at Christmas, I bet he feels like a little orphan."

Louise cringes. I try and smooth things over.

"I'm sure we'll all be on our best behaviour."

"A doctor?" Auntie Val says. She has been listening to the conversation and this has now caught her interest. "Maybe he can look at my back while he's here? You can never get an appointment anymore. You ring up and they say 'Yes, six months on Thursday.' I mean, you'd be dead by then, wouldn't you?"

Mum and Auntie Val start talking about their many illnesses. I then make a mistake and mention Steven, causing Auntie Val to throw her arms in the air.

"Oh, Joan, haven't they let him out for Christmas?"

Mum wipes her nose and sniffles, but there isn't a tear in sight.

"You'd think they would let him out for Christmas, wouldn't you?" she says woefully. "The evil swine there are trying to punish him."

Louise puts her head in her hands.

"Well, our Joan," Auntie Val says, hugging Mum. "You never get used to your baby being dragged from the bosom of your soul, do you? He's such a nice lad. I wish they'd give him a chance."

Mum knocks back a glass of eggnog and wipes her mouth like a navvy.

"That's the trouble, Val, they treat him awful. Oh, let me show you what the little lad has made." Mum and Auntie Val go into the garden to look at the wooden BBQ.

****

The table is set and the food is being kept warm in Mum's forty-year-old hostess trolley. I remember her buying it and the whole of the neighbourhood came in the house to admire it. Mum even offered to hire it to friends and family if they were having a dinner party. The trouble is, nobody ever has a dinner party- not even Mum- so the hostess trolley only comes out at Christmas.

Everyone is sat at the table and we're all chattering at once when the doorbell rings and the whole table goes quiet. Louise stands up and goes to the front door. She soon returns to the kitchen with a tall, handsome man.

"He's black," Pop helpfully mentions.

Louise goes bright red and offers the man a seat. She takes a deep breath and says "May I introduce you to Oliver?" "Yes you may," says Auntie Val with a giggle.

"In that case, everyone, this is Oliver." Smiles Louise.

Everyone is staring at Oliver, then Uncle John says, "We have a doctor in the house."

"I'm Joan." Mum touches Oliver's jacket. "Are you a proper doctor?"

"Pleased to meet you, Joan," Oliver smiles at Mum, "and yes, I am a proper doctor."

"What would you like to drink, Oliver?" Louise asks.

"Thank you, Louise," Oliver replies, taking off his jacket. "Just a water for me."

"Can I have your autograph please?" Mum asks, quickly passing him a pen and paper.

I give Mum a look and nod my head for her to sit down, but, as usual, she won't.

"And one for me," Auntie Val almost shouts.

Oliver is stunned by his new found fame and doesn't know what to say. Louise gently takes the paper off Oliver.

"Gran, you don't really want his autograph, do you?" Louise tries to laugh it off because she's so embarrassed. However, Mum insists that she and Auntie Val do want an autograph, so Oliver scribbles his name on the paper.

Mum seems fascinated by Oliver and suddenly says "You're very tall Oliver, I could do with a length off you."

Oliver nearly chokes on his water. Auntie Val is smiling too and says "The ladies are only small in our family, maybe you could give us both a few inches." Mum nods her head in agreement and Louise's face is bright red.

"Thank you for inviting me to dinner. It's very kind of you," Oliver says, trying to break the ice.

I'm mashing the carrots at this point and I can feel a hot flush coming on. I try not to look at Mum but it's too late, and Mum's voice goes into overdrive.

"Oh Cathy, you've got a right dab on, girl."

Mum then takes a mini fan out of her bag and holds it to my face. All this action sets Auntie Val off.

"Oh, I remember those hot sweats, the night ones were the worst." Auntie Val cackles just the way Mum does. She shouts at Uncle John, "Do you remember, John?" She then turns to Oliver and says, "I was that hot one night, I was wringing wet. John said to me, 'oh, a wet T shirt competition just for me.' He thought I was hot stuff, didn't you, John?"

Uncle John grunts, Mum finds it hilarious and Pop just shakes his head.

"Our Cathy's on the menopause and she's had a really bad time of it recently," Mum confides to Oliver. "Maybe you can prescribe something for her."

"What did everyone get for Christmas?" Louise immediately cuts in, trying to save the moment.

"Same as every year," Pop moans. "It's the same ole shit – socks and hankies."

"I got four Carling Black Label," Uncle John laughs.

"Don't be so ungrateful, you pisshead," Auntie Val looks annoyed.

"Yes John, you ungrateful ole fool," Mum joins in. Pop starts laughing and Mum snaps at him. "I don't know what you're laughing at, you're as bad."

Louise looks worn out and defeated, so I put the carrots in the hostess trolley and chirpily say "I'll serve dinner in a minute, if that's alright with everyone?"

"Stan bought me a Dyson for Christmas," Mum tells Auntie Val, who screams her displeasure.

"A Dyson? I've always wanted a Dyson. I just got some fluffy slippers."

"Look, Val, no lead." Mum pushes the Dyson into the kitchen. Auntie Val screams and it comes out like a loud shrill.

"No lead and no plug? How does it work?"

"Magic Val, pure magic." Mum answers smugly.

"What did you get for Christmas son?" Mum looks across at Oliver inquisitively.

"Nothing," Oliver smiles.

Mum and Auntie Val become really quiet. Then between them they say "Nothing... *nothing*?" Oliver doesn't appear too bothered but Mum disappears out of the kitchen, then comes back with Pop's hankies.

"We can't let you have no presents on Christmas day, can we? Ignore the 'S' on the front of them."

Oliver reluctantly takes the hankies.

"Really its fine, Joan."

"They're mine," Pop protests. "You can't just give my stuff away, you silly ole mew."

"Shut it, Stanley," Mum shouts at Pop.

"I won't shut up," Pop shouts back. "You're always putting me down."

"I'd like to put you down."

"Wouldn't that be nice," Auntie Val joins in. "We could live together then, Joan." Mum smiles and nods her head like it's a done deal. Then Mum and I serve the dinner.

"Carrots Oliver?" Mum offers.

"Not for me thank you, Joan," Oliver declines.

Mum is horrified and puts the carrots on his plate anyway.

"You've never seen a rabbit wearing glasses, have you?"

Oliver doesn't know what to say and I can't help but come to his rescue.

"Mum, don't force people to eat what they don't want."

"All those poor starving children in Africa," Mum says, ignoring me and shaking her head sadly. Auntie Val joins in the conversation.

"Weren't we poor, Joan, when we were younger?"

"Poor? *Poor*?" Mum screams back. "That's an understatement."

"Our mam used to send us to the butcher's for a sheep's head and tell us to ask the butcher to leave the legs on it." Mum and Auntie Val are screaming with laughter and Oliver joins in, he can't help it. Mum smells the gravy and says "Ahh Bisto," then sings "A million housewives every day, pick up the Bisto and say ..."

"Joan," Auntie Val interrupts her. "That's the baked beans advert, not the gravy one."

"I love baked beans," Pop laughs, "but they don't like me, they make me fart."

"Stanley, you're full of wind. I feel it every night in bed," Mum scolds.

"John's the same," Auntie Val adds.

With the dinner over, Pop pours everyone drinks. I can see Auntie Val staring at Louise and Oliver. Then she turns to Mum.

"Aww, don't they make a lovely couple?"

Louise stops talking and answers Auntie Val.

"Oliver is engaged to be married."

"Oh, so that's why you've brought him here," Mum screams. "Quick Stanley, get the Pomagne out of the fridge."

Oliver is staring into space and Louise looks ill. I try to take in what's happening.

"Not to me," Louise shouts over the racket. "He's marrying someone else."

Mum sits down and thinks about what Louise has just said, then looks at Louise with confusion written all over her face.

"You never told us you were going out with a soon to be married man?"

"I'm not," Louise replies tiredly, "and he's engaged to someone else." Louise rubs her brow.

"Mum, leave it, please," I plead with Mum.

"And you're alright with that, Louise?" Mum ignores me and becomes defensive.

"Mum, they're just friends." I'm becoming angry with her now.

"You can't be friends with the opposite sex. I'm not friends with your grandad."

"Thank God," Pop cuts in.

I quickly change the subject, hoping to throw Mum off the scent.

"So, where are you from Oliver?" I ask brightly.

Oliver dabs his mouth with a napkin and replies "Cambridge."

Everyone stops talking and stares at him. Mum's off again. 'So where are your family from?'

"Cambridge," Oliver repeats as I cringe.

Mum looks confused and I'm in such a state that I refill everyone's drinks even though they're still quite full. However, when I look at Mum, her cheeks are flushed.

"Mum," I whisper to her. "Watch how many drinks you're having."

Mum turns on me like a lioness.

"Don't tell me how many drinks I can have." Mum turns on me like a lioness, "I've only had one glass- unlike you."

"Yeah, you've only had one glass but it's been filled up five times." Pop laughs.

Mum turns on Pop.

"Shut it, you alcofrolic. If you can't have a drink at Easter, then when can you have it?"

Auntie Val agrees and for the first time since we sat at the table, Uncle John speaks.

"It's Christmas, not Easter."

"Cheers, to absent friends," Louise Lifts her glass up to everyone.

Everyone raises their glasses back at her. Mum starts crying and turns to Oliver.

"My little boy is absent, bless him," She says through her tears. "Did Louise tell you what's happened to him, Oliver?"

Oliver becomes serious, "Oh, Joan, I'm so sorry for your loss. I had no idea."

I try and change the subject but Mum won't let it go. Also, Auntie Val is now holding Mum's hand in sympathy. Mum starts to become all maudlin.

"I bet he's there on his own; no friends, no presents, no food, maybe just a bit of dried bread and some water. Just looking at four walls all day."

Oliver is confused and whispers to Louise, "So he's not dead then?"

Louise is so embarrassed that she doesn't know what to say, so I interrupt with, "He's on holiday."

"Where's he gone?" Oliver tries to be chatty.

"Manchester," I reply.

"Manchester? How long is he there for?"

"He's on holiday there for about two months, I think," I respond nervously as Louise looks at me with pleading eyes.

"He's never had any luck, that little lad, has he?" Auntie Val whispers.

"Even the car he pinched was glued together by some crook," Mum says.

"There's no justice in this world, Joan." Auntie Val shakes her head.

"Come on everyone, cheer up," I call, chinking my glass. "Nobody wants to hear about doom and gloom."

"I do," Auntie Val interjects.

Louise gulps back her wine as Mum carries on.

"Thank the good Lord for airbags, they lifted him up to safety. When the police got there, he was sat on the roof waiting for them."

"At least he didn't run off," Auntie Val says.

"That's because he was concussed," Pop pipes up.

I get up and quickly sort the mince pies and Christmas pudding out.

"Just a baby pudding for me," Mum calls, as Auntie Val adds "A baby, baby pudding for me please." Mum has to go one better at this point, "A foetus pudding for me." Then, from nowhere, Mum says "Our Cathy has always wanted a black baby, haven't you?"

I can't even look at Mum, I'm so annoyed.

"Why don't you have one now, Cathy?" Auntie Val enquires.

"She's too old Val," Mum sniggers. "Her ovaries have shrivelled up and probably look like sun dried tomatoes by now."

Auntie Val laughs. Louise has given up and is now staring into space with Oliver.

"Cathy, there's a chocolate log in the fridge," Mum shouts to me.

"I did a chocolate log this morning in the toilet," Pop chuckles and Mum shoots him a filthy look.

"Oh, Joan," Auntie Val squeals. "You like that man on the telly, don't you? What's his name? Oh yeah, Morgan MacDonald."

Mum breaks out in a cackle which goes right through me.

"You mean Trevor MacDonald," Mum corrects her and Auntie Val smiles and nods her head in agreement. "*SIR* Trevor MacDonald," Mum adds pointedly, causing Auntie Val to clap her hands. Mum pours more wine and says "Can you imagine waiting for him to come home at night?"

"There'd be no saying, get up the dancers you'd already be up there."

The two of them sound like cackling witches. Oliver raises his eyebrows and smiles at Louise. Auntie Val picks up a piece of turkey, even though she's already eaten.

"That turkey was gorgeous, Joan. Where did you get it from?"

"It's a boneless one from M&S," I inform Auntie Val.

"A turkey with no bones in it?" Mum screams, throwing her arms in the air and causing everyone to jump. "They've sold you a disabled Turkey?"

I sigh.

With everything cleared away, we all sit down with a Port. Mum gets out some masks she's bought from the pound shop. Mum's is a mask of the Queen, whilst she gives Pop one of Charlie Chaplin. Auntie Val's is a Lady Gaga mask and John has a Simon Cowell one. Louise and Oliver have Kate and William, while Mum gives me a mask of Victoria Beckham. Mum makes Oliver and Louise stand up first.

"Thank you for asking Catherine and I for dinner," Oliver intones as he gets into the spirit of things, "We are going to be thrilled to move into Kensington palace."

"Who's Catherine?" Auntie Val asks.

"William and Kate, Val," Mum tuts. "*Prince* William."

"Ah," Auntie Val nods, enlightened.

It's Mum's turn and she stands up and gives a royal wave before she puts on her posh voice again.

"My subjects, thank you for coming here today. The corgis and I are most happy you are here. Last year was a 'horror be bliss' year, but this year will be better when Kate has the baby. Kate will find it easy because she's a midwife."

Everyone laughs.

Pop shoves some peanuts in his mouth then immediately starts choking. Oliver runs over and stands behind him, quickly administering the Heimlich Manoeuvre. We all stand around and watch in our celebrity masks. Doris, the neighbour, is in the garden observing all this.

"You weirdos," she bawls at the top of her voice. "I don't know what you're all doing but you really need to shut the curtains."

I suddenly realise that it looks like Oliver is performing a sex act on Pop and we're all stood around watching.

Pop brings back up the peanuts; he's clearly shaken.

"Oh, I thought I was a gonner then."

"That clairvoyant told me you were going to die," Mum murmurs, astounded. "Oh, well," she adds, recovering quickly, "better luck next time."

Pop tries to regain his posture and sits back down on the chair.

"When I do die, I want you to lock that garage and throw away the key," he instructs Mum with solemnity.

"Why?" she asks, bewildered.

"I don't want any arsehole touching my tools."

"What makes you think I'll marry another arsehole?" she says, rolling her eyes. She then walks over to Oliver and hugs him. "Thank you for saving my husband's life. How can I ever repay you?"

"There's no need," Oliver smiles. "I'm just glad I was here to help."

Mum disappears from the room, then returns with two carrier bags full of medicines, which she hands over to Oliver.

"Gran, what you doing?" Louise asks, gobsmacked.

Mum ignores Louise and says to Oliver "These are medicines your Grandad and I haven't used. Oliver can have them."

I take the medicines off Mum and Louise tries to laugh it off. Fortunately, Oliver does find it all very amusing. Pop and Uncle John go into the lounge with a tin of beer.

****

Three hours have passed and we're now playing, *I Spy.*

"I spy with my little eye," Auntie Val begins, "something beginning with 'K'."

"Cake, Carrots, Candles," Mum rattles off in quick succession. Val informs Mum that she's wrong, as she can only give one answer.

None of us are able to guess what it is and Auntie Val is smug when she says, "Cooker."

"Cooker is a C, not a K." Mum says, getting angry.

Auntie Val ignores her so I try to lighten the mood by joining in with the game.

"I spy with my little eye, something beginning with T."

Everyone looks at each other and the room becomes silent. Oliver puts his hand up like a little boy. "Table?"

I nod my head and Mum and Auntie Val stare at Oliver. The game is going down like a lead balloon so I get up and pour everyone more drinks.

Suddenly, Oliver's beeper goes off.

"Would you excuse me for a minute?" he says to us all. He then tries to get up from the table but finds he can't stand. Louise goes into a blind panic.

"Oliver, are you alright?"

Oliver wobbles from side to side then falls on to the floor. Louise quickly loosens his tie and lays him in the recovery position. As she does so, she gets a strong whiff of alcohol.

"Mum, he's drunk." She looks up at me, confounded.

I'm so shocked, I don't know what to say. Mum looms over Oliver, staring at him.

"How can he be drunk? He's not had any alcohol."

"What's he been drinking, Joan?" Auntie Val asks. Mum takes a look at the bottle he's been drinking from and says, "Water."

Auntie Val takes the bottle and frowns at it.

"Oh no, I put a splash of Vodka in that one," she confesses. "I thought we were going to the pub first and I was determined not to pay those prices."

Mum puts her hand to her mouth and we all stare at Oliver.

CHAPTER 14

All the usual resolutions have been made; it's now the end of January and I haven't stuck to one of them. Jane has tagged on a new one now - I have to agree to go out with her at least once a week. I can't be bothered getting ready and it's so cold outside, but I know Jane will come round and drag me out regardless. Banito is living with Jane now and she says she needs a break from him because he's annoying her. I laugh because it's only been there three weeks since he moved in with her. However, despite her moaning about Banito, I know she's in love with him. I get ready and put on my comfy boots and chunky cardigan – old habits die hard. All I really want is warmth and comfort. When we arrive at the pub, I'm pleasantly surprised to see a log fire burning and people having a good old chinwag. We've only been in the pub an hour when Jane nudges me.

"Cathy, quick, 3 o'clock."

I turn and look at the bar and there's a really handsome man looking over.

"He's not looking at me, Jane, he's looking at you," I state.

"I don't think so," She laughs. Then, before I can stop her, she sprints to the bar. Within a minute, she's back with the man. I feel so embarrassed, I want to run out of the pub. Jane introduces him as Rob and I go all girly as he sits down at our table. After half an hour of making small talk, Jane makes a ridiculous lie about Banito not feeling well and, rather unsubtly, makes her escape. There's an awkward silence before we start talking again.

"Do you come in here often?" he smiles.

I burst out laughing and we both realise how cheesy it

sounds. Rob tells me he's single and was in a long-term relationship for ten years. He has a son who he doesn't see anymore and I feel sorry for him. I skim over my circumstances, although when I tell him I live with Mum and Pop, he starts laughing. I suppose it would seem funny to other people.

It's 11pm and the barman shouts last orders. We've done nothing but chat and I feel a glow as we leave the pub together. Rob drops me off outside my parents' house and pecks me on the cheek. I get out of the car and thank him for the lift home.

"Hey, hey," he laughs. "Aren't you going to give me your phone number?"

I sheepishly scribble down my number for him and dart off inside. Strangely, Mum is still up and I can see that Rupert is wearing a blue jumper.

"What's he got on?" I ask.

"Oh, do you like it?" Mum smiles. "I've knitted it for him. It's freezing out there."

I pour a glass of wine and tell Mum all about my date.

"He's a surveyor, Mum."

Mum repeats what I've said and it comes out as a song.

"Oh, a surveyor. That's a good job, Cathy, and he won't be short of a bob or two."

It isn't about the money, but Mum's right, I know it makes life a lot easier having a few bob behind you. I eventually go to bed but I can't sleep and, strangely enough, I've got butterflies in my stomach.

Rob rings me the day after our date and before I know it, we've been unofficially dating for six weeks. I do fancy him.

There's no great spark but there's something there and I'm willing to hang around for a while to see how it goes. I find myself getting carried away and thinking what if Rob is the one. How would the Freak respond? Not that I'm bothered of course, I just want some justice, a bit of payback and to let him know that I'm finally happy.

Jane is thrilled that I've started dating and on a few occasions we've all been out as a foursome. Banito makes everyone laugh with his broken English and Jane gets really annoyed with him because he isn't picking up the language as quickly as she thinks he should. Rob likes Jane and Banito, which makes it easier all round. The four of us talk about having a few days away and I feel almost normal again. Jane and Tom hated each other, so it was very much divided. I kept Jane as my friend because a foursome was out of the question. The irony is that Tom called Jane 'loose' and said if I went out with her, I would be tarred by the same brush. It's true that Jane is divorced and she has had loads of boyfriends, but that doesn't make her a bad person. Jane is more adventurous than me. To top it all off, Tom said you should only get married once. What a hypocrite!

I think it's defiantly too early for Rob to meet my family, I wouldn't want anything to go wrong this early on. I can imagine Pop saying nothing to him and Mum grilling him like she's in the police. I couldn't inflict that on him yet.

Things are getting a bit steamy and he doesn't seem to mind my wobbly bits and back fat.

"What the hell, Cathy," Jane laughs. "Just go for it."

I figure, why not? I'm a grown woman and single. I can do whatever I want. I go to Jane's so she can help me prepare for my forthcoming shag. I shave under my arms and Jane gets her epilator out while I writhe around on the bed, screaming as she attempts to shave my legs. I'm lying on top of the covers in pain, then she looks at me in a concerned way.

"Cathy, I'm not being funny, but you're going to have to shave or wax… *down there.*"

"Am I really that hairy?" I sit up in shock, only to see Jane nodding at me. I look at the epilator and shake my head.

"You're not using that thing down there. It was bad enough doing my legs."

"Cathy, it's like the tomb of doom down there." Jane stands over me with her hands on her hips. "Even Indiana Jones couldn't hack his way through that."

We both laugh but I feel so embarrassed. That's why I've come to Jane's; the thought of a stranger looking at my lady garden is more than I can stand. Jane waxes the sides of my flue and the pain is excruciating.

"Oh God, help me," I screech.

"God help me," Jane whimpers. "I'm scarred for life."

She then gives the whole area a trim, or 'a short back and sides' as she calls it.

She shows me the strips she's ripped off and it honestly looks like a cat that's been scalped.

"They call them spider's legs, Cathy," she chortles, "but this is like the film *Arachnophobia*… the *revenge.*"

****

After an afternoon with Jane, I feel the need for a couple of nights' rest before I do the dirty dead, so I ring Rob and tell him I'm feeling a little unwell. He sounds concerned but I assure him I'm alright, just a bit run down. I'm in my room, reading a book when I hear voices downstairs. I can't quite make out what is being said so I go out onto the landing to listen.

"What do you mean she's not well?" I hear Mum say. "Have you got her pregnant?"

I fly down the stairs and when I get half way down, I fall the rest of the way. Mum, Pop and Rob come into the hall and find me lying in a heap on the floor.

Are you alright Cathy?" Rob asks as he helps me up.

I'm so embarrassed I don't know what to say, and what does come out of my mouth is complete rubbish.

"I keep getting dizzy spells, that's why I fell down the stairs."

Rob looks really concerned. Pop shakes his head and goes into the lounge with the dog, muttering as he goes.

"She's an attention seeker. Always has been… and she's probably pissed."

"Are you pissed, Cathy?" Mum folds her arms and looks sternly at me.

"No, of course I'm not," I grin out of embarrassment, "I hardly touch the stuff."

Mum walks back into the kitchen, followed by Rob and myself. I'm limping from the fall. Rob and I sit at the table and I'm so nervous that I don't know what to say. I can't tell him to go home but it's too risky to leave him near Mum. Mum stands over us, her arms still folded.

"So, you're Cathy's new fella?" she sarcastically says.

Rob is quite nervous and I feel sorry for him; as he answers Mum his voice is squeaky.

"Err, yeah. I'm … err … Cathy's boyfriend."

Mum laughs and replies "You're hardly a boy."

I interrupt her, "Mum, this is Rob. Rob this is Mum."

Rob gets up and shakes Mum's hand, but when he's finished, she won't let go. Rob is a quick thinker and kisses her hand all gentlemanly. Mum is bowled over and is smiling her head off. She laughs as she says to Rob "Men used to find me irresistible when I was younger. Well, they still do actually."

Rob is clever with his reply and I'm impressed.

"I bet they do, you're a very attractive woman. In fact, you and Cathy look like sisters, not mother and daughter."

I look at Rob and shake my head in amusement.

"All right, Rob," I mouth to him. "Don't' go overboard."

Mum squeals with delight and goes in to tell Pop what Rob has said. I smile at Rob.

"Sorry about Mum."

"Don't worry," he laughs, "My Mum's exactly the same."

I shake my head and say quietly "Nobody has a mum like mine, trust me."

****

It's gone midnight and Mum is still up, talking to Rob. The poor man looks like he's going to fall asleep at any minute. I make hints at Mum to go to bed fall but they fall on deaf ears and she can't shut up. We get onto the subject of Walter and Mum puckers up her breasts.

"Walter was madly in love with me, Rob. The only thing that let him down was that he smelt of raw meat. The smell was awful and even when he'd had a shower, it would still be there. I never slept with him – I wasn't that type of girl. Not like some girls that were around at the time. Anyway, it put me off him. Devastated, he was. Then I met Stanley." Mum's voice trails off as she reminisces and she's quiet for a few minutes, but then she says, "I'd never have been without a joint or a bit of rump, would I Rob?"

Rob agrees with her.

When Rob eventually goes, Mum rounds on me.

"He seems like a nice man, Cathy," she states. "So don't mess it up by acting the fool – honestly, throwing yourself down the stairs at your age. You've always had to show off, just like ya Pop said."

****

It's the night I'm staying at Rob's and I feel really nervous - like I'm a teenager again. I take a long bath, paint my toenails and spray my flue with 'simply delicate' – a feminine deodorising spray that will keep me fresh for up to four hours. I feel sure we'll be getting down and dirty way before that. Over the last few days I've felt a little itch down below, so I can only assume the drought is now over. The other thing that's worrying me is who is supposed to buy the condoms, me or Rob? I've gone on at Louise for most of her adult life about being careful and not having unprotected sex, and here I am not knowing how I should play it. In the end I go to the chemist and buy a female condom, just to be on the safe side.

Rob has cooked a lovely meal and the minute I walk through the door he hands me a glass of wine, which goes down a treat with me. We have the meal and sit on the sofa together. Rob's house is untidy and typical of a man that lives alone. I look around and think that the house would be nice if it had a bit of work done on it and that it would benefit from a woman's touch. I can feel myself getting really giddy as I imagine that I might move in. The minute I finish my wine, Rob fills it up again.

"Are you trying to get me drunk?" I laugh.

"Yup!" he smirks.

After we've eaten the lovely meal, I stand up to go to the bathroom. I'm sure I need to spray my bits again. As I get to the lounge door I can feel Rob gently pulling me back and the more I try to get out of the door, the more he won't let me go.

"Come on, let me go to the bathroom," I smile and say teasingly.

However, when I turn round, he's sat on the sofa at the other side of the lounge, watching me. It's then I realise that the only thing dragging me back is my cardigan, which has hooked itself on the door handle. Rob laughs when I unhook myself. When I come back into the lounge, I sit a bit closer to him and I can feel myself go all girly and silly around him. I pick up my wine and Rob comes towards me. As he goes to kiss me, I slide down the leather sofa and our teeth chink together, causing me to I accidently tip my wine down his back. Rob jumps up because the wine is so cold. I leap to his assistance and try to help him take his shirt off. As I rip away at the shirt, two buttons ping onto the floor. The evening is heading for disaster. Rob changes his shirt and comes back to the lounge.

"Where were we?" he says, smiling.

I giggle but it's more out of nerves than anything else. Rob then kisses me passionately. Well, it's passionate for him, but for me it feels like he's washing a few small bits of clothing in my mouth. Rob takes my hand and leads me to the stairs. I won't go up first because (a) I don't want to look too eager, and (b) I don't want him to see how fat my arse is.

Rob takes his clothes off and jumps into bed, whereas I slowly try to slip out of my leggings and leave my top on until I'm lying flat. Rob tries to rip my top off and as he does, my head gets stuck in one of the sleeves. I'm claustrophobic, of course, and I'm instantly gasping for breath. I pull my top off in a panic, feeling like I can't breathe. Rob grabs a small paper bag and tells me to breathe into it to calm me down. After a glass of water, everything's back to normal. I can't believe the moment has been ruined. Rob puts the TV on and we both watch a film.

****

Jane howls with laughter when I tell her what happened.

"It could only happen to you."

We sit and giggle and then I say, "I'm going round tonight for a re-run, he obviously finds me really attractive."

"He clearly does," Jane says reassuringly. "And why not? He's only human. Just go for it, Cathy."

****

The evening has arrived and the minute I walk into Rob's house he tries to ravish me. I quickly run up the stairs and prepare myself with the female condom. It looks hideous, like a small freezer bag with a ring at one end. At first it's hard to insert, so I get some KY jelly out of my bag and squirt it over the plastic bag. I must have pressed on the tube too hard though, because it goes all over the bathroom floor and I nearly slip on it as I try to clean it up. As I walk out from the bedroom, the top of my legs are squelching from all the gel, and the plastic woman's condom is flapping about like a kite on a wet day. Rob kisses me and then slowly moves to my neck. I forget who I'm with and close my eyes to the pleasure. He then moves down to my nipple and playfully bites it. I scream out in pain, so Rob apologises and moves further down. He tries to separate my legs but I'm so nervous, he can't. It feels like I've got leg irons on. Then he moves to the 'tomb of doom' and I pray that my stomach doesn't look like a white sliced loaf from the position Rob is in. I pull him back up because the last thing I want him to see is a plastic bag hanging out. He gets on top of me then, before I know it, it's all over and I've not even got revved up. Rob rolls over, says he's sorry, and then falls asleep. What a bloody let down! I lie awake for hours, consoling myself that with time and practice it will get better, or at least I hope it will. I'm just pleased I've gone for it and got the whole dirty deed out of the way.

****

I spend the rest of the week in a world of my own, daydreaming about what I can do to Rob's house and planning holidays we can both take together. It's certainly helping me not to think about the Freak and the Fluff, and most days I don't care what they're up to. Mum has taken a real shine to Rob, just as I knew she would. She phones Auntie Val, Doris and all of her friends to tell them what a charmer he is and how he thought she was the most beautiful woman in the world. With each story it gets more exaggerated until it gets to the point where I wonder if Mum is going out with him as well.

Another month down the line and things have slightly improved. Jane thinks the reason it's all over before it's begun, is that he finds me so irresistible and he can't help it. I smile and agree with her. It's a good feeling, knowing you're irresistible to a man.

My parents go to Ireland for four days to visit Auntie Val and Uncle John, so I invite Rob round to return the favour of a cooked meal. It must be awful for a hardworking man to have to cook for himself every evening. I cook a roast dinner with all the trimmings and Rob thinks I'm the best thing since sliced bread. When the meal is finished, he washes up as a sign of his appreciation. Then the two of us cuddle on the sofa, eat chocolates and drink wine. I sit with a smile on my face and my whole body is aglow.

When we finally go to bed, Rob wants me to get on top of him, which I'm not keen on doing because I imagine my face will fall forward and it will frighten him. The thought of my eye bags and jowl sliding off my skull is more than I can bear. I get on top and look at the ceiling, which Rob finds really odd, and I can't stay in that position for long because I'm too fat to lift my heaving body up. I lie down and look at Rob. He's not a bad looking man, he's got a really good job and he finds me very attractive. However, yet again, it's all over very quickly. I go downstairs, pour us both a glass of wine and take it back to bed with us. I want to talk to Rob and try to get to know him better. Was his job exciting and fulfilling? What did he want for the future? I don't get a chance to ask him though, because when I get into bed Rob asks me if I want to move in with him. I'm not ecstatic and it is a bit of a shock, but it's also a relief to finally have my own space.

The next day I ring Jane and she's thrilled to bits.

"I'm so happy for you, Cathy. I knew it would all work out in the end."

****

The following night I stay at Rob's. He's great company and I feel I've got a purpose again. I cook a pasta meal and again, Rob really appreciates it. This is nice and cosy. Even Rupert has found a nice comfy place to sit, on Rob's knee. I sit and smile to myself as I never thought I would meet someone else. It's morning and I didn't sleep well last night because I was thinking about what to tell Mum. I'm moving in with a man I haven't known long and I know she won't be very happy because, in a way, she's got used to me being there. I know Louise will be pleased – she just wants me to be happy. Jane is over the moon for me too. So, all I need to do now is pack up my clothes and move in with Rob. Then I realise that Pop will be devastated if I take the dog. They've both become inseparable over the last year. Maybe we could share custody of him, like you would do with a small child? Rob doesn't live far from Mum, so Pop could come around and get him whenever he wants.

Rob has to go to work so I decide to walk him to his car. He parks it at the back of the house; he says he doesn't want his car to get damaged, which I can fully understand. As we go through a passageway, I see an old red Corsa parked on a bit of waste ground. I don't think for one minute it's Rob's … that's until he unlocks it. I stand staring at the car.

"Is your car in the garage," I ask him in a faint voice. Why did I ask that? He's already sitting in it.

Rob laughs and answers "No, this is it."

"But you're a surveyor; surveyors don't have cars like *that*!" I say, feeling a bit faint.

"This one does," Robs laughs.

I can't let him drive off until I've established what's going on. I draw in breath and ask "What type of surveyor are you?"

"Cathy," he sighs, "why all the questions?"

"I need to know, tell me," I say, panicking.

Rob looks confused.

"I sell cavity wall insulation. I knock door to door. It's not bad but it's all commission based, so some weeks I don't earn a penny."

I can feel my body shaking and the ground suddenly meets the sky. Rob leads me back into the house and makes me a cup of tea. I don't know about tea; I need gin. Rob is confused about everything.

"I don't have to go into work if you're ill, Cathy. I often have days off because I can't be arsed going in."

"Don't you get behind on your mortgage?" I ask in a faint voice.

"Hell no," Rob laughs. "It's rented. I'm always behind on my rent. The landlord has threatened to kick me out about six times. I don't worry about things like that – if he kicks me out, I could go to my sister's caravan at Cleethorpes."

After a long chat, Rob admits that he thought I was rich. It turns out Rob worked in Tom's warehouse years ago and he found out we were separated, so he thought he would have a good life with me. He says he does care for me and he thinks I could make him happy – obviously he means by me showering him with gifts. It seems he thought the reason I was living at home was because I hadn't found the house I wanted yet. I'm too numb to cry or be angry; my whole body, as well as my emotions, have shut down.

I think Rob knows it's the last time he will see me and he sits in silence. I quickly get ready and say my goodbyes.

I drive home in Mum's Skoda and I can't believe what's just happened. I feel angry that he kept the relationship going so he could have a better life; I also feel annoyed with myself that I've slept with him. After an hour of driving around, thinking, I come to the conclusion that I'm no better than him. I'm shallow and, like Tom's mum said, a gold digger. When I phone Jane she disagrees and says, "Why wouldn't you want a better life? You had quite a privileged one with Tom, so why shouldn't you have it again?"

I know from this moment on that I need to make my own way in life, rather than relying on a man. I tried to make it fit with Rob so I could be comfortable again; that's how much I wanted my old life back. Have I got over Tom? I am really beginning to wonder.

CHAPTER 15

Mum comes in from the hairdressers' after her usual wash and set.

"Oh, Brenda's daughter is going through a terrible time at home," she says as she flings her arms in the air. "Her marriage is on the rocks and they've been to marriage guidance."

"Who's Brenda?" I ask, looking at Mum.

"Bridie's daughter, who owns the hairdressers." Mum is clearly annoyed that I don't know this already.

I don't reply. It's a good job too, because Mum doesn't shut up.

"Oh, Cathy, I tell you, her husband took her to see a marriage counsellor and he listed a great big list of her faults," she says. I laugh. Mum doesn't. "The counsellor then askes Brenda what she would change about her husband and she said 'his address.'"

I don't know why I find it so funny but I do and I giggle my head off. I think I'm marvelling in the fact that there's another couple out there who are having it rough, which is sad of me really.

"Oh, I wish I could get divorced," Mum suddenly states.

"Is Brenda the one with orange skin like a Oompa loompa" I quietly ask Mum.

Mum screams, "So she is Cathy."

I laugh and say, "When she dies, she needs to give her body to science and her skin to World of Leather." Mum doesn't want to laugh but she does, then she spots Pop in the garden.

"Stan," she shouts. "Make us something for the local competition at the weekend – it has to be something from the TV years ago." Pop ignores her.

Jane phones to tell me that the Freak has married the Fluff at the registry office. Jane and Banito were driving past the Town Hall when Jane spotted them outside as guests were throwing rice over them.

"It's a pity it's not cooked rice or rice pudding," I say.

We both have a good giggle about it. That's why the Freak was in a hurry to divorce me. I don't know how I feel about them getting married… I suppose it's the final nail in the coffin for me. It's funny, but Louise hasn't mentioned it. I decide to give her a quick ring and it soon becomes apparent that she also doesn't have a clue that they were tying the knot.

"Let them get on with it," is Louise's take on it. Even though I say I'm not bothered, it still makes me feel sad and lonely.

Since Rob, I haven't wanted to date anyone. It's all too stressful for me, and I do wonder if I'll end up an old spinster for the rest of my life. My mind is saying *'Cathy, you don't need a man.'* However, I must be wafting my pheromones about, because when I am in the post office, the man behind the counter asks me to go for a drink with him and he's a lot younger than me. Why not? So I give him my phone number.

The following evening I meet Gary in the local pub. He looks really trendy and wears a skin tight T-shirt which shows off his muscles. I don't want to take advantage of him so I buy the first drink. At about 11.30pm, it appears he definitely wants to take advantage of me and offers me a drink back at his place. For the second time in my life, I throw caution to the wind and go for it. I feel like a real woman and it's doing my confidence a world of good. I've already got over all the embarrassment with Rob so I don't have the same hang-ups like I had before.

Gary's in a rush when he rips my clothes off and I don't complain when I see his bulging muscles. He's so strong and I feel young and slim, which is something I haven't felt since university. Gary and I bonk for most of the night and when I go to the loo at about 4am, I'm frightened of waking him up in case he wants to do it again.

"Cathy," Gary says as he gets up for work and kisses me on the cheek, "Just close the door behind you when you leave and I hope to see you soon."

I'm planning on seeing him very soon, that's a promise I've made to myself. I might start writing letters again so I can go into the post office more often.

Driving back home I feel like a slut, but not in a bad way - it's more in a devilish way and I chuckle to myself as I remember the night before. Gary wanted to play music whilst we did the dirty deed; I thought it was very romantic and told him to go for it. Then, to my surprise, he put on some music that sounded like we were at the funfair; there was a lot of trumpet playing and the odd tambourine thrown in for good measure. It was all very amusing.

When I get home, I ring about a job in a care home and they give me a telephone interview on the spot. I've always been good on the phone, so they offer me a job there and then. I start the next morning.

****

The home is called Garden View and from the outside it looks really nice; it's a large Georgian house that has been converted into a home for the elderly. There's a huge advertising board outside the home with a picture of a woman sitting in a rocking chair; on the other side of the board is a man sitting in a wheelchair. Underneath it says: 'Join in the fun and rock and roll.' It makes me giggle.

Once inside the home, the smell of urine is overwhelming and it takes me a minute to catch my breath. There's a large lounge area and patients are sat on chairs, nodding off. One or two of them smiles but the rest snarl and mutter to themselves.

The matron gives me a guided tour of all the bedrooms, the dining hall and the two lounges. In the smaller lounge there's an old lady that is in a really deep sleep. When she wakes up and sees me, she asks "How old am I?"

I look at the Matron, who whispers, "Ninety one."

I repeat this to the old lady and she weakly says, "No wonder I'm so tired." It makes me smile and I suddenly feel really sorry for them. Was this going to be me one day, all alone in a care home with no visitors other than Louise? The thought makes me shudder. The Matron laughs when she takes me into what's called 'the boudoir.' She tells me that George and Tilly think they're married, so they insist on sharing a double bed. The room is full of tack and there's a small bar area at the end of it. On Tilly's side of the bed lies a pink nightie and a pink bed coat. On George's side are some striped blue pyjamas. Apparently when their children visit, they don't know whose they are, so they call them all 'child.' As we walk along the corridor to the office, I see a little old lady dressed in a pleated skirt and a lemon jumper. She greets me and asks me my name. I'm about to answer her when she excuses herself and walks into the office to answer the phone. Matron looks at me and laughs.

"That's Tilly, she thinks she owns the nursing home and she's convinced she and George bought it years ago."

This makes me chuckle and I realise I could have some fun working here.

****

Later that afternoon, I go into a room at the end of the corridor to check on a man called Roy. When I walk in, he starts over-exaggerating about the pains in his legs. I bend down to look at his legs and they do look sore and swollen.

"It's just old age, Roy," I say gently.

He looks at me and he's clearly annoyed.

"You don't know what you're talking about," he snaps at me. "My other leg's fine and that's exactly the same age."

I can't help but laugh, which makes him more annoyed with me.

It's 5.30pm and my feet are killing me. I've never done a proper day's work in all my life, not like this, and I know I'll fall into bed later and pass out. At 6pm, I put on my coat to go home. Then the Matron calls me into the office. *'Maybe I'm getting the sack already?'* I think to myself. I don't get the sack and instead, she tells me what a good job I've done on my first day.

"You'll get used to the patients, Cathy," she smiles at me. "Some of them are easy to deal with and some of them are unconscious, and remember this: your warped sense of humour will come out in a job like this."

I laugh and make to leave, but before I can get through the door the Matron calls me back.

"Cathy, there's a phone call for you."

I run back in and answer the phone.

"How did it go today?" Mum's voice asks eagerly.

Mum, I'll be home in a minute so we'll talk when I get in," I quietly answer her, feeling quite a fool that my mum is phoning up.

Mum won't leave it, though.

"Cathy, I need you to ask if they've got any vacancies for ya Pop. Also, ask them if we get a discount with you working there. He's drove me mad today."

I can't get off the phone quick enough

****

It's the morning after and, as I pull up outside the home, there's complete chaos. Staff are running around the grounds and it's clear they're looking for someone. I get out of the car and shout over to Ruby, a larger than life Jamaican woman.

"Ruby, what's happening?"

"George and Tilly have taken the pool car and have gone off somewhere," Ruby shouts back. "Cathy, get back in your car and see if you can see them."

I jump back in the car and drive up the road. I've been gone a good ten minutes when I spot George and Tilly coming out of a supermarket loaded up with shopping. I leap out of the car and run over to them.

"Where have you been? Everyone's been so worried."

"We needed to get supplies for the home." Tilley looks at me like I'm mad, "A business doesn't run itself you know, whoever you are."

I make a quick decision to get in the back of the pool car and go back to the home with them. I can't take the chance in case they go off somewhere else.

I ring the home to tell everyone I've found them and to

explain what I'm doing. After driving along the main road for a few minutes, Tilly screams.

"George, you've just gone through a red light."

"Oh God, am I driving?" George looks at Tilley in shock.

My heart is in my mouth as I close my eyes and pray.

****

When I get back to the home and everything has settled down, work commences. I'm already tired and hungry and it's not even lunchtime. I go into the kitchen to make a coffee for the nurses and whilst I'm there, I notice three old ladies sitting at the table. One of them gets up to look in the fridge, then turns to the others.

"I can't remember if I was going to make a sandwich or get the mayonnaise."

"I do that all the time," one of the other ladies laughs, "I go into my bedroom and I've forgotten what I went in for."

"I don't have that problem," the third lady joins in with a chuckle. She knocks on the wooden table, then says "Oh, there's someone at the door," before getting up and going to answer it. It's like watching a TV programme and I'm mesmerised.

At lunch time I spend most of the hour feeding patients, only for them to spit it back in my face. I wonder how long I can stay at a job like this. After all, I get enough hassle off Mum and Pop and right now I feel like I'm on 'old' overload.

****

It's 3pm, I've only had one cup of coffee and I desperately need a pee. My bladder feels like a Winnebago water carrier and every time I try to get a break, someone shouts at me to do something for them. At 4pm, Mum is on the phone again, but this time it's a real concern because the ambulance has taken Pop to hospital. I quickly tell Matron what has happened and fly out of the building.

When I arrive at the hospital, the nurse tells me that Pop's had a funny turn and collapsed on the kitchen floor. Mum looks in a right state and cries when she sees me there.

"Oh, Cathy, thank God you're here! I didn't know what to do."

I give Mum a hug and we wait for the doctor.

"What will I do if anything happens to him?" Mum cries. I reassure her that he'll be fine and he's in the right place.

"You took your time, didn't you?" Pop exclaims the moment he sees the young Asian doctor.

Thankfully, the doctor smiles and carries on with the examination.

I want the floor to swallow me up and it's gone right over Mum's head. When the doctors have done their rounds, Mum and I head off and promise Pop we'll be back in the morning.

"No need," Pop shakes his head, "I'll be home by then."

We both walk out of the hospital and I know Mum doesn't want to leave him. I take Mum for a bite to eat and as soon as we get the food, Gary the body walks in, in his post office uniform. The uniform isn't at all flattering, but it's the body I'm interested in. He winks at me and I go bright red. When we've finished the meal he beckons me over.

"'Hey, Cathy, how about coming back to mine?"

I'm very flattered but say "I can't. I've got Mum with me and my Pop is in hospital."

"No worries," Gary say with a shrug of his shoulders,

"Maybe another time."

I'm not under any illusion where Gary's concerned and I know I'm just a shag to him- maybe he likes older women. I'm taking it for what it is.

****

Pops seems chirpier the next day and he says he determined to come home. I try and persuade him to stay in but he is even more stubborn than usual. Mum brings him his favourite sandwiches, which are potted beef on white bread. Then she talks to him like he's a small child.

"Here you go, you little love, eat them up and they'll make you strong."

"Shut up, you silly mew." Pop pushes her hand away. "You're not talking to our Steven now."

****

It's day three and as we walk onto the ward, we can hear Pop shouting for the nurse. An unkempt man is in the bed next to him, and Pop is trying to grass him up because he's had two dinners.

"Nurse, nurse, he's had two dinners! Look, one is under the bed!"

The nurse assures Pop that it doesn't matter and that sets him off on a rant.

"People want everything for nowt. It shouldn't be allowed."

Mum agrees with everything Pop says. By the time the doctors come round to take more blood, Pop is still moaning.

"I'm like a bloody pin cushion, leave me alone."

Thank God they ignore him.

The day after, Mum and I arrive on the ward but Pop is nowhere to be seen.

"Oh, Cathy, what's happened to him?" Mum panics. "What if he's dead?!"

The nurses reassure Mum that Pop isn't dead, he's just gone missing.

"Missing? I say, "How can he be missing?"

The nurse looks at me with a stern face and replies "Your father is a very difficult man and will not do as he's told. We've had security looking for him and now we'll have to wait for him to turn up again."

"So he's gone before?" I'm shocked.

"All the time." The nurse folds her arm, "He's always going off somewhere and we can't take responsibility if anything happens to him."

Mum nods her head.

"He's a pain in the arse, always has been. This is what I've got to put up with, week in and week out."

The nurse walks off, so Mum and I go outside to see if we can find Pop. Within a minute, we see him in an electric wheelchair and he's whizzing across the car park. We both stand open-mouthed. When he reaches us, he smiles and asks "How long have you two been here?"

"More to the point," I sigh with a mixture of relief and impatience. "Where have you been?"

"I've just been to the pub for a few pints," Pop laughs.

I can't believe what I'm hearing and Mum starts shouting

at him.

"Stanley, you're a bloody nuisance, and don't blame anyone else if you wake up dead tomorrow." Mum's formerly pallid face has now gone bright pink but Pop just laughs.

****

It's the weekend so Louise has come home to visit Pop. I think Mum is glad of the break, as she looks tired and drawn. We arrive at the hospital just after lunch and, as usual, Pop is moaning.

"I want to come home. They're cruel to me in here and it stinks of pee."

Louise tries to calm him down by telling him he's in the right place and that he needs to get better. Pop pulls a face like a naughty child. It's coming up to tea time and some of the other patients are having a curry.

"They're getting better treatment than me, they've sent out for a curry," Pop points at them.

The next day, Louise and I are back to visit and Pop isn't in his bed again. I look at the nurse. She doesn't say a word and just points to the other side of the room. Pop is sitting with five other men and they're all playing Crib for money. Pop looks up and smiles.

"Oh, Cathy, Louise, I'm having a game with me friends and I'm winning! Also, I've had a curry for me dinner; all I had to do was ask for the Asian menu. Me friends helped me order it."

The doctor comes over and tells us that Pop has been diagnosed with a stomach ulcer and that they're allowing him to go home tomorrow.

"Mr Mathews," the doctor shouts over to Pop. "Can you

come back to your bed please?"

Pop tuts and slowly walks over to his bed. The doctor tries to help him get inside the bed but Pop won't get in.

"I'm not going back to bed. I'm not an old man and I haven't finished me game."

The doctor pulls the curtains around the bed and sits on the chair.

"Mr Mathews, you have a stomach ulcer. So no spicy food from now on. I notice you had a curry for your lunch but no more when you get out. Also, NO alcohol."

"You're not to tell me what to do," Pop laughs," I'm a man in my seventies and if I want a curry and a pint, I'll have one. It's the only pleasure I have."

Even the doctor looks tired.

"As you wish, Mr Mathews, but I warn you, you will become really ill if you ignore my advice."

Pop won't leave it.

"I've never been ill in my life."

The doctor shakes our hands and walks off. I feel sorry for the doctor because I know how difficult Pop is.

****

Within a day of being home, Pop is back in the pub with his cronies. It doesn't matter what Mum says, he won't listen to anyone. It's the day of the village competition. Mum and I walk around all the houses to see how the neighbours have decorated their homes. Mum has left strict instructions with Pop that he's to decorate the front of our house by the time she gets back. We've been out for about an hour and as we approach our house, Mum is leaning forward to try and see what Pop has done. She can't see, so she breaks into a run. When we're outside, Mum stares at the bench at the front of the house. It has an empty suitcase on it with a sign on the front saying, 'Man in a Suitcase.' Next to it is a note which reads 'The invisible Man'.

"Stanley, where are you?" Mum shouts at the top of her voice. "I'm gonna kill you."

When we go inside, we find Pop has gone back to the pub. Mum sulks because she knows she won't get first place. All afternoon, people congregate outside the house and laugh at what Pop has done; some of them even take pictures. Pop comes in from the pub and Mum is just about to start on him when there's a knock on the door. Mum answers it and a lady from the local church hands her a shopping voucher for fifty pound and a rosette. She congratulates Mum and tells her that she's won 3rd price for humour and originality. Mum can't wipe the smile off her face as she walks into the lounge.

"Do you want a drink, Stanley?" she says, looking at him.

Pop can't believe what he's hearing and can't bring himself to answer her.

The nursing home has paid me while I was off and I feel very guilty. However, they have also said in a kind letter that they need someone more reliable and because I am living with ailing parents, they have had to let me go.

CHAPTER 16

It's a couple of weeks before Mum has the courage to talk to me about what is bothering her. She starts off by beating about the bush.

"You know we love you, Cathy, and, well, the price of fish - and we don't begrudge you fish or anything really ... when you're a pensioner, it's hard love. I know you had a very extravagant life with Tom and ... I think you need to watch your weight though and...."

"Mum just say what you want to say," I sigh then I smile at her but she seems uneasy. Pop interrupts.

"Cathy, what your mother's trying to say is that you seem to be eating a lot of food in the house. Like she says, we don't begrudge you anything but we're pensioners and can't afford all the food you've been eating."

I am shocked to the core and stand with my mouth open. All the food *I've* been eating? I've been eating at Jane's a lot. What do they mean? I'm quite hurt, so I go to my room and think about what I have been eating. Before long, Mum comes in.

"I'm sorry love, I don't want to upset you, but I bought a pound of ham and that's gone. There were two loaves of bread and twenty four packets of crisps too, not to mention the chocolate and all your Pop's beer: all in two days."

I'm shocked and need to defend myself.

"Mum, I may have had one ham sandwich in two days but I don't eat crisps and I wouldn't touch Pop's beer. I don't drink beer."

Mum sits on the bed and thinks.

"Maybe you're sleep eating, Cathy."

I have to admit it's a possibility, although I've never sleepwalked before. Well, not that I know of.

After another few days of food going missing, we're all puzzled. I even go to Jane's for a night and food still goes missing, so that throws the suspicion to Mum and Pop. Pop completely dismisses it could be him and he blames Mum.

"Joan, I know Cathy's getting chubby, but you're going in the same direction."

Mum is furious and shouts at Pop.

"Since you've retired, Stanley, you've been a right pain in the arse. I've got twice as much nastiness and only half your pay."

"Come on Reggie," Pop says, picking up Rupert's lead. "Let's go for a walk."

Mum puts the kettle on and all I can hear from her is fecking this and fecking that. For once I feel uncomfortable at home.

****

Day four and we've run out of food. I go to the supermarket and replace what has gone missing. As I'm walking around the supermarket I think to myself, can I really be stuffing my face with food in the night as a sort of comfort? I then wonder if it's Mum and Pop and neither of them know they're doing it, so I buy cream cheese and smoked Salmon - foods I know they both detest – to try a little experiment. I also buy small bags of nuts and salads which only I eat.

Sure enough, the following day, all the ham, bread, crackers, cheese, crisps and chocolate bars have gone. I jump up and down in the kitchen. Now I know it's not me. This sparks a whole new debate. If people sleepwalk and raid the fridge, do they eat the foods they love or is it any food? Mum decides it's so serious that she'll go to the doctors about it all. I've no idea why the doctor has to be informed. Mum comes back with no solution at all. We're all sitting in the lounge watching TV as the news comes on.

"Good evening," begins the presenter.

"Why do they say good evening and then bring you a shed load of bad news," Pop laughs.

Mum agrees, then squeals.

"I know what it is," she announces. We both look at her expectantly. "We've got a ghost! Oh, how lovely."

"Don't be silly woman," Pop shakes his head. "There's no ghost in this house."

Mum's not convinced and keeps looking at me. I can feel myself getting paranoid. Pop gets up and goes into the kitchen to eat some left over stew. Thirty minutes after eating it, Pop starts laughing, and once he's started we can't shut him up.

Mum is annoyed.

"Stanley, stop it, you mad old fool."

After ten minutes it's getting on my nerves, so I decide to go to bed. However, I wasn't expecting Mum to follow me and get in bed with me.

"I can't sleep with him, Cathy, he's gone mad. He's having some kind of breakdown and he's taking me with him." Mum has a light bulb moment. "Maybe he caught a bug in hospital? The clairvoyant did say I was going to lose him and it hasn't happened yet. Maybe this is it? He's like a death boomerang – when we think he's going to go, he comes back."

I shake my head, as I can't believe the nonsense that comes

out of Mum's mouth.

****

It's around 2.45am when I hear a banging at the front door. We hear Pop's bedroom door open, then Mums screams.

"Oh, good Jesus, Cathy, the ghost has come for us." Mum starts praying for our lives. I look at her and put my finger to my lips so she'll be quiet. Then we hear an almighty bang and a huge draft rushes through the house. Mum is terrified and I tell her it's just Pop opening the front door. Who can it be at this time in the morning? We hear voices, so Mum and I get out of bed and stand on the landing to hear what's happening. We can hear another man's voice and a radio. We both race down the stairs only to find a police officer standing in the hallway. The policeman nods at Mum and I out of courtesy, then Pop shows him into the lounge and we follow. The officer has a search warrant and his two other colleagues search the upstairs of the house.

"They've come for ya Pop," Mum whispers to me.

"Why?" I whisper.

Mum leans into me.

"Years ago, when we had no money – well, nobody had any money – Pop stole some coal from the local coal yard. Ever since, I've been waiting for them to arrive."

I can't take in what mum is saying.

"Mum, they wouldn't come for him over fifty years later."

Mum's not sure and whispers, "Some cases are never closed, Cathy."

The officers come down the stairs and ask if any of us have seen or heard from Steven. We are all totally confused and shake our heads. Mum jumps up.

"I hope that scum bag in prison hasn't beaten my boy up again or he'll be getting another beating off me."

"No, Mrs Mathews, Steven has absconded with another prisoner," explains one of the officers.

Pop shakes his head then bursts out laughing. The officers don't know what to say. Mum runs into the kitchen to get Pop a drink of water and the officers follow her. She turns to them and meekly says "I don't know what's wrong with my husband, Officer."

I follow Mum into the kitchen. One of the officers walks towards the kitchen window sill and touches one of Mum's plants. He rubs a leaf, smells it and then looks at his colleague. Without saying anything to each other, one of them turns to Mum and says "Is this for your own consumption, Mrs Mathews?"

Mum looks confused.

"What do you mean 'for her own consumption'?" I ask.

"Does she grow it for her own consumption? It's a simple question," the officer repeats the question slowly to me.

"Oh, I grow everything myself," Mum smiles, "and don't you think I've got green fingers? You should see the greenhouse." With that, we all walk into the greenhouse and it is full of beautiful plants with lovely green leaves. We can all hear Pop laughing inside the house. The other officer radios for back up, and within a few minutes Mum is read her rights and is frog marched into the back of a police van. I scream for them to leave her alone and try to get them off her at every opportunity. This results in us both being arrested and Pop waves us both off at the door, still laughing his head off like the laughing clown at Blackpool Pleasure Beach.

****

It's 6.30am and a new police officer walks into the interview room.

"Come on, Cathy, come clean with us. Did you think you could hide behind two old people? Your parents! How low is that?"

"I've told your colleagues I can't remember where the plants came from and I have no idea how come there are so many in the greenhouse," I reply with a hefty sigh. "I don't even know what they are."

The officer laughs and starts to chomp on a really crispy apple, which annoys me.

"Cathy, there's no way two old people use that amount for their own consumption. Who are you selling it to?"

I feel really weary and long to get to Mum. I try to be nice to him as I plead.

"Look, please, I really need to speak to my mum."

"I bet you do," he laughs.

"It's not like that," I snap back as I get annoyed, "I'm wondering what you're saying to her."

He sits down and becomes serious. His voice is stern.

"Like I've said, I bet you are."

I stand up and the officer bangs his hand down on the table.

"Sit down."

"I demand to know what questions you're asking her and what she's saying to you," I shout back at him.

"She's singing like a canary," He says as he walks out of the room. "When you're both done with the duty solicitor, you can confer with each other... oh, and by the way, your father's here. He's been to the station to report you two as missing. He can't remember a thing about last night. He came in here wobbling around like Bill Hayley doing *Rock Around the Clock*. We asked him if he was drunk and asked to take blood from him. Turns out he's still smacked up to his tits. Shame on you."

I want the officer to stay so I can ask him what he is talking about. What does he mean 'smacked up to his tits?' This is like a living nightmare.

****

When the duty solicitor arrives it takes him two hours to fathom out what's happened, and then we are free to go. Steven is still on the run and that's why the police went to the house in the first place. Then, of course, they found Mum's stash. Pop tested positive for cannabis and Mum had been using the dried herbs to cook with. Mum's in the back of the taxi with Pop.

"It couldn't have been catnip, could it?"

"No Joan," Pop laughs. "I'd have been rolling around on the floor in ecstasy if it was."

Mum cackles and I have a headache from hell.

We all walk into the hallway and Mum puts the kettle on. I decline any tea and go to my room to see if I can get rid of this awful headache and get some sleep. As I pass my parents' room, I can hear faint laughter coming from it. When I open the door, there's no one there. I slowly walk to Steven's door and listen; it's silent. I slowly open the door and find Steven in bed with a tray full of food, watching *Mr Bean* with his headphones on. The look on his face is of total shock and he doesn't know what to do. I shake my head, then a rage comes over me.

"You little scumbag! Have you any idea what you've put us through?"

He tries to run past me but I block his escape. Then the idiot shouts down to Mum.

"Mum, Cathy won't let me pass."

Mum and Pop run up the stairs. Pop tries to hit Steven and Mum is screams for him to let go of him. Steven sits back on the bed like a cornered rat, then Mum rushes to him and cuddles him tightly.

"Are you hiding from that nasty man?"

"Which one, Mum?" Steven looks puzzled.

"The one that gave you a beating when you were in prison," Mum kisses his head.

"Oh yeah," Steven laughs. "The one you belted."

Mum smiles and nods. I swear what happens next freaks me out. A man's face appears from under the bed, and it seems to be eating a cheese sandwich. We all stare at the man and, sure enough, it's the one Mum gave a good slapping to. We all turn our heads to the side to get a good look at him. He slowly emerges from under the bed and sits on the edge with Steven.

"Well that solves the riddle of the missing food," Pop points out.

"This is my friend Pete," Steven says. "He's helped me escape."

I can't believe what I am hearing and seeing, so I challenge Steven.

"Where were you both when the police arrived?"

"We were both in the loft." Steven points to the ceiling.

I'm furious because of everything that's already happened.

"I'm phoning the police," I announce. All of a sudden, Pete jumps off the bed, grabs a load of sandwiches and runs down the stairs with Steven in tow.

"Don't go, son," Mum shouts after Steven. "I'll hide you."

I chase them both onto the drive shouting for them to get back in the house. At that moment, Doris arrives in a taxi with her shopping and looks on in disgust.

"What the hell's going on in there now?"

Steven gets in Mum's car and his jailbird friend gets in the driver's side. Rupert runs out of the house and onto the drive as Pete is about to reverse and screech off. I can hear Mum gasp as she watches the dog nearly go under the car.

"Oh Jesus, the dog," Pop yells.

I sprint into action and, coming to Rupert's rescue, I grab him before he goes under the wheels.

CHAPTER 17

The garden looks beautiful and I feel really happy here. I look up at the sky and let the sun shine on my face. Louise comes back from walking Rupert, and Tom puts the new BBQ together. I prepare the food and shout for Mum and Pop to come into the garden. It's much less of a burden now they live with us and it doesn't all fall on my shoulders. I miss Jane – I never thought she would move to Italy. Even Josh has gone with her because he met an Italian girl who works there as a waitress. We eat the BBQ and after a few rosé wines and some yummy food, it's time for bed. I sink into the king-size mattress and, with Tom's arms around me, I fall into a deep sleep.

I can hear the birds singing and a slight breeze is blowing through my hair. I feel slightly drugged and I can there are noises around me that are unfamiliar. Voices and things being clattered in the distance. I get a whiff of disinfectant and wonder if Mum's mopping the kitchen floor. I can't make out where I am, so with all my strength I try to open my eyes. It takes me a few minutes to focus and I see Mum's face staring at me.

"Cathy, you're back," she whispers. I haven't got a clue what's she's talking about. Then she starts shouting, "Nurse, nurse come quickly."

I see a young nurse looking at me. She immediately takes my pulse and says "I'll get the doctor." Mum holds my hand. Within a few seconds the doctors are all around the bed, staring at me and shining lights in my eyes. I want to ask where I am but no words will come out. Two nurses sit me up in the bed whilst the doctor tells me what's happened and he reiterates that my parents have given the doctors a full report of what happened that night. As the story unfolds, I get flashbacks of me running out of the house to save Rupert from being run over. Apparently, I slipped on ice and the car backed over me, then it tried to speed off and dragged me up the road for about a hundred yards. I sustained a broken arm, two broken fingers and slight head injuries. They didn't know the extent of the head injuries when I arrived at the hospital, so they put me in a state of induced coma for just over a week, then they dealt with the injuries and slowly brought me round. In the accident, my skull had taken a good shaking and there were splinters of bone in my brain. Nothing too serious and thankfully not life-threatening. The doctors say it will all heal in a matter of months.

Mum is sat crying and I can't comfort her because my body is still so sore. By the time the evening visitors arrive, I have a cup of tea and a small slice of toast. Pop files in with Louise and his eyes are full of tears. Louise has been by my side everyday with Mum. Pop tells me that Steven and his friend were sentenced in court the day after and they've both been given extra sentences because of what they did, and for once Mum didn't try and protect Steven. His friend Pete got two years extra for stealing a car and leaving the scene of an accident and Steven was charged with aiding and abetting and was given an extra six months in prison. The judge told him that he was lucky he not to get the same sentence as the perpetrator.

"They should be grateful they weren't charged with attempted murder." Pop says, shaking his head.

It's hard for me to take all this in and I get tired very quickly. Mum and Pop go home, but Louise stays and reads a book whilst I drift in and out of sleep.

The following morning, Jane arrives. I stare at her because, in my head, I think she's gone to live in Italy. The nurse tells me it's all normal and people take themselves off into their own little world when they're out of it.

After four days, I'm let out on the condition I get complete bed rest.

"She's getting full bed rest I can assure you of that," Louise laughs.

"And a full English breakfast," Mum laughs too. "Poor girl's nearly wasting away."

That comment makes me happy: wasting away.

Walking in the house is very comforting and, with my arm still in plaster, I feel happy to be at home. Mum and Louise waste no time in waiting on me.

I've been home about an hour when Mum comes to sit next to me.

"The police came and took my stash of plants; cleared me out, they did. I think they've sold them on the market and they've not given me a single penny."

It's good to see Mum on form and I feel quite tearful every time I think of the accident. Mum gets all emotional and says "Things could have been a lot worse. You could have died."

****

Four months down the line and the accident has made me evaluate my life. I enrol on a private course for flower arranging. The course is for four weeks and Pop has lent me the money so I can get started. I feel I need to get my teeth into something and make something of my life. I don't want to dwell on the past anymore- it's time to move forward.

The course is being held at the back of a busy shop in the centre of town, and it's very hands on. Lydia, who owns the business, says it's the quickest way to learn the trade. I think this is really up my street and I remember Polly used to spend hundreds of pounds on flower displays. Christmas was no exception, when all her friends were sent table displays as presents.

Lydia is a really nice young woman and starts by giving me some valuable advice.

"Cathy, florists are known as the silent psychologists or, as I was taught, the three wise monkeys: see no evil, speak no evil and hear no evil."

I laugh but she shakes her head and says "Cathy, you'll see and hear it all if you work in a florist, so discretion is the key word at all times."

On my first day, Lydia shows me how to make a basic bouquet and by the end of the week I can do button holes, wedding bouquets and table displays. I'm getting on well with the other girls and I love going out in the van to do deliveries. I can feel my life changing every day and my confidence is reaching new heights. I never knew going to work could be so rewarding and it is certainly changing me as a person. I love the buzz of the shop and people coming in and out telling us all the local gossip. Even my parents say they've noticed a huge change in me over the last couple of weeks. I've lost weight and every morning I put a full face of make-up on and prepare me for the day ahead.

****

When I reach my final day, Lydia says she's sorry to see me go because I've been a lot of fun and got on famously with the customers. She gives me a massive bunch of flowers, a certificate, and a card signed by all the girls with 'Good Luck' splashed across the front of it.

When I get home, I'm on cloud nine as I tell Mum and Pop about the compliments I've received. I assume Pop is only half listening because he's reading the paper, but after a few minutes he folds it up and looks at me.

"Cathy, don't go and work for anyone else; you'll be a wage slave forever. You've trained in an upmarket shop, make the most of it."

"Pop, are you serious?" I ask, shocked at what he's just suggested.

"You'll never have any money working for someone else," he says earnestly. "Put the hard work in for yourself and you'll reap the rewards."

"It's a great idea," I admit thoughtfully, "but I don't have the money to start up a business."

"Go and look at that shop that I saw in the paper," Mum squeals with excitement. "I was going to open it as a haberdashery shop, but your Pop won't let me."

Pop shakes his head and carries on reading the paper.

****

The following day, Jane meets me for lunch and I tell her about what Pop has said.

"Can you get a bank loan?" she asks me.

"No," I say, shaking my head sadly. "I can't. I've got bad credit from all that crap with the Freak."

Jane sighs and goes to the bar to get us both a drink. When she sits back down, her face lights up and she says "I could lend you the money."

"How?" I ask, screwing up my face.

Jane becomes really excited and almost squeals.

"I've got the money from my parents' house. It's just sat there in the bank." Jane is more than thrilled. "Honestly,

Cathy," she continues, "I would love to lend it to you."

I can't take it all in. We have lunch and I think my heart is going to burst with excitement. When we leave the pub, we drive up to the shop Mum has told me about. We look at it from the outside then Jane rings the agent. Jane's a cool cucumber when she wants to be and I listen to her chatting on the phone.

"No, we need to look at it now. We're going on a business trip tomorrow." There's a slight pause, before she continues, "This shop has been empty for years. Do you want to rent it or not?"

Jane and I go to the estate agents and they give us the keys for the shop on the High Street. It's filthy dirty and the outside definitely needs to be painted. It's hard to get through the door at first because there's about two years of mail behind it. It smells a bit musty but a good airing and a splash of paint would freshen it up wonderfully. Beyond the front shop area we discover a room at the back, along with a separate kitchen and toilet. We walk back into the main shop area and Jane asks "What do you think?"

"It could be made lovely and in a way it's perfect," I say, looking at the double frontage, "but the shop's too big. It would take a lot of stock to fill it and if it didn't have much in, it would look stupid."

Jane sits on the window sill deep in thought.

"I know what you mean, Cathy, it is big but the rent is reasonable."

I sit on the other window sill and then I have a thought. I scream at Jane like we're a couple of kids.

"Jane, why don't we share the shop? Split it down the middle with an archway? You could get back into making your cakes."

Jane squeals with joy and we both bounce around the shop like children, hugging each other.

We head back to my house to tell Mum and Pop, armed with a bottle of Champagne. They thinks it's a fantastic idea and I feel like I'm going to burst with happiness.

****

Two weeks later and we've got the keys for the shop. Josh has been roped into helping clean and paint – Jane says it's the only way he can earn his keep – and Louise has taken a week's holiday to help. Everyone is cleaning and decorating; the radio is on loud and music from the seventies fills the shop with happy vibes.

Within a week, the phone line is connected and we've bought two second-hand cash registers off the internet. A local builder has constructed the archway to divide the shop into two and, with every hour that passes, the shop looks better and better. We both put posters in the shop windows so that we can start taking orders and customers will know we're opening up. I go to Jane's and we order a curry and some wine to celebrate our new businesses. The signs are going up tomorrow and our opening day is Saturday. For the whole evening, all we talk about is what we're doing in the shop. There's no talk of men; it's all positive and to do with us.

****

It's the day before opening day and we both unveil the signs. Mine is called *'Wake up and Smell the Roses.'* This is a bit of a dig at Tom because he always used to say to me, 'Cathy, wake up and smell the coffee.' Looking back now, I realise how derogatory he was with me.

Jane's shop is called *'For Cakes' Sake'* because Jane's

favourite saying is, 'For God's sake." We both have a good giggle and we know the names will be a conversation starter. As we stand on the main road and admire the shops, we see motorists pointing and other people staring out of nosiness; many laugh at the names we have chosen. Jane and I buy a little white van between us and Jane employs Banito as our driver. One half of the van is a sign written with Jane's business and the other half is a sign written as mine.

****

It's opening day and Mum has insisted on coming to the shop to help out. Jane has three cake orders that are going to be picked up today and one is being delivered. I have orders coming from all over the place. I didn't want to go cheap and cheerful, like Lydia had taught me 'Don't do cheap flowers, you're not a garage'. I appear to have a few classy customers and one lady, called Lady Meadows, orders a hundred and fifty pounds worth of flowers to be delivered today. Her address is 'The White House' on Lindley Green, which is a very posh part of Yorkshire.

Mum has given herself the title of 'customer service manager' and every time the phone rings she grabs it and chats to customers. When my phone doesn't ring, she answers Jane's phone. It's mid-morning and Jane is getting fed up with Mum, because she answers her phone and says, "Hello, cake hole." So Jane gently steers her back into my half of the shop. Mum then runs to answer my phone and spends a good five minutes just chatting about everything and anything with the caller.

"Oh yes, come in for a cup of tea anytime, we'd love to see you. We've got some lovely things in the shop. Aww, take care of yourself love. Bye."

"Who was that?" I ask her.

Mum shrugs her shoulders and replies, "Just a nice lady, like me."

****

It's 4pm and Jane is on the phone taking an order while Mum makes cups of tea and cake for us all. I sit down behind the counter and Mum sits next to me.

"It's been busy today, hasn't it, Cathy?"

I nod as I take a large bite out of the cake.

"Mum, it couldn't have gone any better. I'm really pleased."

"This is gorgeous cake," Mum mumbles as she tucks in.

Suddenly, Jane screams at the top of her voice. I run into her shop with my mouth full of cake.

"What's wrong?"

Mum is behind me. Jane points to a blue teddy bear cake that has two great big pieces taken from it.

I look at Mum.

"Mum, you haven't? Please tell me you didn't cut into that cake." However, it's obvious to everyone that she clearly has. Jane is distraught.

"That was an order for a christening tomorrow."

Mum doesn't know what to say as she tries to stick her piece of cake back onto the teddy. It looks a right mess. Jane has rosy cheeks now, something she always gets when she's stressed. I try to help.

"Jane, I'll stay behind and help you make another one."

Before she can answer me, a customer comes into my shop.

I stand behind the counter, smile and say "How can I help you?"

"I want a bouquet of flowers please," The man says sheepishly.

I walk around the shop with him and he points to different flowers to be included in the bouquet. It only takes me a few minutes to do the arrangement but I have to keep an eye on Mum, who is trying to comfort Jane in the back room. When I pass the flowers to the young man, I ask, "What would you like on the card?"

He answers without hesitation "I want 'congratulations' and 'I hope it's mine'."

I quickly write out the card and he pays and leaves the shop. I go into the back and tell them what's happened, in a hope that it will cheer Jane up. It doesn't. Instead, Mum just pipes up "She must be a right dirty cow."

Jane and I stay behind and make up another cake. While we're waiting for it to be iced, we chat about her and Banito.

"I do love him, it's just that I can't spend all day, every day with him, and he drives me mad," explains Jane, softly.

"The customers love him," I laugh. "He's very charming and the women love his accent."

"I know, Cathy," Jane grins but then heaves a sigh. "He keeps getting lost though. It's costing a fortune in diesel." As if on cue, Banito walks into the shop. "Talk of the devil and it will appear." smiles Jane.

"I no devil, Jane," Banito looks confused and upset by the comment, so Jane tickles him.

"You're my little devil, Banito. Come here and give us a kiss."

I watch the two of them being silly and I long to find someone who I can love the same.

****

Another day begins and I've asked Mum not to come in today so at least we can have a fairly normal day. My first customer is a woman who has a face like thunder. She picks up a small basket of flowers and passes me a delivery address. All the time she's in the shop, she doesn't make eye contact and she doesn't speak. She quickly writes out a plain card. I tell her the price of the flowers and she hands me a credit card. When I read what she has written on the card, my blood goes cold. It's says: *'You're not going to live until Christmas'*. She then walks out of the shop talking to herself.

Jane screams with laughter when she looks at the card and says "What a nutter." I think so too but I remember Lydia's words to me - *'See all and say nothing.'* I go out the back and start making up bouquets of flowers.

It's early afternoon and Jane and I are having a cup of coffee. Mum walks through the door and my heart fills with dread. Jane laughs. Mum's brought us both a sandwich and a cake as a way of saying sorry for eating Jane's order.

"It's fine, Joan, don't worry about it." Jane hugs Mum.

That's Mum's cue to start taking over again. I decide to have a gentle chat with her.

"Mum, please don't get involved. I'll deal with the customers."

"Oh, Cathy, you know me, I'm not one to interfere," she laughs.

I roll my eyes and carry on cutting flowers for a delivery.

We're just about to close the shop when a man runs in and

begs us to help him. Mum is the first on the scene to ask what's happened. The man gets his breath then tells us he needs a bunch of flowers urgently. I select about ten flowers and start to wrap them in clear paper.

"What have you been up to?" Mum asks him in a playful way.

"I've slept with my girlfriend's sister and she's found out," he goes bright red.

Mum gasps, runs over to gather more flowers and roses, and then slaps them on the counter. The flowers have more than doubled and I stand there with my mouth open. Jane comes in to see what all the fuss is about. The man gestures for me to hurry up so I quickly wrap the flowers and he hands me fifty pounds.

I'm just about to say it's too much when Mum interrupts.

"There you go, lad, get gone, and if you take my advice, there's a chocolate shop further on." The man runs out of the shop and Mum starts sweeping the floor. Jane can't speak for laughing.

Mum has formed a few friendships from answering the phone and now there isn't only Mum coming to the shop, but three of her new friends are hanging out with her in the back. There are endless cups of tea and the clattering of false teeth as they chat amongst themselves. If I tell Mum once I tell her a thousand times a day, 'DO NOT eavesdrop on conversations and DO NOT repeat what you do hear.' This is like telling a deaf person to listen carefully while you whisper to them. I've asked Pop to try his best to keep her at home but she won't listen. It's early afternoon and Mum decides to go home; she's tired but she won't admit it. She shouts through to Jane.

"I'm going, Jane. If I don't go, I can't come back."

I can hear Jane sniggering and laughing in the back. Mum has only just got out of the shop when she sees a neighbour and shouts "Edna, come over here! I've got something to tell you." Mum then comes back into the shop with Edna and they both go out the back. I hear my name being mentioned several times and when I ask Mum why she is hell bent on telling everyone my news, she becomes annoyed.

"There are other things to talk about other than you, Cathy. That's the beauty of being in a shop: all the gossip we hear is new gossip."

There's no one in the shop and I really lose my temper with Mum.

"If you don't stop gossiping, I won't allow you to come in the shop anymore. Do you understand?"

Mum is furious and grabs her coat.

"If you want to be like that, Cathy, I won't let you have a bath at MY house." With that, she walks out of the shop talking to herself.

I put my head on the desk and say to Jane "What the hell am I going to do with my mother, Jane?"

"I have no idea," she shrugs.

****

A few days later, a young man comes into the shop and asks for twelve red roses to be delivered. He looks about seventeen years of age and he's a bit scruffy looking. I tell him the price and he agrees. I then ask him whether he would he like to pay cash or card. He looks at me and seriously says "Cash on delivery."

"Will you be at the premises when they're delivered?" I ask.

"No," he shakes his head.

"Who will be there?" I ask politely as I take a deep breath.

He looks at me like I am stupid and replies "My girlfriend. That's who the flowers are for."

Jane stands in the doorway to listen. I can't get my head around it so I ask him outright.

"So your girlfriend is paying for her own flowers?"

"Yeah."

Jane's got her head down and I know she's laughing. I lean on the counter.

"I'm sorry," but I can't send flowers out without a payment," I explain softly. "She may not want to pay thirty pounds."

"She won't mind. I've ordered them and it's the thought that counts."

When he leaves the shop, Jane and I look at each other.

"Jane, kill me now, I can't cope."

****

We've been open for exactly five weeks when I see Tom walk past the window. I hear Jane say loudly, "Oh no, trouble's here."

I can feel my heart racing and when he steps inside the shop, he stands and stares at me

"How are you, Cathy?"

I can't answer him because my mouth is so dry and my hands are trembling. Tom then looks around the shop and smiles. "I didn't think you had it in you, Cathy, well done."

I try to ignore him but he's now standing in front of me. I take a deep breath and say, '"What do you want Tom?"

"He probably wants to buy flowers for his tart," Jane shouts from the other side of the shop. Toms laughs. This annoys her and she stands in the doorway so she can look him in the face. She almost spits at him. "You're hard faced enough to come into your ex-wife's shop. Do you want flowers? Maybe you've got a new girlfriend?" Tom's rash starts to develop. I stop what I'm doing and stare at him. Then a gush of water covers him and he's standing in front of me dripping wet. Mum has come out of the back, lifted some flowers out of a bucket and thrown the water over him.

"Oh no, I didn't know SHE was here," he groans, looking at Mum.

"I bet you didn't," Mum screams at him. Tom wipes his face with his hankie and leaves the shop. Mum puts her hand on her hips. "The nerve of that fecking man."

Tom coming into the shop shakes me for a couple of days and I have to try my best to get back on track. I didn't think after all this time that he could still de-rail me like that, but he has. Jane calls him every name under the sun since he's been in and I have to laugh at her because I know she's right. I just hope and pray he doesn't come back in and I can't help wondering what he came for. Jane thinks he came in to nosy at the shop.

****

We've just opened the shop one morning when a young lad comes in and only buys three flowers. How he wants me to 'bulk them out' I have no idea. When I ask him what he wants on the card he says: 'Drop your drawers and the flowers are yours'. I know it's unprofessional of me but I fall about in fits of laughter. What makes it funnier is he doesn't know what he's said. . For the rest of the day, Jane and I laugh every time we look at each other. This is by far the best job I've ever had.

CHAPTER 18

One thing I need to do to move on completely with my life is to visit Steven in prison. Mum's still annoyed with him and tries to persuade me not to go but I feel I need to. I want him to realise how serious it is; what he and Pete did. He needs to realise he could have killed me or left me with severe head injuries. Mum refuses to make the appointment, which shocks me, so I decide to ring the prison myself and ask for a Sunday visit.

The passes arrive a few days later so Mum and I go to meet Steven.

"I'm going to give him a good hiding when I see him," she says on the way there.

"Please don't, Mum," I beg. "This is something I need to do, otherwise I don't think I'll ever speak to him again."

When we arrive at the prison we're searched. Then a prison officer comes over to me and says that the governor would like a word with me before we see Steven. I find this a bit odd but I follow him anyway. Mum makes herself a cup of tea. The officer knocks on the governor's door and I walk inside. The governor is standing, looking out of the window and the officer introduces me. The governor turns round and we look at each other, and in all my life I have never seen such beautiful blue eyes on a man. He points to a chair opposite him and introduces himself as John. I smile and shake his hand. We stare at each other for a few seconds until I feel stupid and have to look away.

"It's a very brave thing to do, Cathy," he eventually says with a sigh. "I think it will help all concerned, and I need to make you aware that Steven is full of remorse. I know that doesn't make it better. I just want you to know that he appears to be a changed man."

I don't know how I feel about this new information, so I ask, "Am I supposed to feel guilty or sorry for him?"

John raises his eyebrows in surprise.

"Oh, no, that's not what I mean. Steven has done wrong and he and his friend are being punished for it. He was re-sentenced as you already know. Not only is he doing more time, he's had no privileges or wages and his friend has been moved to another prison."

I sigh because I really don't know where this is going. John looks awkward for a moment then says "Do you know you're mother has refused to visit him?" I nod my head sadly.

"Yes, she's still angry at how he behaved."

"Some people can change," John tells me earnestly. "It often just takes something serious to happen and it shocks them to the core. He's not all bad. I just thought I would warn you. Oh, and he's lost an awful lot of weight too, so perhaps you can prepare your mother."

Before I leave the office, I catch a glimpse of John looking at my wedding finger. I shake John's hand and leave.

****

We are shown to a sparse room and Steven is sat near the window with an officer by his side. He's painfully thin. When Mum spots him, she runs over and slaps his head.

When Steven shouts "Ouch" and holds his head, she slaps the other side of it.

We both sit down and Mum starts. I've never heard her so displeased with him. Her face is twisted and she snarls at him.

"You, young man, are a disgrace. You could have killed Cathy with your childish behaviour."

Steven stares at me and when he sees the faint scar on the right side of my face, his eyes fill up with tears. I'm not at all moved by him.

"Steven, it's about time you took responsibility for your own life and realise there's consequences for your actions," I begin honestly but gently. "What you did was extremely foolish. What would you have done if it had been Mum or Pop that that you had backed over and dragged up the road?"

Steven starts to cry softly again and I feel like belting him myself.

"Stop crying or else I'll give you something to cry for," Mum says, poking him.

The officer next to Steven sniggers.

"Cathy, I'm so sorry, honestly." Steven speaks in a quiet voice. "I know it's no excuse but I was drugged up at the time and full of adrenaline."

I come at him again.

"So how would you have felt if, when you came down from your high, you had found out I was dead?"

Steven doesn't want to listen to any of it and puts his head down.

"I'm telling you, lad," Mum shouts. "When you get out of here you're grounded for six years." Steven doesn't answer Mum back so Mum thinks of something else. "And you owe me for a new bumper for me car, not to mention all the food you and that rug rat ate."

The prison officer raises his eyebrows and grins. He's so shocked at what Mum has said. I look at Mum incredulous.

"Mum, we're talking about something serious, not a bumper or food."

"You can't get them anymore," Mum mumbles and folds her arms. "That car is an antique and worth a fortune."

Steven takes hold of Mum's hand but she moves it.

"I'll find the money, Mum," he says in a sheepish voice. "As soon as I get out."

"Darn right you will."

Steven then turns to me.

"I don't know how I will ever make it up to you, Cathy."

I lean forward and look him straight in the eye.

"You can make it up to me by behaving yourself from now on. Stop being so stupid and childish."

Steven puts his head down again and that's where it stays until we leave.

When we leave the building, we're just about to get into the car when I look back at the large ugly prison and wonder how anyone would want to be in there and keep re-offending. Then suddenly I notice something out of the corner of my eye and, as I look at the window, I see John looking out at the car park. He briefly waves so I smile and give him a little wave back.

On the way home I wonder if Steven will change his life and think about what he's done… or will he always be a complete idiot? Mum must have tuned in to my thoughts as she says "Cathy, I've just had an awful thought. I don't think Steven's my baby. He can't be. Maybe they got him mixed up at the hospital."

I try not to laugh out loud but I'm finding it difficult. When we get home, the comment starts a massive debate. Mum tells Pop her thoughts and he listens to her indulgently. Then she goes into a panic.

"I'm going to get back onto the hospital to find out where my baby is. I was out of it, wasn't I Stan?"

"I don't think that's possible, Joan," Pop says as he shakes his head.

"I saw a film once called *Switched at Birth*. Yes, that's definitely what's happened." Mum stops and thinks for a moment. "Oh, Stan, just think, we've fed someone else's child all these years and took him on holiday. Maybe we'll get some compensation."

Pop looks deep in thought, then says, "Maybe he's your baby but he isn't mine?"

"How dare you, Stanley!" screams Mum, going berserk, "I'm not one of the trollops you used to date. Do you remember Jean Jones? She was a right whore and a dirty stripper. She'd do anything for money."

The memory is too much for Pop and he smiles to himself.

"That's why you never had any money Stanley," Mum looks at him and continues, "You were probably spending it on her." She walks into the kitchen and slams the door. I sigh and go to my room.

****

Monday morning and Jane and I are back in the shop. Jane tells me about the wedding she did over the weekend and says that she's starting to do balloons on her side. I think it's a marvellous idea. It will turn us into a one stop shop for people. We're already finding that when people order flowers or cakes, they use the second half of the shop too. It is a win-win situation for both of us.

The first customer I have is a really young lad who only has eight pounds to spend on flowers. I give him a few extra to bulk it out and on the card he wants me to write: 'She's just a friend. It was YOU who I took to Greasy Joe's, not her'. When he leaves the shop, Jane and I look at each other and say "Aww."

As the week goes by, we get busier and busier. It's fantastic, but really hard work; even Banito is feeling it and Jane tells me that most evenings he has fallen asleep on the sofa. Jane and I have regular customers but Fridays and Saturdays are always our busiest days; this Friday is no exception. It's late morning when a man rings up with a complaint.

"I'm not happy," he declares. "I've just moved in to a new house and I've received some flowers with a card that say: 'Rest in peace'."

My blood runs cold as I frantically check the order book. After only a minute, I realise that Banito has got the flowers mixed up and that there's a funeral nearby with flowers that have 'Congratulations on your new location' written on the card. I apologise to the man and promise to call him back.

I get in the van, race to the cemetery and pray the service hasn't started yet. I finally locate the funeral party and discreetly change the card. When I stand up, one of the mourners comes over to me.

"How do you know Victor?" she asks.

I'm frozen to the spot because obviously I don't know him. I don't know what makes me say it, but I blurt out, "I'm Cathy from the flower shop on the High Street, I thought I'd come over and offer my condolences." The woman is so moved, she shouts to other members of the family.

"Oh look, Cathy from the flower shop has taken time out

to come here to pay her respects. How wonderful that you've run that extra mile," she gushes as the other mourners smile and look on.

I can feel myself going bright red.

"Well, we like to be loyal to our customers."

The ladies stroke me like a dog, then they all file in to the crematorium. I run towards the van and I'm flustered and hot. Just before I get to the van I see an old man crying by a grave and my heart goes out to him. All he keeps saying is, "Why did you have to die... why?"

I have to go over to him and offer my support.

"I'm so sorry for your loss," I say as I kneel down next to him. "Was it your wife, a child or grandchild?"

"No," he replies looking up at me. "It's my wife's first husband."

I don't know what to say so I slowly get up and walk backwards to the van.

****

When I get back to the shop, Mum's there and she's almost shouting at a young man.

"No, no, no! A single rose means you think she's cheap. Buy her a dozen."

"I did try to stop her." Jane looks at me and sighs.

When the man leaves with a dozen red roses I turn to Mum.

"Mum, what are you doing, bullying the customers again."

"I'm not bullying them." Mum's annoyed "I'm trying to get you more business and I'm helping them stay in love."

"Mum, I'm trying to build up a good reputation," I explain as I take her to one side. "People will buy what they want."

"I'm only trying to help," Mum says as she gets in a strop and walks out of the shop. I feel really bad.

I've just locked the shop door and gone into the back when I hear someone tapping on the glass. I sigh and say to myself "There's always one straggler." As I walk towards the door I see John the prison governor. My face lights up when I see him. He smiles and says "Hiya Cathy, can I have a word."

I open the door and we both stare at each other for what seems like ages.

"What can I do for you?" I have to ask.

"I've had your Mum on the phone asking me to do a DNA test on Steven and she won't believe me when I tell her I can't do it."

"Oh no, I'm so sorry. She's always been like this," I reply as I burst out laughing "She's now decided that Steven isn't her son," I explain and John laughs at this. I suddenly realise something and narrow my eyes at him suspiciously. "How did you know where to find me?"

"Steven told me," he admits and breaks out into a cheeky grin. There's another moment of silence and we both look at our feet. John speaks first.

"So, can you tell your Mum she'll have to go to the doctors for the DNA test?"

We both laugh again and John leaves the shop.

****

When I get home, I try and explain to Mum that the prison can't do a DNA test and she needs to go to the doctors when Steven's released. It's no good me telling her that she's being silly because she goes crackers and starts shouting and waving her arms around. Mum has always been the same and if she's made up her mind to do something, no one can change it. Mum screws her face up and she's deep in thought.

"I can't take him to the doctors, Cathy, they're in on it. It's a conspiracy - like area twenty-seven."

"Area twenty-seven, where's that?" I ask, totally confused now.

"She means area fifty-one," Pop shouts in from the lounge. "It's a secret location in America."

I go to the fridge and pour a glass of wine when Louise walks into the kitchen and flings her arms around me.

"Oh, Mum, how's the shop going?"

Before I can answer her, Mum interrupts.

"Louise, I know you'll understand, being a midwife. I've lost my baby."

"Sorry, Gran, I don't know what you mean?" Louise looks blankly at her.

"Oh, it's nothing, Louise." I try to laugh it off but Mum gives me a dirty look.

"What do you mean, Cathy, 'it's nothing'? Someone else is living with my baby. I might be a Grandma for the second time for all I know." Mum sniffles and blows her nose. "He's probably been crying for me for forty-seven years, poor little sod. I might have to go on one of those telly programmes to get a DNA test."

Louise looks at me and I haven't the strength to say anything.

Louise hears the whole sorry tale from Mum. I know Louise doesn't want to laugh but I can see her shoulders shaking and her face is going red because she's trying to keep it in.

"The worlds gone crazy, Rooney," Pop says to Rupert, "but I know one thing, you're Pop's little boy, aren't you?" Rupert is licking Pop to bits and he's loving every minute of the attention.

****

Four days later, John walks back into the shop. He stands around looking awkward.

Are you going to buy flowers or cake, or shall I kick you out and make room for real customers?" Jane asks brazenly as she walks through from her side of the shop. John laughs and walks around the shop.

"Wow, he's a bit of alright" Jane whispers to me. I go bright red and laugh. John is there for a good half hour and Jane can't stop laughing. I can't look at her because she will set me off too. Then Jane walks over to my side and picks up six peonies out of a bucket. She hands them to John and giggles.

"Here you go, John. Give them to Cathy later when you take her out for a drink, they're her favourite."

Now it's John's turn to go a crimson colour and I feel a flutter of excitement. Sure enough, John pays for the flowers and, as he gets to the front of the shop, he turns back to me.

"I'll pick you up at seven, is that okay?"

I nod my head. John smiles and shyly says, "Dinner - my treat."

"Jane, he doesn't know where I live," I suddenly turn to

Jane in a panic.

"Of course he does," Jane laughs. "Your bloody mental brother is in the prison where he works."

****

John picks me up from my parents' house. He doesn't come in, he just sits in the car and beeps the horn. When Mum sees him she goes into a panic.

"Cathy," she shrieks. "The prison man is outside. Oh God, do you think that little feck has run off again?"

I try to calm her down and say "No, he's come for me."

Then Mum runs out of the door and up to John's car, screaming like a banshee.

"Go away, you're not taking my Cathy to prison. You already have one of my children and now you want the other? You're like the child catcher in Shitty clitty bang bang."

John is in shock and I try to catch my breath as I explain that he's not come to take me to prison but to take me out.

Mum looks confused. "Why?"

"Because," I sigh, "we want to have a meal and a drink together."

Doris has come out to the front of her house so she can nosy.

"Doris," Mum shouts. "Take his registration number so we can call the police if our Cathy goes missing."

Doris runs into her house and gets a pen. I need to get away from Mum so I jump in the car and tell John to drive off. As I look out of the back window I can see Mum and Doris jotting down the car registration. When we have driven a few miles up the road, John looks at me and we both burst out laughing.

We drive into the country to a lovely pub and find a little nook in the corner. John tells me he lost his wife eighteen years ago when she was in her late thirties. After two all clears, the cancer came back and she died following a short illness. I really feel sorry for him and I tell him I can only imagine how he felt. He asks me if I have been married and I roll my eyes and laugh.

"Now that's another story John."

John seems intrigued so I tell him a little about Tom leaving me and having a son with the Fluff. John's jaw drops and he can't understand how anyone could do that. Come to think of it, I have no idea either. I also tell him about my meltdown and how I burnt all of Tom's things.

He roars with laughter and says, "Serves him right, he'll not mess with you again."

"He won't get the chance, John," I snort.

We have a beautiful meal of paté, chicken in a white wine and dill sauce and we both share cheese and biscuits. I don't feel awkward eating in front of John; he's very easy to be around and throughout the meal we chat about our lives.

John tells me he has no children, which again is tragic for him as he and his wife would have like to have them. My heart goes out to him.

"John, I feel like I want to give you a hug." I don't know what makes me say this, it just slips out of my mouth.

"Go on then," he laughs enthusiastically.

I don't, but I do stroke his hand and he seems really moved. We get onto the subject of my parents and he howls with laughter; so do I. It's funny when you look at things from a different angle. One thing we don't talk about is Steven and for that I am grateful, as I still don't know how I feel about what he's done.

When we walk to John's car, he reaches into the boot.

"Oh, I've got something for you," he says and passes me the six Peonies he bought earlier at the shop. On the way home we put on songs from the seventies and both sing along to the music. He drops me off at home and when we pull up, we see Mum looking out of the window.

"Oh no, she's spotted you," I say and we both have a chuckle.

Mum then appears at the door, stares at John and shouts "Have you been to see Steven without me?"

"Of course we haven't, it's nearly midnight." I yell back.

She starts walking towards the car so I quickly peck John on the cheek and thank him for a lovely meal. I get out, gently take Mum by her arms and lead her back to the house.

As Mum goes inside, I turn and wave to John. Once we get in the house, there are questions from Mum.

"Why are you with that man? Has our Steven done something wrong again and you don't want me to find out?" She pours herself a sherry, then continues, "Why were you in his car?"

I know I won't get to bed unless I tell her, so I take a deep breath and say, "I've been for a drink with him."

"Why?"

"Because I wanted to, Mum, just leave it."

"So that's where you were when he asked to see you when

we visited Steven. You went in the office and asked him out."

"I didn't ask him out," I retort.

I try and edge my way up the stairs but Mum follows me all the way to my room. I sit on the bed and she plonks herself next to me defiantly.

"I know you're lonely, Cathy, but if you've asked him out, he'll think you're lad mad."

"It was just a drink, nothing more." I'm exasperated now.

After eyeing me up and down for a moment, Mum goes wordlessly to bed. I then lie in bed, look at David Cassidy, and smile.

"David, do you think I've done well? I mean, getting over the pig and the trollop was hard for me, but I've survived an accident and I've opened my own business."

I swear David's smiling at me and I can hear him in my head.

"You're the best, Cathy, you've shown everyone."

I thank him.

CHAPTER 19

The minute I walk into the shop, the phone is ringing. I answer it and it's John calling to say he wants to see me again tonight. When I come off the phone I can't stop smiling. I can't wait for Jane to get in, however, when she does arrive she's in a foul mood. She tells me that she and Banito were dressing up and play acting to bring a bit of fun into the bedroom and she put on her old paramedics uniform. It was a bit tight by her own admission but when she went into the bedroom to seduce him, he laughed and said she looked like a large Brussel sprout. I want to laugh but I daren't. Jane has flatly refused to speak to him since last night and says she won't speak to him for another few months. I agree with Jane because you can't reason with her when she's in a mood. An hour after we open the shop, Banito comes in begging Jane for forgiveness.

"Jane, I lush you, please speak to me. You're breaking my heart."

Jane dismisses him and he walks off with his head down. I feel sorry for him but maybe he has to learn a harsh lesson about what you can and can't say to women.

I tell Jane about John wanting to see me again and she says "Has he got any mates for me?"

"You know he didn't mean it, Jane," I laugh. "He probably wasn't thinking."

Mum hears the whole conversation and comes into the shop.

"Oh, Jane, Stanley used to be a bit kinky," she states. I put my fingers in my ears and gently hum because I know if I tell Mum to be quiet she'll totally ignore me. She carries on. "One day he asked me to keep my boots on in bed. I said no way, they're dirty. I'd been around the market in them, Jane." Mum laughs at the memory. "I wouldn't mind, Jane, but they weren't very flattering – they were ankle boots. I looked a right bugger in them." Jane bursts out laughing while Mum starts cleaning up and says, "Bloody men."

It's afternoon and, for the first time in ages, the shop is quiet. This gives me a chance to do some jobs and put some stock out. Jane and I can hear Mum talking in the back.

"My memory is really bad," she almost shouts.

"How bad is it?" one of her friends encourages her.

"How bad is what?" Mum replies, and this is met with much hilarity. Jane has her face on the counter and she can't look at me for laughing.

"Oh, God I love her."

"Love her," I repeat acerbically. "She's a bloody nightmare."

"At least you've still got her here, Cathy," Jane says and becomes sad. I nod. I have to agree that I don't know what I would do without her, even though she drives me mad at times. I'm clearing out the shop window for new stock and come across some candles that have gone a bit discoloured. I walk into the back and give Mum and her friends a candle each. They're so happy that you'd think I'd given them a thousand pounds, and Mum is beaming as she kisses me.

"Cathy, thank you. They're gorgeous."

****

The night out with John is nothing but fun. We go ten pin bowling and I hardly knock any skittles down; on the other hand, John is showing off and hits a strike on almost every turn. I haven't laughed and felt so giddy from fun for a long time. As we leave the bowling alley, John takes hold of my hand. I wonder if he wants to hold it or is simply trying to guide me across the road.

On the way home, we stop and grab a burger and John laughs his head off when I tell him I've worked at the burger bar.

"Cathy, I can't imagine you working here." He then chokes on his burger when I tell him the story about Fanny coming into the burger joint, and his eyes water as he guffaws. I think to myself it's funny now, over a year down the line, but at the time it was awful. When we leave and walk to the car, John gets hold of my hand again, so I know it's intentional, and for the first time in years my heart skips a beat. As John takes his jacket off and puts it in the back, I spray my mouth with freshener. If my feelings are right, I'll be getting a good snog any minute now… and snog we did. We are sat in the car park like a couple of teenagers, giggling and kissing. When I get home Mum looks at me like I've committed a terrible crime and I am some dirty woman; it was wishful thinking for me. When I get in bed I tell David all about my night out with John. I can see David is a bit jealous but if this carries on like I hope it will, David will have to get used to it.

"Who are you talking to?" Mum demands from the bedroom doorway.

"No one," I sigh, but Mum gets down on her hands and knees and looks under the bed.

"Mum, what are you doing?" I ask as I sit up.

"I thought you'd brought that governess home with you."

"Mum, what do you think I am a man-eater?" I can't believe what she's saying. She just raises her eyebrows and leaves the room.

****

Jane, of course, wants the lowdown on everything and even Louise rings to see how things are going. I'm walking on air and I haven't felt this good since my university days. My new found confidence is shining through and I am on form as I run the shop. Even Mum and her friends aren't bothering me anymore; so when Mum walks in with one of her friends, I smile at them both. They don't even acknowledge me and carrying on talking.

"Yeah," Mum says to Lilian. "Her husband dropped dead. He was digging up a cabbage."

Lilian stops in her tracks, puts her hand to her mouth and gasps.

"What did they do?"

Mum looks Lilian in the face and says earnestly, "They had cauliflower instead." Then they both walk into the back room.

"That's the joke I told your Mum last week," Jane grins. "She thinks it's real. I haven't the heart to tell her it's a joke."

A customer comes in as Jane and I are laughing. The customer beams at us.

"I always love coming in here. The place is always full of laughter and it's a pleasure to chat to you both."

A bit later on and I'm talking to a customer outside the shop. I can hear Mum mumbling to herself inside.

"Mum, who were you talking to?" I ask when I come back in.

"No one." Mum looks sheepish.

"Mum, I've just heard you." I state as I put down a bucket of flowers.

Mum thinks for a minute and then just shrugs her shoulders.

Later on in the day, one of our regular customers comes in the shop and starts laughing.

"Cathy, I love your answer phone message, it did make me laugh." After buying two bunches of tulips, she leaves the shop and I run to the phone so that I can listen to the message. It's obvious that Mum's recorded it. So that's what she was up to earlier - I should have known. Jane joins me, we play the message and sure enough, it's Mum's voice.

"Hello, it's Joan. I can't get to the phone right now, as I'm away from my desk. Leave your name and number then wait by the phone until I call you back."

"Can you believe that Jane?" I ask, shaking my head.

"Anything's possible with Joan," She laughs. I quickly record over the message and we sit down for a well-earned coffee.

John and I have been on seven dates and tonight he's asked me to stay at his place. Mum demands I come home and Pop thinks it's all very amusing.

"So, what time will you be in?" Mum demands as I leave the house.

"If you're not in bed by 10pm, come home." Pop shouts out.

"I won't be back tonight, Mum. So don't wait up." I walk to John's car and I know Mum is giving him a filthy look from the door.

She's not happy at all and the next thing I know, she is walking behind me, heading towards John's car. She taps on his window.

"Don't you be fertilizing my daughter."

John is speechless and doesn't know what to say. Mum looks at me as I quickly get in the car and we drive off. I wave to Mum but she doesn't wave back.

****

John's place is a 1930s detached house, and when I walk inside it has a lovely homely feeling. John pours us both a glass of wine and we sit on the sofa. Before I say anything, John says he wants to tell me something. For a second, my heart misses a beat, and I wonder what he is going to say. He takes a deep breath.

"This wasn't my marital home, Cathy," he explains, "and nothing in the house belongs to me and my late wife." I stare at him and he carries on talking. "So I don't want you to feel uncomfortable and think you are staying in another woman's bed."

I don't know what to say and I feel a little embarrassed. I try to reply with a joke to soften the mood.

"Who said I was staying in your bed? That's a bit presumptuous."

"That sounded awful, didn't it?" he laughs.

I laugh it off and he puts his head down. I feel sorry for him but he continues. "The only thing I have is a picture on the landing."

I take John's hand in mine.

"John, you have every right to have pictures of your wife, but thank you for being so thoughtful."

John squeezes my hand and goes to pour more wine. When he comes back in the lounge he's quite chirpy.

"To be honest, it was a relief to move from the last house. It had too many memories, both happy and sad."

I don't know what to say and I can feel my eyes fill with tears. I try my best not to cry in front of him and make him feel worse.

We order a takeaway and settle down to watch a film. We've only just finished our meal when Mum rings me on my mobile. Her voice is still abrupt.

"Cathy, I think you should come home tonight. It's not right, staying at different men's houses. Folk will stop coming in the shop."

I walk into the kitchen clutching my phone and assure her that no one will be in the slightest bit bothered about me.

Before she hangs up she says "What about God?"

"What about him? I say, starting to get annoyed, "it's got nothing to do with him."

Mum hangs up on me and I'm relieved she has. It's funny because Mum always brings up God when she can't win an argument or she wants her own way.

Sleeping with John doesn't feel at all awkward. Granted, there are no violins playing or sounds of waves crashing against the shore. It's a gentle and loving experience and I don't try to hold in my stomach; I don't even cringe when he sees my fat arse as I go to the bathroom. I don't go completely nude but the shirt is very short. John says I'm a real woman and for the first time in years I feel like one. It's the morning after and John brings me breakfast in bed. I'd never had that with the Freak because he worked and I stayed at home; he took it for granted that I would automatically make all the meals. This is a new experience for me and I'm loving every minute of it. When John takes a shower, I walk onto the landing and look at the picture of his wife. She certainly was really pretty and she had a beautiful smile. I try to imagine the grief John must have felt when he lost her but nothing I can think of seems adequate. John comes out of the bathroom and I jump. I'm a bit embarrassed because he's seen me looking at her picture.

"I can take it down if you want," he offers.

I follow him back in the bedroom and give him a hug.

"I don't want you to take it down. Why would I?" John smiles at this and I have to ask "What was her name?"

"Lucy," he sighs, "it was Lucy."

"A pretty name for a pretty lady," I say and head for the shower, but all I can think about is Lucy with John. What were they like together? Where did they holiday? What was their first house like? The curiosity is taking over my mind and I have to get a grip and remind myself that John is seeing me now and that this is a new chapter in both of our lives.

John and I decide to go shopping at a local shopping centre that's just opened. When we get there it's packed, so the first thing we do is have a coffee. I drag John around make-up and perfume counters and he never once complains. When I see a top I like he promptly pays for it. I can't believe how happy I feel and every time I look at him I get butterflies in the pit of my stomach. Could I be falling in love? I hope so.

We have a fabulous day out and I insist on paying for a meal in the evening. Since owning the shop, I've got my own money and it feels good being able to pay my way. We drive home in silence; not that awkward silence, a silence that feels good and no words are needed; it just feels good to be in each other's company.

When John drops me off, Mum is looking out of the

window again and I can see her mouth moving. That can mean only one thing – she's arguing with Pop.

When I walk in the lounge, Mum has her hands on her hips and it's clear she's still in a bad mood.

"Everyone is treating this house like it's a hotel," she yells, "and you, Stanley, have a serious drinking problem."

"I've only had two pints, woman." I hear Pop shout from the kitchen, "I'm not an alcoholic. Alcoholics go to meetings, I go to the pub."

"Oh, feck off, Stanley."

That's my cue to go to bed and get ready for work in the morning.

****

The following evening we finally get to meet Louise's new boyfriend. I miss her so much but I don't bother her because I know she works long hours and she has her own life to lead.

"At long last we meet Mathew," Mum announces the moment they walk through the door.

Louise looks really nervous around Mum, and who can blame her? Mathew shakes everyone's hand, then he kisses me on the cheek.

"Hey, what about me?" Mum squeals and taps her cheek, ordering Mathew to kiss it. Pop looks him up and down then carries on reading the paper. We all go into the kitchen and I put the kettle on. I watch Mathew as he speaks to Mum and he's very patient with her. He's a handsome lad with light brown hair and lovely brown eyes, he's also quite muscular. I look at Louise, raise my eyebrows and smile at her. She lifts up her thumb and I lift up mine as a sign that everything is going well. They only stay a couple of hours - I think that's all they can stand. Mum asks them if they're getting engaged and if so, when will they be married. She then starts talking about babies and I think it is all a bit much for them both. We wave them off at the door and Mum says "Isn't he a lovely lad? If I'd been a couple of years younger I would have gone for him myself." I look at Mum and she chuckles.

****

I stay at John's most weekends and this Sunday morning we both decide to book a week in Greece. Jane is gobsmacked.

"Cathy, it's going really well isn't it?"

My face is beaming. I know I can take a week off because Jane will run things and I have also employed another florist called Jodie. She is lovely and very good at her job. I really can't believe my life is going so well.

Another long day over and at 5.30pm, I bring all the outside displays back into the shop. Jane has gone early because they have cakes to deliver. As I put the last bucket down on the shop floor, I turn around to find Tom standing there. This time I'm annoyed.

"What?" I snap.

Tom grabs hold of me and tries to kiss me. I immediately push him away and wipe my mouth.

"How dare you?" I demand crossly. "What the hell do you want?"

"Cathy, I need to speak to you … please." Tom grabs my arm.

Part of me doesn't want to listen to him but part of me does. Tom looks really worried which intrigues me.

"I'll be over in a minute." I say, pointing to the pub across the road.

Tom exhales and the relief almost immediately lightens his face. Now I really want to know what's going on.

When I walk in The Nelson, Tom has already got the drinks in and he's sat by the window. He sheepishly smiles at me and I can see he's extremely nervous. I sit down, but when he doesn't speak for a few minutes, I become agitated.

"What do you want?"

Tom takes a deep breath and says, "Cathy, I've made a terrible mistake leaving you."

I don't know what comes over me but I howl with laughter. Tom doesn't know what to do and stares at me.

"What?" I stammer, when I have my breath back. "You've come over to the shop to say you regret leaving me?"

"In a nut shell, yes," Tom says, hanging his head. "I do regret leaving you. It's not turned out like I expected it would."

I can't find a word in the dictionary that could describe Tom's cheek. Tom tries to laugh it off by saying "I'm glad your mother's not here," but I don't find anything amusing about this and I say nothing. There's an awkward silence between us and every couple of seconds, Tom tries to either touch my face or my hand. And every time he does so, I move away from him. Tom gets up to get more drinks and I grab his jacket.

"Not for me, I'm not wasting my time here with you. I've better things to do."

Tom's breathing is laboured as he replies to me.

"Cathy, I'll get us another drink then I'll come clean with you."

I watch him at the bar. He's not the Tom I know; he's lost a lot of weight and he looks really tired. I know when Tom is stressed, as I've seen it many times before. I'm intrigued to know what's going on with him and I know I definitely don't have the feelings I had for him before. Tom comes back from the bar but this time he's got a brandy and a beer. *'Oh dear, things must be bad,'* I think to myself. He swigs his brandy in one go.

"I've just found out that the little lad isn't mine after all," he blurts out.

My face lights up and I want to relish this information and bask in his self-pity. I have to admit I'm really astonished by what he's just said, but I don't show it. Tom is searching my face to see what my reaction is, but I don't have one. I feel stunned and a little bit in a daze. However, I keep calm and pretend to be all concerned, so that I can get all the gory details out in the open.

"Oh no. What happened?" I whisper.

Tom forgets he's talking to me and babbles on about Fanny deceiving him. He takes another sip of his beer and draws in a deep breath.

"Simon went into hospital to have his tonsils removed," he explains, "and there were complications. He needed blood and when they tested him, he had a rare blood group. It's AB positive, which is very rare."

"No, then what happened?" I gasp.

Tom takes another swig of beer.

"I know Frances hasn't got a rare blood group because she donates blood and we once had a conversation about it, and I know I'm positive. It got me thinking, so I did a DNA test when Frances wasn't at home."

"How did you do a DNA test at home?" I ask.

Tom is now feeling really sorry for himself and carries on with the story.

"I did it with a swab and paid privately for the test."

"What a terrible thing to find out," I act really shocked.

"'I know, Cathy."

I gulp my drink, so Tom goes back to the bar. I'm not going anywhere; this is far too exciting and better than anything on the telly. He soon returns with the drinks.

"So, I take it you confronted Fanny?" I widen my eyes as I ask him. It has completely gone over his head that I've called her 'Fanny' and he carries on talking.

"Awful, it was. She just shrugged her shoulders and said that she thought he was mine. I don't believe her and I know she's tricked me all these years. I've lost the love of my life."

I interrupt Tom and ask "The love of your life, who's that?"

"YOU, you, Cathy." He looks hurt as he answers me.

"Oh," I take another sip of my drink.

"Will you be able to forgive me, Cathy?" he carries on.

"Of course I forgive you, Tom." I nod my head.

The colour in Tom's face comes back and I actually hear him sigh.

"Thank God for that," he whispers. I rub Tom's hand and he smiles. He is still shaken when he says "She want's half of the company."

"What?" I almost scream. "The cheeky whore, how dare she?" Tom's head is bobbing like a nodding dog; the ones you see in the back of people's cars. I can't let it go. "How awful for you, honestly, my heart goes out to you."

Tom cocks his head to the side and smiles faintly.

"Oh Cathy, what a wonderful woman you are."

"Yes, I know I am," I sip on my drink and nod.

"Why, oh, why did I ever consider having an affair when I had you at home?" He's going for bullshit overload now.

"I know, Tom. You know the saying though – you went for a bit of scrag-end and you had fillet steak at home." This is going well for me.

"I know, Cathy, you're right," Tom says.

I stand up and put on my coat. We leave the pub and Tom links my arm as he walks me to Mum's car.

"I'm going to buy you another car, Cathy, as soon as all the financial mess gets sorted," He says as we reach the battered old Skoda.

"Oh, Tom, you don't have to," I drop my bottom lip and make it quiver.

Tom's chest puffs out and he looks like a gorilla showing off his strength to a female. He puts his arms around me.

"There's something I need to ask you, Cathy, it's a huge favour."

"Anything for you, Tom," I smile.

He is acting very suspicious and he beckons me to his car. I'd forgotten how lovely the Range Rover was, and it still smells of leather. Tom takes a deep breath and takes some papers out of his jacket pocket. We're sat in the car like a couple of detectives on the lookout for someone.

"Cathy, these are deeds to a Villa I bought in America

years ago," Tom blurts out. "I don't want Frances knowing about it because she'll want half." I'm shocked and it shows in my face.

"If she's been to the villa, surely she knows it's yours?"

"Nope," Tom smiles and shakes his head, "I never told her I owned it, I told her we were renting it."

I look him up and down and it truly sinks in what a horrible man he is. Tom notices the look on my face.

"Please forgive me for hiding them from you, Cathy."

It takes a minute for it all to sink in, so I get hold of Tom's hand.

"Of course I forgive you. It's all in the past, Tom, let's move on."

Tom sighs, which is over exaggerated. I smile and he gives me a hug.

"I knew I could count on you, Cathy," Tom takes out a pen and hands it to me. "Sign here, Cathy. If I put it in your name, she'll be none the wiser. She's got a brother who runs a detective agency so I don't want him snooping around."

I read the deeds and although I don't understand all of them, they clearly state that he does own a detached house in America.

I sign the forms and give the pen back to Tom – he looks so relieved.

"Cathy, take them to the solicitors in the morning and he'll witness it. Then tomorrow night, you can give them back to me."

I put the deeds into my handbag and promise to take them to the solicitor the very next day. I get out of Tom's car and

Tom does a silly little jig and says "See you tomorrow, same time, same place." I laugh through gritted teeth.

****

The following morning, at 9am on the dot, I'm in the solicitor's office. Richard Dawson, or 'dick head' as everyone refers to him, is making smarmy remarks.

"Cathy, Cathy, how good to see you. You're looking very well and pretty as always. To be honest, I was shocked when you and Tom separated." He snorts a few times, which knocks me sick, then he carries on with the conversation. "Oh, yes, I would have gone there myself but, you know, you don't do that to an old pal, do you?"

I pretend I don't know what he means and say, "Gone where?"

"You know," Richard laughs and replies, "You and I, a bit of hanky-panky… but now you and the good man have sorted things out, I'll never get my chance." I laugh hysterically and it's totally over the top. Richard signs and stamps the deeds.

"Do you want me to give those to Tom? I'm meeting him for lunch." He smiles at me.

"Oh, no, I'm looking forward to seeing him tonight," I laugh.

"I hope you'll get a room," Richard snorts again. I laugh hysterically and Richard thinks he's the dog's bollocks and just so funny.

****

The day can't go quickly enough for me and I'm glad we're busy – it takes my mind off the meeting I had with Tom. Jane can't believe what's happened at all. Throughout the day, she keeps saying the same thing: "Who'd have thought there'd be another big secret he kept from you. That man's got a nerve." I can't agree with her more and I can't wait for the evening to arrive. I lock up the shop and walk across the road to the pub.

Tom's already there, with a bottle of champagne on ice.

"Are you trying to get me drunk?" I ask, pointing to it.

"That was the idea," Tom laughs.

I chat about how busy the shop is and Tom hangs on my every word. He nods, laughs and says "God, my wife, a business woman. I'm so proud of you."

"Your ex-wife, Tom," I correct him.

"Not for long," Tom laughs. I smile but I don't say anything. We both drink the Champagne and I'm giddy; more from the mood than anything else. After an hour Tom leans into me and says "Shall we book into a hotel?"

"Why?" I laugh.

"You know why," Tom replies playfully.

We finish the Champagne and I put my coat on. We walk to the car park holding hands. Tom doesn't see Mum's car and asks "Where's the witch's Skoda?" I take a deep breath and stare ahead.

When we get to Tom's car, he points to the 4x4, opens the door and nods towards the car seat.

"What are you doing?" I look at him.

"We're booking into a hotel," Tom laughs.

"I don't remember saying I would book into a hotel with you," I say, putting on a confused expression.

"Stop playing with me, Cathy, you little minx," he chuckles.

"I'm not playing with you, Tom." I say with a blank face, "You asked me to do something for you and I've done it."

Tom becomes nervous and shuffles from one foot to the other. I love to see him this agitated.

"You're right, Cathy." He says, "We can't rush it – I need to court you again from the beginning." I don't say a word and stare at Tom's face. Tom is now very nervous as he says "Oh yeah, the deeds, have you got them on you?"

"Yes, I've got them, thanks." I stare at him with my face poker straight.

"Cathy, give me the deeds," Tom screams like a little girl.

"The deeds? You mean MY deeds?" I lean on the 4x4 and smirk. "Oh, don't worry, they're safe."

"Cathy, don't do this to me … please." Tom goes from being hysterical to pleading. "Tom, I did what you asked." I sigh and speak slowly to him, "Why are you reacting like this?"

"Cathy," Tom jumps up and down. "I need those deeds back." He grabs my handbag and tips the contents out onto the floor. He's surprised when monopoly money and a small gold property falls out of my bag. He looks at me with such hatred. "Give me those deeds."

"But Tom," I talk to him in a patronizing way. "They're MY deeds. You gave them to me."

"You Bitch!" he screams, red-faced.

"Now, now, if you call me names I will go to your wife and tell her what you've done. Do you understand?"

Tom looks like he's going to collapse and screams like a wounded animal. I walk over to him and try to soothe him. "There, there, Tom. I feel your pain. That's how I felt when you left me. Horrible, isn't it?"

Jane and Banito get out of the van and start clapping. They've been waiting in it to keep an eye on me and when Tom sees them, he is furious.

"Oh, I thought you'd be in on it, you bitch," Tom shouts to Jane. Jane laughs, then before we know it, Tom is flat out on the floor. Banito has punched Tom so hard it knocks him flat. Tom doesn't know what's happened and looks at Banito.

"And who are you?" Tom asks in a husky voice.

Banito leans over Tom and says, "Banito, Jane's husband. Don't ever call my wife a bitch again. Next time I will kill you."

Tom is shocked and Jane links Banito's arm, I can tell by the look on her face she's impressed by how manly Banito is.

"Oh, Banito, fighting for my honour, wait until I get you home," she whispers.

Tom scrambles to his feet, gets in his 4x4 and screeches off. Jane, Banito and I just laugh and laugh.

****

The morning after and I've just opened the shop when Tom walks in. He looks like he's slept rough and he hasn't had a shave. His eyes plead with me.

"Cathy, please give me the deeds. I know you're only playing with me, teaching me a lesson and I deserve it."

"But Tom, I'm not trying to teach you a lesson." I say as I look him straight in the eye.

"Cathy they're all I've got until I sort out this financial mess." Tom looks like he's going to cry. "I need them. The building society has come after me for the shortfall from when they took the house back."

I lean on the counter and look him square in the eye.

"I need them too. Remember, Tom, you left me with nothing. I lost my home, my car and my dignity. You took that away from me and then you had the cheek to give me five hundred pounds a month, so you would look good in court."

"Cathy," Tom pleads with me. "I know what I did was wrong and I'm sorry, please forgive me."

"I have forgiven you, Tom, but I can't forget," I say honestly. "You didn't deceive me for just a year; it was for over thirteen years. And now, just because Fanny tricked you, you want to worm your way back to me. You weren't thinking of me when you left, were you?"

Tom is looking more defeated by the minute and he hasn't really got a reply to what I've just said. He makes one last attempt to try and cuddle me and I shout to Jane, who is in the back with Mum.

"Jane, unleash Mum."

Tom runs out of the shop before Mum gets hold of him.

Jane and I talk about Tom on and off all day. She can't believe the nerve of him, but I can. At 6pm, Tom is waiting in the car park for me and, again, he gets out of his car, walks over to me, and pleads and pleads with me. I turn around and poke my finger in his chest.

"Come near me again, and not only am I going to the police to report you for harassment, I'm telling Fanny you're stalking me and then she will take you to the cleaners, won't she?" Tom is defeated and gets in his car. I drive up the road in Mum's Skoda.

That night I have the best night's sleep I've had in years

and I truly feel refreshed.

The days go by and I don't give the house in America much thought. Both shops are packed with customers and the minute we get a break I turn to Jane.

"Jane, I haven't heard from John for five days."

Jane thinks for a moment.

"Maybe he's busy, Cathy."

I shake my head.

"No, I think he's gone off me."

"He won't have gone off you. Why would he?" She gives me a hug.

"Jane, you know my luck with men," I sigh.

"I think you're reading too much into it, Cathy."

She may be right but I have this awful feeling it's over and I can feel my heart breaking all over again.

A week goes by and I go from feeling elated at what happened with Tom to the depths of despair because John hasn't contacted me. I check my phone every time I get a break in the shop. On one occasion, a man phones the shop and for a moment, I think it's John and my heart misses a beat. Jane and I go for a drink after work and I don't know why I bother because I'm not at all good company.

"Why don't you phone or text him?" she asks gently.

"Jane, I can't." I shake my head, "The thought of being hurt again is too much, I couldn't bear it."

Jane looks worried and I don't know what to do with myself.

That night, when I'm in bed, I ask David Cassidy what he thinks.

"David, should I text him or phone him?"

David's answer is loud and clear to me.

"Cathy, phone him and text him. We're in the twenty-first century, it's not up to a man to do all the running these days."

I know he's right so I send John a message and try to sound cheerful in it:

> *Hi John, hope you're well. Not heard from you. Are you busy? The shop's really busy at the moment, I haven't had a minute to myself. Anyway, call me when you can.*

Another few days pass and I'm in a right state. The pain I felt when Tom left me is there and I can't console myself. I'm becoming paranoid and every night for a whole week, I drive past John's house. Some nights his light is on and I long to knock on the door; other nights the house is in darkness and I know he's at work.

After four weeks of trying to be chirpy in endless texts and phone calls, I finally crack and sob my heart out for hours. What's wrong with me? Why do men do a disappearing act? Am I being punished for something? Should I have gone back with Tom when I had the chance? At least I know him and his many faults. I know I'm being unreasonable but my mind is all over the place.

I'm having a sad moment in the shop when Richard Dawson walks in.

"Who's been a naughty girl then, upsetting my good old friend Tom?" he snorts.

I can't even be bothered to answer him. I just shout to Jane "Jane, unleash Mum." Mum comes from the back room and throws a bucket of water all over Richard. It is the only time I smile. As Richard leaves the shop I shout "Bye, Dick head."

He is furious and threatens to sue me but Mum shouts "Get to the back of queue, you ugly feck."

****

It's Sunday morning and I'm lying in bed wondering what John is doing when my mobile rings. It's a number I don't recognise but I answer it in case it's a flower order. It's Tom and he's furious. I was just about to put the phone down on him when I hear him say something about Louise, so my ears prick up. Apparently, he and Louise have had a row and he thinks I've poisoned her mind and turned her against him. I jump out of bed and scream back at him.

"How dare you blame me? Blame yourself - you're the one that's messed up. She's no respect for you, Tom, and that's your fault."

I slam the phone down on him and I'm livid. Within ten minutes, Louise rings me to tell me what happened. Apparently, Tom rang Louise and said he thinks she should make more of an effort to meet up with him. Meanwhile, she was acting like she didn't care. Louise went berserk and it all came out; she told him exactly what she thought of him and how she was disgusted with him for lying, not only to me but to her too, for most of our married life. The house in America was the final straw. Louise let her true feelings be known to Tom and he couldn't handle it. One of the things she threw in his face was America. When she was young, she'd asked him for years to take her to Disney World in America and he'd always said no, claiming that he hated America. Things come flashing into my mind and I'm starting to remember more and more.

CHAPTER 20

It's been nearly six weeks since I've heard from John. I've not only texted him every day, I've put a note through his letter box and I still haven't heard from him. The whole dating game has changed from what it was years ago, and unfortunately I don't know the rules anymore. Is it because I slept with him and he thinks I give it out too quickly? Am I too fat? Have I got a no personality? Maybe my lot was Tom, but look how that ended – he didn't want me and that's why he had an affair. I feel so low and nothing anyone does or says makes me feel any better.

I'm sitting in the garden and it's a gorgeous day; the birds are singing and I should be really happy. I have my own business, I'm earning good money and I now own a house in America, but I'm still not happy. Am I really that shallow that I need a man to fulfil my life? Why can't I accept that I will be on my own forever? At least in a few months I can afford to get my own place. I wonder about the house in America: what is it like, how big is it? Knowing my luck it'll be a rundown shack with tramps living in it. Mum comes out and sits on the bench with me. She doesn't talk, she just gets hold of my hand and looks around the garden. After a few minutes, Mum gets up, kisses me on the cheek and says "Come on, Cathy, chin up." However, when she walks away, she mumbles, "Chin up, both of them." I'm too fed-up to be annoyed and I start giggling to myself.

I decide to book a flight to America for Louise and me, so I can look at the house I now own. At one time I would have been totally loyal to Tom and I wouldn't have dreamt of betraying him, but not anymore. He betrayed me and I have no remorse for keeping the deeds to the house. After all, it was his idea.

I book the tickets online and I'm flying in a few days' time. My assistant is more than capable of running the shop and Jane is there to help. I really need a break and perhaps it will help me get over John. Louise is over the moon and I've promised her I will take her to Disney World. A break will do us both good and I will enjoy spending time with her. Mum has decided all by herself that she's coming with us and, when I book the tickets on line, she gets Doris's grandson to hack into my computer and find the site I have just used, so it's no coincidence that she is sat next to us on the plane.

We arrive at the airport and go straight to check in. Mum waves her hand at the check-in clerk and says "It's not cheesy jet is it?" The girl smiles and assures Mum it isn't. When the bags are safely through, I buy us all a drink. When I come back from the bar, Mum is nowhere to be found and a panic comes over me. I tell Louise to watch the drinks and handbags as walk out of the bar to look for her, but she's disappeared. A couple of minutes later and I spot her in duty free, having a full makeover. I tell her where I am and she promises to join us as soon as she's made-up. After twenty minutes, I'm getting edgy and anxious. I go back to the counter, where I find Mum armed with freebies.

"That madam wanted me to buy creams and products off her, but I told her I need to try them out first," she explains as we return to the bar. I don't answer her. I order more drinks and we sit patiently for our boarding call. I hate flying and I feel sick as soon as we board. I thought a few drinks would calm me down but it hasn't. I wretch a few times but I've had nothing to eat, so it comes up as gas.

"You're not pregnant are you, with that man in prison?" Mum says loudly, causing everyone to look at me.

"How can I be pregnant at fifty-five?" I whisper.

"Oh yeah, your ovaries are shrivelled up."

A man sat in the opposite aisle laughs. Louise doesn't know what to do with herself so she buries her head in a book. Mum hasn't sat down yet and she asks for a sandwich and a drink. The stewardess tells her it will be along later. Mum is smiling her head off.

"Oh, Cathy, it's so exciting to fly through the air. You wouldn't think something this big could float."

My stomach turns. Eventually Mum sits down but she fidgets and goes from reading a magazine to trying to read a book. She's too excited to sit still and I feel like I've got a naughty child at the side of me. I really wanted to come with Louise and spend some time with her and I feel I need time away from Mum – not much chance of that. I feel guilty thinking about Mum in that way but I can't help how I feel. Louise listens to her music and is content to sit and have a rest.

I look out of the window and see all the clouds in the sky. I wonder what John is doing right now. Maybe he's got another girlfriend? Maybe he was a serial shagger? I wish I could pull myself out of this mood and stop torturing myself, but I'm finding it really hard.

The drinks are served two hours into the flight, and when the stewardess comes over Mum says "It's hot in here, love, can you open my window." The young girl giggles and I pretend I haven't heard what's been said.

We're three hours into the flight when the meal comes. Mum looks at the food and says "How have they cooked that on a plane?" I try and explain to her but she isn't listening. When we finish eating, Mum dabs her lips with a napkin. "That was nice, Cathy. There wasn't much of it, but it was nice." When they clear away the food containers, Mum jumps up and starts helping the stewardess stack the plastic containers on the trolley.

The young girl thanks her and tells her she doesn't need to help. Mum sits back down, reaches into her handbag and gives the girl a pound coin as a tip. The stewardess looks at the pound and asks "Do you want to purchase something from the bar? Everything is free on this flight."

"No, love," Mum cackles. "it's a tip for you, and if you think it's not much money then you need to go to the pound shop – ooh, the bargains they have in there." Mum goes on to list all the things she has bought from there and the stewardess smiles and walks off, so then Mum starts telling me.

"Mum, I know what you buy, I live with you," I whisper.

Mum gets all stroppy and folds her arms while Louise keeps her head firmly in the book.

Half an hour later and Mum goes to the toilet. After fifteen minutes, she's still not back. I get up out of my seat and go to look for her. There's no one in the toilet but I can hear Mum talking to someone.

"Are you gay? Oh I love gays. Can I come to your wedding? Oh, our Cathy's just got divorced, he went off with another woman. She has no luck with men. Maybe she should get a nice gay boyfriend like you."

I look around the cabin's blue curtain and Mum is talking to a young man. He smiles and at me and says, "I love your mum."

"You cheeky monkey," Mum squeals with delight. We go back to our seats and I close my eyes; my stress levels have gone through the roof. Mum notices a woman in the next aisle with a pair of support tights on. She gets up, walks over to her and asks, "Why are you wearing elastic tights?"

The woman quietly speaks to Mum, who then returns to her seat and sits down. When she sees the young steward she shouts "Can I have some tights? I don't want to get deep throat thrombosis."

The young steward howls with laughter and Mum cackles. People on the flight start to giggle and I quickly order another large G&T.

I must have fallen asleep for a while because when I wake up, Mum has gone again. I panic and go looking for her but this time she is nowhere to be seen. Louise goes to the back of the plane and I search the front. I wonder to myself how a person can get lost on a plane. I walk to the front of the plane and a man asks, "Are you looking for an old lady?" I nod. He points to the cockpit and says "She's in there. She was knocking on the door for ages until they let her in."

I ask the stewardess to get her, and when they open the door, Mum is sat in between two pilots.

"Can I have a go?" I hear her say. "I'm a brilliant driver." The pilots laugh. The stewardess talks to Mum and then points to me. Mum gets up and thanks the pilots.

"Thanks for teaching me how to fly, I've never been on a plane before." Then, to my horror, she kisses them both on the cheek and says "See yer later, cock." We get back to our seats and, when I tell Louise what's happened, she can't believe what Mum's done. Mum is such hard work, I thank God when she falls asleep.

****

We arrive at the airport and wait for our luggage. They're very efficient and we're in the taxi in no time. Mum is mesmerised by America.

"Can we call off at Disney World on the way there?" she calls to the taxi driver, who just laughs. Thirty minutes later and we arrive at a gated community. I get out of the taxi and walk into the gatekeeper's office to collect the keys for the property. I then return to the taxi, who drives us a few yards up the road and drops us all in front of a large detached house.

"Oh, Cathy, it's gorgeous – fit for a queen," Mum squeals.

Louise is a little bit in shock as she shakes her head "Mum, it's fabulous."

There's a double garage and the front lawn is beautifully maintained. I open the large oak door and step into a massive hallway. Mum normally can't walk far but today she's running from room to room like Billy Whizz. The taxi driver brings the bags into the hallway and I pay and tip him. Louise runs up the stairs like a little girl and, for a moment, I feel great anger at Tom for depriving her of the chance to come here when she was younger. I look at the magnificent kitchen and there's every appliance you can imagine. Then I hear Mum scream. I run out the back and there, in front of me, is a beautiful kidney-shaped swimming pool. My face lights up as I realise that the whole of the outside space is unbelievable, with large pots containing little palm trees, beautiful tables, chaise lounges and sunloungers. Louise has heard Mum scream and is now standing next to us. "Wow." is the only word that she can say.

We unpack and sit by the pool. The sun is beating down and I slowly close my eyes and relax. John immediately comes into my mind and I wish he was here with me, basking in the sun. Louise is on the phone to Mathew, telling him how gorgeous the house is. After an hour it's too hot to sunbathe so I wander around the house. I still can't take in how big it is. Everything is clean white with just a touch of colour in the lamps and pictures. You can tell it's a rental property because it lacks the personal touches that you get from having your own house.

In the evening, we all get a taxi and go out for a meal at a nearby restaurant. The food is delicious, the staff are very friendly and we get complimentary drinks. Mum starts talking to people in the restaurant, and after ten minutes she's speaking in an American accent. She's walking around saying, "Have a good day," and "Howdy." The American people think she's great; personally, I know she's barmy.

We get back to the house and I put Mum in bed because she's really tired. Louise also goes to bed and I think the flight has taken it out of us all. I go to the main bedroom. It feels funny being in this big house and I feel like I'm on holiday or secretly sleeping in a house I shouldn't be in. As I lie in bed, my thoughts turn to yet another bit of deceit from Tom. How on earth did he buy a house and let it out for several years, and I never knew about it. I think Tom is capable of anything and that thought makes my blood run cold.

I fall into a deep sleep which I obviously need, as I'm both mentally and physically exhausted.

I wake up and I feel really refreshed. Mum is already awake and swimming in the pool with Louise. I look at them for a few minutes and see they're really enjoying themselves. I look at Mum and think that it's such a shame to get to her age without having visited another country. Tom and I have travelled to places all over the world and at the time I took it all for granted.

I decide to have a good look round the house again, because I couldn't take it all in yesterday. The house has four bedrooms – two with walk-in wardrobes and two ensuites- two sitting rooms, a kitchen and utility room. The gardens are beautiful and lush. As I walk around the house I wonder what

Tom did with all the rental money.

Later that day, I decide to hire a car and go to the property rental company that used to rent out the house for Tom. I know which one it is because there are leaflets all over the house and I've already phoned and spoken to them. I've not gone into details, I've just said I need to discuss the house with them. Louise decides to stay behind and sunbathe, so I take Mum with me. Mum and I drive to the rental property agents and when we get there, it's huge. Also, not only do they rent houses but they sell them as well. We go inside. I sit down and Mum sits next to me. The woman who deals with the rental side of things is Jill and she sits down and asks how Tom is.

"We've not seen him for a good eight months," she says. "He's such a nice man. When he's over on business he always brings cakes and wine in for us."

I smile but inside I'm thinking, "I bet he did, the little snail."

"He's not really a nice person," Mum cuts in. "He left our Cathy for another woman and…"

I laugh and give Mum a look to be quiet. I then realise it may not be a bad thing that Mum has just said this, as it sort of breaks the ice as to why I've got the deeds.

"Unfortunately Tom and I have got divorced," I reveal, "and I've got the house in Kissimmee as my settlement and I've decided to sell it."

"Oh, I'm so sorry to hear that," Jill replies.

"Don't be, it's fine," I smile.

Jill smiles sweetly, which knocks me six.

"We didn't know Tom was married, though," she says in a

girlish voice. "He was always asking one of us out, and we know he had an affair with the manageress here. She's left now."

I smile but my teeth are locked together. Mum gasps and almost screams, "The dirty fecking dog."

"I need a valuation to sell." I interrupt Mum.

"I'll be there in the morning and I'll dig the notes out." Jill almost sings, "Tom bought the house off us from a plan about twelve years ago. It's a very saleable property and the fact it's on a gated community is even better."

We go back to the house and have some lunch, then for the rest of the day, we all visit the large shopping centre and have a good look around the shops. Mum's getting tired so I hire a scooter for her to whizz around the shops in. She loves it and says she's going to buy one when she gets home. Most of the clothes and shoes are really inexpensive but Mum still says they're not cheap enough. In the end I buy Mum a beautiful blouse and, although she tells me not to, she seems really pleased with it. Louise has bought so many clothes that she can't carry any more bags, so we all head back to the car.

Driving along the roads in America is a joy. The traffic just flows and there's no jams like there are in the UK. We end up in a Mexican restaurant and once again, the staff are lovely; they even put a Mexican hat on mum and start singing to her. She's in her element from all the fuss and one older man says to her that she's a lovely English Rose. She cackles, which amuses him. Even one of the younger men chats up Louise and she laughs it off. Funnily enough, nobody chats me up but I don't care because I am well and truly over finding a man. A couple of times I think about John but I have to push the thoughts to the back of my mind.

I buy all of us a cocktail and they serve it with a sparkler.

Mum's face is a picture and I can't help but take a photo of her. We drive back to the house and sit by the pool with a glass of wine and Mum is beaming from the day out. I look at her and wonder what I would do without her. I start to think about what the house may be worth and I get butterflies in my stomach.

"Let's have a little bet, what do you think this house is worth?" I say to both of them.

"Oh, Cathy," Mum shrieks, "it's worth a million pounds at least."

"I hope so Mum," I laugh.

"I wish we could stay here and live in the house, just you, me and our Louise," Mum sighs wistfully.

I feel sorry for her. I know she loves Pop, they've been married forever, but I also know she gets lonely and longs for adventure. Mum and Pop have really struggled financially all their married life and when they were children, they didn't have anything.

Louise says she doesn't have a clue what the house is worth, so she guesses it to be around one hundred and fifty thousand pounds. We all lie and bask in the sunshine but my thoughts are about John. What has gone wrong? Why is he ignoring me? I sit up and get us all a cool drink of juice, and as I walk into the kitchen I get a terrible feeling that John has met someone else. I don't know where it comes from but it is just there in my head. I sit at the breakfast bar and feel sick to the pit of my stomach. This doesn't't' feel like the break-up with Tom, but it's a very close second. I can't take any more hurt and rejection – my mind can't cope with it. I sit in the kitchen until it goes dark. Mum goes to bed early and I think she's a little tipsy. Louise and I sit by the pool and talk about her future and she tells me that Mathew is the one. I'm so happy I could burst. My little girl, being in love and possibly engaged! I tell Louise that not all men are shits and she needs to put what her father did to one side. Louise sits on the edge of the lounger.

"I can't get over dad doing this to us. All that stuff with the house and car was bad enough; then to find out he has a son, then he doesn't. I've no respect for him and I never will."

I can fully understand what Louise is saying and she is old enough to know her own mind.

We all have a good night sleep again, so when Jill the estate agent comes round to view the house, we're all fresh and ready. Jill works her way around the house with a pen and clipboard. She talks quietly to herself as she makes notes. When she is finished, she sits at the table with us all. She gives me an estimate for 450,000 US dollars and she roughly works that out to be £300,000 in sterling. I can't believe what it's worth. My mind won't register what's happening. Mum screams and starts dancing.

"We're rich, we're rich."

Louise is speechless.

"Do you want to put it on the market, Cathy?" Jill gently asks.

"Yes please, Jill." I slowly nod my head.

When Jill leaves the house, I sit by the pool and try and take it all in. Louise beckons for Mum to join her in the lounge and I know Louise realises I need time to take it all in. I think of the money. I can pay Pop back and I can pay Jane for my half of the business. It's a good feeling... so why do I feel so sad?

After an hour, Jill rings me up to tell me that the house is fully booked for rental for the next six months so any rental payments will come straight to me. She also tells me she thinks the house will be snapped up by an investor. I'm over the moon. We stay by the pool and drink champagne for the rest of the day and in the evening, we have a BBQ. Mum sits back on her sunlounger and says "Oh this is the life."

****

The next day we end up at Clearwater, a beautiful beach with fine white sand. Mum can't stop smiling.

"Oh, Cathy, I feel like royalty. How the other half live, eh?"

In the afternoon, we all swim with the dolphins. Louise can't wait to get in the water but Mum is reluctant. Eventually she gets in and after a few minutes, she's stroking the lovely dolphins. I take pictures so we can show Pop because I know he won't believe she actually did it. We spend the afternoon on the beach and I try and read some of my book, but I can't concentrate. I look at the white sand and turquoise water and watch Mum and Louise paddling in the sea. For a moment, I wonder if I should sell the shop and come and live here in the house. I know Mum would live here but Pop wouldn't - he hates the heat. Every time Mum's suggested they go abroad, Pop has made up an excuse that all his vegetables on the allotment would die if he didn't go there every day.

We drive to a steak house where the food looks delicious. At home, Mum and Pop don't eat what I call good quality food, but here Mum polishes off a 10oz steak, fries, sweetcorn and bread.

"Cathy, I'm stuffed," she announces leaning back in her chair, but when the waiter offers her a dessert she says "Oh, go on then, I'll just have a few bites." She then eats all the New York cheesecake with no problem whatsoever. The restaurant has a band on when we've finished our meal; a country and western singer comes on and we all end up singing along to the songs and dancing to Tammy Wynette.

****

The following day is Disney World and I don't know who is more excited, Louise or Mum. Again I hire Mum a scooter to stop her from getting tired. I can't abide fast rides so Louise goes on a couple of them alone, while Mum and I cheer her on. Mum does go on a ride with Louise – the giant teacups that spin around – and when she gets off, she looks drunk, so I tell her to take it easy and help her to get back on her scooter.

"Steady on," she cackles, "I'm enjoying myself and nobody is going to stop me."

Mum and Louise have pictures taken with Mickey Mouse and I buy them both Mickey and Minnie Mouse stuffed toys. The theme park is so hot, every now and again a machine sprays water over everybody, which is very much appreciated by all. The problem is, within a few seconds were all hot again. It's the last night and we go out to a restaurant that looks like a burger bar from the 1950s. It has black and white tiles on the floor and bright red stools in front of a highly polished stainless steel bar. There are old-fashioned drinks of Coca Cola in a glass bottle, sarsaparilla and all kinds of milkshakes. When the burgers arrive they are delicious and really big, but we all manage to clear the plates.

Louise takes photos of the house so that she can show Mathew when we get home, then she goes upstairs to phone him. Mum and I sit outside and she asks me what went wrong with John. The whole thing comes flooding back to me and I try my best not to go all maudlin. I skip over it all and say I don't think we were right for each other.

"I quite liked him," Mum says, to my surprise, "He was very handsome." I laugh and think to myself how I like him too, it's just a pity he doesn't feel the same way. Mum tells me about Walter, the love of her life. At first I feel uncomfortable listening, but then I think *'Hang on, Mum's been young once and I already know that Pop isn't her first love'*. Mum tells me that she was madly in love with Walter but she played too many games and listened to her mother, who used to say things like, "Treat 'em mean and keep 'em keen." Mum took it to a whole new level and was horrible to him. Walter was heartbroken and mithered Mum for months. He even got down on one knee and asked her to marry him. Mum admits she loved the attention and turned him down. Then he stopped knocking at the door and waiting for her at the end of the road and Mum was confused and tried to get him back but he wouldn't entertain the idea. Mum was a real looker in those days and wasn't short of male admirers. She fell for Pop because, in her words, he was a cheeky chappie and made her laugh. They did bicker even then but she mistook that for banter. Within months, Mum found out that Walter had met and married someone else, so Mum married pop. I'm now seeing a side of Mum I've never seen before and my heart goes out to her. All that bad advice from Gran has cost Mum her first real love.

****

The following morning the taxi arrives to take us back to the airport. I smile when I think about the beginning of our trip and Mum lining up five suitcases in the hallway for a five day vacation. We had to unpack quickly and in the end, we put together one case between the two of us. Mum says "Howdy" to the taxi driver and when he drops us off she says, "Have a nice day." Everything is shipshape with the American airline and we've boarded before we know it.

Once the plane is in the air, Mum and I fall into a deep sleep. Louise is listening to her iPlayer. A few hours into the flight and we're woken up by children crying and people talking loudly. We've hit turbulence and the plane is swaying from side to side. It takes Mum a minute before she realises what's going on and when she does, she screams.

"Oh, sweet mother of God, help us. Help the youngest first and then the old people. God, you can take the others when you want."

People are looking at Mum. One man shouts, "Shut up, you're frightening the children."

I try and calm Mum down but I can't. She gets out of her seat and runs down the aisle shouting "We're all gonna die. Oh God help us!" She bangs on the door of the cockpit and shouts "Let me in, I want to know what's happening." I'm chasing her up and down the aisle and she won't let me take her back to our seats. She's screaming. "I'll never get back on a plane ever again. It's not natural, this great big fat thing floating around in the sky."

Mum runs back to the seat where we're sitting and grabs my handbag. I pull it back and calmly say "Mum, what are you doing?"

Mum becomes really agitated and says "I want to phone your pop. I want to tell him I'm sorry for calling him a useless feck before we came away." A young steward gives her a brandy in the hope it will calm her down. Mum makes the sign of the cross and puts her hands together in prayer. One passenger sitting in front of us is so annoyed, he indicates that Mum should have been tranquilized before we got on the plane. This results in me having a row with him and this provides more entertainment for the rest of the passengers. I get Mum another brandy and we sit in our seats and I hold her hand. The trip back home is the longest one I have ever taken.

We eventually land and go to wait for our bags. On the way out, Mum warns the passengers that are waiting to board that it's not safe to fly and some of them look horrified as they try to get away from her.

The taxi pulls up outside my parents' house and Pop is stood at the door, smiling at us all. Pop appears to have missed us, although he says he hasn't.

"Have I 'eck missed you, you've only been gone five days."

Mum is acting all sophisticated, telling Pop what a worldly well-travelled woman she is. She then tells Pop that she nearly died on the way back, that the plane was tipping upside down and that she felt like a pilot in the red arrows. She then explains to him what a rock she was to all the other passengers and how she'd calmed them down. Pop shakes his head; he doesn't believe a word she's saying. Mum has bought Pop a baseball cap that says 'I love America' and a plastic man holding the American flag. Pop says it's all tack but later that afternoon, he puts on his baseball hat picks up his figure and heads for the allotment with the dog.

Later that evening, we all have a fish and chip supper. Mum's new worldly ways have left her sophisticated and she is now open to buying food from takeaways. I tell Pop about the house going on the market and he's delighted.

"Well, Cathy, there's nothing he can do, it serves him right. It back fired on him." Then Pop laughs his head off.

"That's what the women in this family are like." Mum laughs,

Louise shows Pop the pictures she's taken on her phone and, although he pretends he's not interested, we can see that he is. I still haven't taken it all in and it all feels very surreal. I know as soon as it's sold I can pay everybody back and get a place of my own, so that pleases me.

The next day I open the shop door and Jane's already there. She throws her arms around me as she sees me.

"Cathy, I've missed you." I've missed her too and I've bought her a few fake bags home and she's over the moon with them. Jane is acting a bit strange and I can't put my finger on what's wrong. Then John makes an appearance from the back room. He walks towards me carrying a cup of coffee. My heart is beating so fast that I think it may come out of my chest, but I'm also very confused as to why he's making coffee in the shop. John puts the cup down and throws his arms around me. I stand as stiff as a board, not knowing what to do. Customers start to come in the shop and John says "I'll meet you tonight in the pub over the road, we need to talk."

I'm bewildered and when we get a quiet moment, I have to ask Jane what's going on. Jane tells me that she went to the prison and sat in the car park until she saw John leave work so she could confront him. To my horror, she then tells me that John said he had come to see me weeks ago in the shop and that he saw a man put his arms around me and kiss me. Then, the following evening, he saw me go into the pub and when he looked through the window, I was laughing with the same man. He also told Jane he'd seen me leave the pub with him and we linked arms to the car park. Jane said she'd explained the whole story to him and explained the man was Tom, my ex-husband, and that I'd gone along with a plan for revenge. The relief on my face is enormous and I burst into tears.

"I like playing cupid." Jane say as she hugs me. I laugh with relief.

****

John and I iron out everything and we are closer than ever. I wish I'd told him more about Tom, then it wouldn't have got out of hand. I thank God Jane told John what had happened, as he obviously thought I was seeing another man. I'm also really glad that he didn't cancel the holiday we planned to together, so that's still something to look forward to.

It's a month since we made up, so John takes me to a lovely Italian restaurant and we chat and laugh our way through the meal. It's 10pm and John lifts up his hand to the waiter. I presume he's asking for the bill but when the waiter arrives, he's carrying two glasses of Champagne. John gets down on one knee and asks me to marry him. I can't answer because I am completely speechless. It sounds like everyone in the restaurant is holding their breath and when I do answer, it comes out as a squeak.

"I will"

Everyone cheers and I can feel myself welling up. John puts a beautiful solitaire ring on my finger and, courtesy of Jane, it fits perfectly. We both go back to my parents' house to tell them the good news. They're both still up and I'm so excited, the minute I walk in the house, I blurt it out. Pop gets up and shakes John's hand and Mum kisses us both on the cheek.

"I'll get the Pomagne from the fridge," Mum says as we sit down. We all have a glass of cheap bubbly and Mum starts getting excited.

"Are you having an engagement party?"

It isn't something I haven't thought about yet and I look at John.

"No we're not," he says smiling. "We're going to get married as soon as we can. When you've met the one, there's no point in waiting."

I'm wrapped in a warm glow so I'll go along with anything at the moment.

"If you're going straight for the wedding, I think I might buy myself a designer dress from that designer, Steven Hawking," Mum squeals.

"Mum, you mean Steve McQueen, the designer that Kate Middleton likes," I laugh. "They're very expensive, though."

Mum thinks for a moment.

"I think I'll get something a bit cheaper then."

Everyone is thrilled about the wedding and I start to plan the day. With only five weeks to go, there's a lot to sort out. At first, Mum is furious that she can't be a bridesmaid with Louise and Jane. However, it only takes a minute for me to tell her that the mother of the bride is the person everyone will be looking at.

****

The morning of the wedding is as chaotic as I knew it would be. Pop is vacuuming Mum's hair – she says it's getting on her nerves because it keeps falling out. As usual, Louise is the sensible one and is getting everyone organised. Pop brings his old MG midget out of the garage, ties ribbons to the front of it. It's polished to within an inch of its life.

When Mum makes an appearance into the lounge she looks lovely, even though nothing matches. My dress is quite plain with lace on the chest and arms. It could be worn on most occasions. Mum has bought a blue skirt, a cerise jacket with a black camisole top underneath and the yellow hat she has on is massive. I can't believe my eyes and Louise is trying her best not to laugh. Pop looks handsome in a grey suit and pink shirt and tie.

Mum and Louise go off in the wedding car and Pop and I have a glass of Champagne. Pop kisses me on the cheek and says "Are you ready m'lady?"

"I'm ready." I laugh.

We get in the MG Midget. Doris comes out of her house, along with other neighbours, to see us off.

"I'm right behind you, Cathy." Doris yells. I wave at her and Pop and I fly along the road with the roof down. People cheer as we drive past and when we pass the shop, loads of customers are lined up to wave at us.

"See you all later," I shout at them.

We're at the traffic lights on Becket Street when we see a police car pull behind us and an officer gets out of the car. For some unknown reason, Pop puts his foot down, so the police officer jumps back in the car, puts his siren on and chases us up the road. Pop laughs and shouts out to me.

"I hope they don't catch us, Cathy. I've no license, have I?"

In all the confusion and giddiness, I'd forgotten that Pop had his licence taken off him. I feel faint with the shock. When we get to the second set of traffic lights, the police car comes to the side of us and signals for Pop to get out of the car. He is just about to speed off again when I plead with him not too. Pop sits in the car and the policeman gets out of his to ask Pop to step out onto the pavement. I go to pieces and worry that the day will be ruined, so I step out too.

"Officer, I know Pop was speeding but please don't fine him," I plead. "He was only trying to get me to the registrar in time. I've been let down by another car company so Pop is my only hope of getting married."

The officer eyes us both with suspicion and tells us to be on our way. He looks at Pop and says "Go slow, Sterling." We get back in the car and drive off. That was a close call and I shake my head at Pop for not reminding me about the license.

When we arrive at the registrar office, I'm a nervous wreck and everyone else is already there. I feel more nervous than I did when I got married years ago. John smiles at me and my stomach turns with excitement. Pop is so proud walking me into the room and Louise and Jane are right behind me. Mum is stood on the left with Auntie Val and Uncle John. When I get to the registrar, John winks at me and I smile back. However, when the registrar speaks, he has a lisp and he can't roll is 'R's. I start giggling which sets John off and the pair of us are stood with our heads down and our shoulders juddering from laughing. I look to the left and see Steven handcuffed to one of the prison officers. He sees Mum and waves at her but she doesn't wave back.

When the ceremony is over, we kiss.

"Our Cathy paid for the wedding license, therefore she now owns you John," Mum shouts. "That's what I did with Stan. It's like buying cattle and expanding your wealth."

Everyone laughs. Auntie Val looks at Uncle John and says "That's where I went wrong, letting you buy the license." Uncle John shakes his head.

The ceremony's over, so we head to the cricket club where we're having food and drinks. Steven has to go back to prison with the officer and deep down, I'm pleased that John allowed him to come to the wedding on a special pass.

Once inside the cricket club, everyone gasps as they see an array of flowers, paper lanterns, cakes and fancy cups for tea. There's wine on every table and baskets full of goodies to eat. It looks like a tea party for adults. The atmosphere in the room is fantastic, and when I look at John I feel so proud to say he's my husband.

When we do the speeches, John stands up and says "I want to thank Cathy's Mum and Dad for Cathy." Everyone in the room is really moved by this.

Then, when Pop stands up, he says "Right, any man who has a key to our house must give it back now, because Cathy is now taken." Every male in the room, including Banito, comes to the top table and drops a key into a small box in front. Everyone is in hysterics and Jane gives me a look because she knew what was coming.

Louise does a speech too, which I don't expect.

"I can't tell you how happy I am to see Mum so happy," she says. "Mum has been my rock over the years and has taught me right from wrong. I respect her and I also admire her. She's a strong woman and I'm really happy she has found a man who really loves her." Louise raises her glass: "To Mum and John."

John is clearly moved and I have tears in my eyes. Mum is beaming and she's talking to Auntie Val. From the bits of conversation I hear, it appears that Mum thinks Louise has said the speech directly to her, which is comical.

We go outside for some pictures and Mum is lording it in her outfit. John whispers to me "Your mum is so eccentric, but I do love her."

Mum hears John and hugs and kisses him.

"John, if you want to know what Cathy will be like when she's older, look at me," she whispers. John raises his eyebrows at exactly the same time as the photo is taken.

The End.

ABOUT THE AUTHOR

Carol Kearney lives in South Yorkshire with her husband and daughter. Her own story is one of surviving against the odds. Since losing her mother to cancer at the age of ten, Carol avoided hospitals like the plague until just a few years ago, when doctors told her she was highly unlikely to survive bronchial pneumonia and a misdiagnosed pancreatic cancer. "It was during this time I started to chant in my mind that I was going to get better, because I had not fulfilled my dream to write a book. And the more ill I got, the louder the chanting got," laughs Carol. She's been writing ever since.

Carol has attended two *Arvon* writing courses on script writing and also went on two courses at Tilton House in Sussex, which were run by Nicola Larder (Tiger Aspect), Eleanor Moran (BBC writer and producer)

Snap Cackle & Pop is Carol's first of what we at Wallace Publishing hope will be many.

Printed in Great Britain
by Amazon